Enough

Enough

—— A NOVEL BY ——

Rachael Kirkham

authorHOUSE®

AuthorHouse™ UK
1663 Liberty Drive
Bloomington, IN 47403 USA
www.authorhouse.co.uk
Phone: 0800.197.4150

Published by AuthorHouse 10/22/2014

ISBN: 978-1-4969-9461-5 (sc)
ISBN: 978-1-4969-9460-8 (hc)
ISBN: 978-1-4969-9462-2 (e)

Contents

Chapter One: The Context...1

Chapter Two: The Explosion: Part One.. 13

Chapter Three: The Aftermath 31

Chapter Four: The Respite 53

Chapter Five: The Explosion: Part Two... 77

Chapter Six: The Spiral... 109

Chapter Seven: The Incident 155

Chapter Eight: The Questions.. 191

Chapter Nine: The Truth 217

Chapter Ten: The Future 231

CHAPTER ONE

The Context

I am what you might describe as a high-functioning fuck-up. Although I carry on living a full and useful life, I can never escape from the nagging doubts and criticisms in my head. Most of the time, I can keep it under control but every now and again, everything explodes and I ruin everything. It's scary and I really don't understand it. I go from being a loving, caring, respectful person to being the world's biggest bitch. I shout and scream, I say the most unimaginably awful things to the people I love most in the world and then I remember absolutely nothing about it.

My lovely Mum - who has witnessed this happening far too many times for my liking - says it's like I disappear when it's happening. My eyes are blank, my usual reasoning goes out of the window and I become somebody who nobody recognises. When it's all over I have a terrible sense of doom, a sense that something awful has happened, yet I have no idea what it is.

Over the past couple of years, I've systematically alienated pretty much all those I most care about. It always feels as though the next time will be the fatal blow, when they'll run out of patience and leave me to my own devices. So far though, I've been lucky. We go through a period of remorse and reconciliation and then carry on. Believe me, I don't take this understanding and love for granted. I am eternally grateful. And eternally ashamed. I've tried to get help but so far, nobody can help to understand it or, more importantly, to stop it happening.

And that's not all. I sometimes find life completely unmanageable and just want out. I reach the threshold where I've just had enough: enough of being me and enough of being unable to escape from my own head. When this happens, I shrink into my own world and isolate myself. The world keeps turning during these times and I keep doing all of the things that I need to do to make life keep working. It's just that there is very little joy in it and I remove myself from the very people who can bring some of that joy back. Not really a winning strategy, eh?

The most ridiculous thing about all this is comes when you know what I do for a living. I am a motivational speaker and trainer, helping the people I work with to overcome their self-doubt and negative self-belief to become the person that they most want to be. Most of the time, I feel like a complete hypocrite: I know all the theory but can't apply it in my own world. Even though I know it works. I've seen the difference it makes to people and the new world it opens up for them. I'm lucky: I love what I do and I find real value in it. I just wish that I could use it myself. The difference is, I see value in the people that I work with. I struggle to find the same level of value in myself.

But I'm getting ahead of myself. There are more conventional ways of starting a conversation, aren't there? Shall we try again?

Hi. It's good to meet you. My name is Eve. I live in Manchester with my boyfriend Carl and our cat, Jess. We've been together for almost eight years and have established our own little family. Neither of us is interested in having kids – I'm not sure that either of us is sufficiently responsible to be responsible for a new life – but our cat is our little girl. We live a fairly quiet life, watching lots of films, going to gigs, enjoying good wine and spending time with good people, but it's a life that makes us happy.

It's an interesting process, 'starting again' and meeting someone new in your thirties. By this stage, you have a much clearer idea of who you are, how you want to live and what's right for you. I'd been in a fairly destructive relationship for about five years in my twenties. Then I woke up one morning, gave myself a severe talking to and decided that the time had come (actually, the time should have come about three years earlier but hey ho...) to move onwards and upwards. I spent several years as a single girl, half of it living like a nun and the other half in very un-nun-like behaviour, before I felt ready to give all that love stuff another go.

Like most people these days, I turned to the internet to find somebody. Now that was a serious eye-opener. I soon learned that men who sent you a picture of their genitalia as their next point of contact after 'hello' were not ideal candidates for a meaningful relationship. I kissed a few frogs and rejected more than a few toads and was on the verge of giving it up as an interesting experiment but not the right way for me, when my friend George stepped in.

We were both a bit fed up with work and so decided to spend the day skiving together. We met for lunch, shared a bottle of wine and put the world to rights. George is a remarkable person to have in your life. His 'left of centre' way of experiencing the world makes him a wonderful catalyst for new ideas and new ways of thinking. His love and support is unswerving and the situations in which he finds himself are a constant source of debate, soul-searching and downright hilarity. This is the man who, in his recent past, started his own political party to fight corruption in his local Council, designed a website for his local brothel and conquered the world of eco-friendly cleaning products. He's also the man who takes the time to understand my mental health issues, becomes an instant enemy of anyone who has wronged me and makes me smile when I need it most.

After lunch, we wove our way back to his house and settled in for the afternoon. One of his lodgers at the time was a renowned Manchester drag queen and I spent a happy half-hour trying on the shoes and costumes spread across George's living room. Later, while we were outside enjoying the sunshine and a skilfully rolled joint, George told me that it was time I found myself a good man. I told him about some of recent experiences of online dating (including the self-styled music producer who, after giving me a lift home – all of ten miles – asked me for petrol money) and told him that I'd given up on it.

This is where George sprang into action, got my logon details and set about finding me a suitable chap. His criteria were just what I would have chosen: a fine head of hair (preferably red), a good education, more than a passing interest in music and film, no kids, something interesting to say about himself, a sprinkling of self-deprecation and a quirky sense of humour. After nearly an hour's tireless searching, he presented his shortlist. Carl was at the top. I was impressed. Being an abject coward, I didn't want to contact him like some brazen hussy. Instead, I added him to my 'favourites' so he'd know I was interested. Sure enough, the next day I had a message from him.

We quickly realised that we liked each other and were soon spending lots of time together. After just six months we moved in together. That's when the real learning took place. We'd both lived on our own for a number of years and both had our own ways of being – and our own beliefs about how frequently to do the washing up and what to do when the laundry basket's full. However, these details are pretty inconsequential compared with the fact that we share the same values plus an overriding care and respect for one another.

Soon after we moved in together, Carl had a bit of an early mid-life crisis. He worked in an office, doing a job that he hated with a passion. He hated the pretend matiness which went hand in hand with constant back-stabbing and career plotting. He says he's never been particularly ambitious where the career ladder is concerned, but always prided himself upon doing a good job and doing what's right. Just like his father, he has a deep-seated resistance to injustice and intolerance. When there's battle to be fought, he'll fight it – regardless of who his opponent is and how important they might be. As a complete coward when it comes to conflict, I admire this bravery and his need to take a stand. My approach is the complete opposite: I put my head down and hope it will go away. When it doesn't, instead of facing it head-on, I let it fester to the point that it becomes all-consuming and I explode. Having said that, Carl's approach doesn't always work either. He's been known to get into some absolute humdingers at work with people who have a big say in his career progression. Personally, I'd rather have my brave warrior on the side of what's right than someone who gets a company BMW.

After a particularly passionate exchange with his boss, Carl came home one day and said, "Fuck this for a way to live your life. I'm going to be a driving instructor." And that's exactly what he did. He trained up and then set up his own business. Looking back, it makes sense. One of Carl's favourite things in the whole world is to criticise others' driving. I don't think that we've ever taken a single car journey together when Carl hasn't shouted at other people on the road and explained in very colourful language why they are completely inept. He also has remarkable attention to detail and, most of the time, a great deal of patience. He just needs to work on his rapport building skills. After wondering why so many of his learners (of both genders) left their lessons with him in tears, we worked together on his feedback techniques and ways of softening his language in a way that made his learners build their confidence. He's still not completely convinced that saying, "There are some opportunities for us to work together to improve your parallel parking" is better than, "Well, that was pretty shit wasn't it?" but the results speak for themselves – fewer tears, higher pass rates and more customers. He seems much happier now he's made that change and become his own boss. I've just had to remind him that I'm not one of his learners and he doesn't need to pass comment on everything I do when I'm behind the wheel…

Over the years, we've both grown in our understanding of one another: our quirks, our foibles and our passions. Even though I'm a lifelong Spurs supporter, I developed an affection for Carl's beloved Leeds United. We've even been to see the two teams play one another, and survived the ordeal. He even managed not to gloat when Leeds won. I've been introduced to the world of American zombie TV series and the myriad websites reporting on the bargains of the day, although I can't get too excited when somebody finds a supermarket that's reduced the price of its toilet rolls by a whopping 10p. Carl hasn't quite come around to my secret passion for 70s sci-fi series, Blake's Seven. I still watch it in private and hide the DVD box sets behind the more socially acceptable titles.

I think that maybe Carl has his own mental health issues. He suffers from excruciating self-doubt, putting barriers in his own path without really knowing whether the barriers are based in reality or a in his fears. More than once, he's stopped himself from doing something because he's so worried about what might happen. He imagines the worst and then paralyses himself with the fear of what might go wrong. Then, having worked it through, he eventually realises that many of his fears are imagined and that he's missed an opportunity. One of the things I have failed at during our time together is getting him to believe in himself – in his talents, creativity and resourcefulness. I wish that he saw himself as I see him. He is a remarkable man and I wish he could believe that.

Carl has helped me to explore my mental health and to try to understand what's happening. He's been with me through some of my darker and more explosion and stuck around to help pick up the pieces. Believe me, he has copped for it more than anyone else and I think he'd be well within his rights to walk away and leave me to deal with it. I'm thankful every day that he hasn't chosen to do so. He's one of the main reasons that I need to find a way to get better and move on – on to an easier life where I don't hold my breath every time I'm around other people and worrying that the next explosion is just around the corner.

So, that's Carl. And you've briefly met George, so maybe it's time to introduce you to the rest of the 'significant others' in my world who you'll no doubt meet along our journey. My other dearest friend is Anna. We've been friends for fifteen years – there for all the twists and turns, the good stuff and the not-so-good stuff. We met at a mutual friend's wedding - the two singletons who no-one really knew what to do with! After a couple of minutes of polite chit chat with the others around the table, we realised how much we had in common and spent the rest of the event talking, talking and talking – about music, about films, about men.

The following weekend, we went out - to the Indie Night at the nightclub above Woolworth's in Warrington. You know it's going to be a good night when your new friend jumps up to dance to all the songs that you love. You know it's going to be a pivotal night when that same new friend helps you to ward off the advances of a random bloke with a unique line in flirtation. When we both heard him utter his enticing chat-up line, "My name's Keith and I'd like to snog you but I've got a broken jaw,"Anna winked at me and whispered, "Just follow my lead…"

She pulled herself up to her full 5'3" height, folded her arms and said to Keith, "My girlfriend is not interested. She's here with me so kindly take your broken jaw away from us." Then she kissed me to complete the effect. Poor Keith. It worked, though.He went. Probably gave him something to think about later as well…

Over the years, Anna and I have had adventures together; we've done a tour of the Far East and Australia, each moved house on the same weekend and shared our introduction to Johnny Depp as Captain Jack Sparrow when we went to see the first *Pirates of the Caribbean* film together. When I was having problems with my evil ex, I'd pack my cat into his travel case and we'd go to stay with his Aunty Anna for a few days.

In a lot of ways, Anna and I couldn't be more different. I have flitted through a very eclectic career, ending up as a freelance consultant who goes wherever the work takes her. Anna is a Chartered Accountant, working near to home and surviving the personality clashes and petty office politics that seem to haunt corporate life. I've never really been able to manage my money. Anna has a spreadsheet on which she records every pound she spends and projects how much she can spend in the months to come. I have to remind myself to check my bank account every few weeks, and I just live in hope that I'll make it from one month into the next. I love cooking. Anna doesn't. She even manages to burn the chocolate she melts for our Pancake Day pancakes.

What I love most about Anna is her true generosity of spirit. She'll go to the ends of the earth to help the people she cares about. Once, on our travels, we were in a revolving restaurant, high above the city. I got a bit confused and couldn't work out where my handbag had gone. When we realised that, while we were revolving, the place where I'd dumped my bag was not, she leapt up to find it. It took her a while and she apologised to the table she upset in retrieve it by telling them that her friend was 'a little intellectually challenged' but she came back clutching my bag. The other thing I love about her is that, no matter how ridiculously I behave she always finds a reason why and defends me to the hilt. On some occasions, I think her faith in me is a little misguided but I love her for it.

My parents have been a huge influence on me in so many different ways. From them, I inherited a set of values which abhor injustice and discrimination, cherish peoples' various gifts and bring kindness to others. I have also inherited a strong musical taste which tends towards the noisy and irreverent. Some may call it indoctrination. They have a tape of me singing all the words to *Bohemian Rhapsody* when I was three years old. My first gig was with them – David Bowie's Glass Spider tour at Wembley. Later, in my teenage years, I would go to the same gigs as them but, given how uncool it was to acknowledge one's parents' existence, I'd always make sure that I was stood over the other side of the room. Now, we share music discoveries and go to gigs together. I even stand next to them these days!

My folks live close enough to enable us to spend time together, yet far enough not to live in each other's pockets. We talk regularly and share news as it happens. They are a fantastic advert for marriage – more than 40 years together and it's still obvious how much they fancy one another. I think that one of the tricks is that, however much they love and value their children, they have always made time for themselves and their relationship.

One of my biggest regrets is the hurt I've caused my Mum and Dad over the years through my scary explosions. Some have been aimed (unfairly) at them; others have happened when they have been around. Of all of the people who don't deserve my awful behaviour, my parents are pretty much top of the list. To my eternal gratitude, they have dealt with these situations by talking me through events and trying to understand what is going on for me. They have encouraged me to seek help and then supported me every step of the way when I find it.

I'm one of two children, both girls. My sister, Sarah, is a good few years older than me. I often wish that she would acknowledge that I have grown up and am no longer "Little Evie, my little sister". Although we look a little similar, Sarah and I are so different that it's hard to believe that we're related. Even as children, I'm told that, while I was making up dance routines to ABBA classics (I'm very thankful that this was in the days before camcorders so there is no shameful record of these that can be wheeled out at family events), Sarah was making scrap books of her dream wedding. While she cared for her dollies and treated them like her own little babies, I gave mine punk hairstyles then pulled off their heads and never touched them again. Actually, there was one exception. I remember when, as a nine-year-old, my best friend Emma Jenkins (bit of a tearaway but intoxicatingly cool and streetwise) told me about the facts of life and demonstrated this using my Sindy doll and her brother's Action Man. I'm not sure I believed what she was telling me and couldn't look Sindy in the eye from then on.

But back to Sarah. Sarah's life has turned out to be uncannily like the scrap books she made as a child. At 23, she married Ronald ("Ronald, not Ron – that sounds far too *Eastenders*") in a fairy-tale wedding. As a gawky teenager, heavily into goth music and goth clothes, the idea of being put in a pink frilly dress was too much to bear. I sulked all day and only smiled for the photographs because Sarah threatened to stamp on my foot with her stiletto if I didn't. I compromised by wearing the pink dress for the ceremony and the meal and then changing into my black jeans and Sisters of Mercy T-shirt for the evening. Funnily enough, there are no photos of me from that bit.

Sarah and Ronald continued in their quest for the perfect life by bringing two children into the world – Primrose and Harvey. They bought a 4-bedroomed, detached house in the suburbs and made a life for themselves there. While Ronald spends his days as a Senior Health & Safety Inspector (always interesting when he comes to our house and lectures Carl about the unsafe sitting of our central heating boiler), Sarah is a Medical Receptionist at her local doctors' surgery. She gave up work until the children were old enough to go to school but soon got back onto the career ladder and, as she proudly tells anyone who will listen, is now "second in command to the Practice Manager herself".

The kids are growing up and are well into their teenage years. Primrose now refuses to answer to her full name and insists on being called Rosie. I kinda understand why. She is obviously a disappointment to her mother who was hoping for a prima ballerina or show jumping champion as a daughter. Rosie wants to be a social worker and work with underprivileged kids. She recently got her first tattoo –a small butterfly on her shoulder blade – and then endured the silent treatment for over a week. She is a confirmed rock chick and we often swap music. I just thank any god that's listening that she's come through her formative years without succumbing to the pop media machine that has brought us the delights of Justin Bieber or One Direction. I love the fact that she has found her own path and doesn't just want to blend in. For a sixteen year old girl, she has remarkable clarity of vision about what the world should be like and the contribution that she wants to make. I applaud her and also admire her for moving away from the path mapped out for her.

Much to the chagrin of her mother, Rosie and I spend quite a lot of time together. She comes over for weekends and I've been helping her with exam revision. We talk – a lot. She's really trying to find her place in the world and often feels slightly out of the step with all that's around her. I can empathise– maybe too much. I wish I could tell her that it'll go away over time but... I can see her taking exactly the same path as me, revelling in the fact that she's not 'normal' and going out of her way to shout her difference from the rooftops. She shouts it with her clothes, her hair, her choice in films, her whole way of being.

Her political views are decidedly left of centre. Whereas I agree with most of what she says, I did speak up in our debate about solving the country's problems by introducing a Communist state. The great thing is that she listens and forms her views through learning and discussion. I've encouraged her to try to listen to her parents' right wing attitudes and discuss (rather than simply railing against) them. Yep, like most other people on this planet of ours, I can give it out but I can't always follow it. I am regularly accused of leading her astray but I prefer to think of it as opening her mind and letting her form her own opinions.

Harvey has become used to the battle of wills between mother and daughter. He keeps his head down and stays in his room, playing on his Xbox and listening to dubstep. He's been trying to educate me – "Auntie Eve, it's the ONLY music people are listening to these days and better than anything else" – but I'm afraid I just don't get it. At almost 14, Harvey is at that awkward stage in a boy's life when things are starting to get hairy and his voice has a mind of its own. He's also discovering girls. Gone are the days when his only love was his football team. Now, his love for the beautiful game has been replaced by a lust for all things female.

We had an interesting conversation recently when he asked me about how girls think, and how to impress them. I didn't know how to answer. I know how I thought at that age but I'm not sure that I was typical of my peer group and I'm not at all clear how my experiences would translate into the teenage world of today. He was worried that he wouldn't be cool enough or street enough (whatever that is) for the girls he was interested in. Just like his sister, he's trying hard to find his feet and find his place. Unlike his sister, he isn't immune to peer pressure and wants to fit in. When I suggested that he just be himself and the girls who are right for him would like him for who he is, he snorted at me derisively and told me that I knew nothing. I couldn't disagree.

Believe me, I don't go out of my way to court trouble and piss Sarah off. It doesn't give me pleasure. Well, not often. I love my sister because she's my sister. I just wish that we could find a way of moving a little closer towards each other's worlds. I try to do it by building meaningful relationships with my niece and nephew and supporting them as they grow and develop. I don't always get it right and I haven't quite learnt when to talk and when to shut the hell up. I don't want to court controversy, I just want them to grow up with their own thoughts and ideas – rather than ideas passed down (or, in the case of their peers, across) from someone else. When I talked to Sarah about this, she told me that I just couldn't help myself, that I always need to play the rebel and the renegade. I wish that she could get past her enduring image of me as a teenage goth and accept me as a fully-functioning adult.

I guess that's what's at the root of our problems: we have very different maps of the world. From my perception, it seems as though Sarah wants to keep her world close, so she can control it and make sure that things happen the way she wants. I find that idea restrictive and the best way to ensure that life stays the same and stagnates. From her perspective, I go out of my way to be 'alternative' and buck the trend. I fully accept that, just as Rosie is doing now, I used to do just that. These days, though, I do what comes naturally, and that's not often the accepted convention. One of Sarah's favourite causes is the fact that Carl and I are not married. We've been together for seven years and convention dictates that we should be making a 'real commitment' to each other; in her eyes, a 'real commitment' means marriage and children. I have explained that we love each other and are planning to be together for the rest of our lives but don't feel the need to 'prove' it to anyone through marriage. Sarah simply rolls her eyes reminds me that my biological clock is ticking and that I'm running out of time to reproduce. Tick away, oh biological clock.

Where Sarah and I do come together is our feelings for our parents. While we have different relationships with them, we are united in our love and affection for them. It's good to know that we share something. I envy Anna and her relationships with her two brothers. They like being together and choose to be together. They are friends as well as siblings. Anna holds a prestigious place in Sarah's regard: Anna is the only one of my friends who has her approval.

"Anna is such a sensible girl with a valuable career, so unlike some of the other hippies and creative types that you seem to like." Anna thinks this is hilarious and plays on her high profile in Sarah's perception. She's even been known to act as mediator between us.

What Sarah seems to miss is the richness that those 'hippies and creative types' bring into my world. Having people who, because they inhabit such a different place, can transport you from the everyday to another world where people think and act differently is a wonderful thing to have. They've chosen a different way to live yet share the same values with you. I have to admit that, when life gets a bit too much, I escape into their 'alternative' haven. I never quite feel as though I fit in – I immediately feel very 'square' and mundane – yet I revel in being a different version of me when I'm around them.

One of my very favourite members of this alternative haven is Guy. Guy and I were briefly in the same sixth form class until he left to move with his family to Devon. I think we both worked out quite quickly that we liked one another but couldn't necessarily work out why. We didn't spend too much time together but I do remember going on one adventure with him to see my favourite band at the time, Dogs D'amour. I was crazy about them. I loved their bohemian styling and their irreverent lyrics. For a while, I styled my own look very much on the lead singer.

Guy and I lost touch as we both went onto university but were reunited by one of the early websites that enabled you to look up people you used to know. Guy moved up to Manchester and became a cameraman for a couple of big TV stations. He lived in a series of communal houses across the city. They may not have been the cleanest or tidiest of places, but they were always a hotbed of ideas where people and their ideas were accepted. Over the past ten years or so, we've drifted in and out of one another's lives, spending concentrated periods of time in close contact and then spending time when we both know that we're still there but not really seeing one another.

On my last birthday, Guy gave me the most amazing gift. A couple of days after my birthday, I woke up to find a video link from him on Facebook. I almost didn't open it as when Guy's not got too much work on the books, he spends far too much time on Facebook. I'm so glad I did, though. The message that went with the link was: "Hey, Eve! Remember when we went to that gig together in 1989? Bet you never thought they'd be singing *Happy Birthday* to you…" It just so happened that Guy was asked to film a Dogs D'amour gig the night before and, when it was over, he asked them to sing to me for my birthday. It totally made my day. And that, for me, is the true delight in these relationships – those unexpected and unprompted moments of joy which leave you smiling all day.

So, Sarah, I'm sorry that you find it easier to badge some people as 'hippies' and dismiss the contribution that they make to my world. Maybe your life is enough without those moments which lift and delight you. Mine is not.

Chapter Two

The Explosion: Part One

One of the traditional events in December's social calendar is the annual get together of the 'Uni Girls' which, as the name suggests, is a group of us who were at University together. We have spread across the country but choose a place every year to meet up and catch up. This year, it's Birmingham. A few of the girls are based around the West Midlands but it's an overnight stay for me. I'm sharing a room with Alex who's coming up from London. Alex is often my partner in crime, a kindred spirit. Although she has two lovely daughters who she loves very dearly and of whom she is enormously proud, she despairs at the posturing and one-upmanship of what she calls the group's 'yummy mummy brigade'. When the brigade starts to boast about the achievements of their feted offspring, Alex usually grabs me and heads for the nearest bar.

I have to confess that my enthusiasm for this event has waned over the years. The people from this group of friends I particularly like and relate to are friends of mine outside of the Uni Girls: the others, I see just once a year when we all meet up. It's a really mixed group, as I guess it would be almost 20 years after we left university. Peoples' lives have taken such different paths. Many of the girls are now wives and mothers, others are divorced, some are militantly single and two are now together and planning a civil partnership next year. For some of the group, 'Uni Girls' Night' represents their one chance in the year to let their hair down and go wild without husband and kids around. For some of us, it doesn't have quite the same significance.

Even though I have known these women for many years, I've found myself becoming increasingly nervous and agitated in the days and weeks leading up to the get-together. It's fairly typical behaviour: I've never been great in big groups and find myself fading into the background, unwilling to shout loud enough to be heard over the chattering. I don't know quite where my place is in the group. As well as the yummy mummy brigade, we have the 'career girls'. I used to be one of them, working all hours to progress in my job. I did too. Then, about ten years ago, I decided that I was climbing up a greasy pole that didn't take me where I wanted to go. I wasn't a good corporate bunny, didn't want to play the political game or join any of the opposing gangs that seemed to grow in every organisation I worked for. I wasn't easy to employ or manage and so I went out and did it for myself. So, not a yummy mummy, and not perceived as a career girl anymore. Not maternal enough to be included in the children chat (not that I mind about that!) and not corporate enough to be involved in the tactical discussions about the next promotion. Thank Crunchie for Alex!

Over the past few years, Carl has watched me becoming more agitated before these December events and has asked me why I do them, what I get out of them. Great questions to which I'm not sure have an answer. I don't enjoy them and I wind myself up something chronic in the days leading up to them, yet still I go. When I've tried to analyse why, the best that I've come up with is that I feel obliged to be there and don't want to be the one who starts the fragmentation of a long-standing group. Hmmm... Would I want somebody else to be there purely through a sense of obligation? Would I want somebody else to spend days fretting about it and then spend the whole event holding their breath to the point where they can't relax and can't be themselves? No and No.

Most years, we take advantage of hotel chains' pre-Christmas events put on to bring in the punters. Not my first choice – the idea of a pre-processed meal, a cheesy tribute act and a load of company Christmas do's, full of people who don't usually choose to socialise together but are thrown together and bow to the social pressure to be the life and soul of the party. What's wrong with finding a nice restaurant where we can have a good meal and good wine? Still, I have no room to complain as I have doggedly dodged the responsibility of organisation since the night I organised at a Stereophonics gig and it went down like a lead balloon with half of the group. Also, events like this tend to give the people that want to the opportunity to go wild, drink too much, have a good dance and flirt outrageously with the sales reps from the assembled companies.

This year's extravaganza is an 80s revival night at a big hotel in the middle of Birmingham city centre. The round-robin email from this year's organiser, Barbara, has instructed us to 'come dressed as you did when you were 15'. She's pointed out that day-glo is back in fashion and has given us 'useful' links to designer collections that 'incorporate the fun of 80s fashion into a more sophisticated look'. I have to admit to a bias here. Barbara is my least favourite member of the group and is pretty much the antithesis of everything I hold dear. Over recent years, she has insisted on being called 'Babs' as she thinks it gives her a cooler edge. After the number of times that we have heard her saying, 'Oh, call me Babs, darling', Alex and I refer to her as 'Call Me Babs'.

Call Me Babs didn't quite finish her degree. She was studying Media Studies when she met a rich but slightly dull man during the Christmas holidays of her third year. When she found out that she was pregnant two months later, she left her course and got married, moving into his house in Southport. She hasn't worked since. She is now a confirmed homemaker with three kids and a beautiful house of showhome proportions. Her proudest achievement was being featured in *Home & Gardens* magazine last year: she brought a copy for each of us to last year's event.

With the time that she has on her hands, Call Me Babs has become a true fashionista, scouring the high-end magazines to identify the season's must-haves and ensure that she is permanently on-trend. Sometimes, she looks absolutely stunning. Sometimes, the phrase 'slave to fashion' takes on a whole new meaning.

I'm getting ever so slightly bitchy now aren't I? Sorry, that's another of my worst habits. When I'm feeling under pressure, I sometimes go on the attack. My principle of valuing everybody for the gifts that they bring goes out of the window and I become ultra-critical and judgemental. It's one of the trigger signs that tell me that all is not well in the world of Eve. It's a horrible, shameful habit and not one that I like in any way. When I notice it happening, as well as making myself think positive things about the person that I've found myself berating,

I check myself to work out what is causing it. So let's try and work out what's going on now in this moment… I'm nervous about meeting up with everyone, I'm steeling myself for the judgements from Barbara and I'm trying to get myself in the right frame of mind to be sociable and try to relax.

It's not that I begrudge Barbara her lifestyle or the benefits it brings her. It's not a choice that I would make but it works for her and that's okay with me. What I do begrudge is the judgement she makes of others and the way that she likes to make it known that her money and fashion knowledge make her superior. I like to buy clothes because I like them, regardless of the cost. I've never been able to justify in my own head spending hundreds of pounds on anything and have always railed against the need to be wearing the right labels. If I like something, I like it because I like it and not because it's by the designer du jour. I've developed a style which Carl describes as 'stylish with a twist'. I love the French-inspired style of La Redoute and find myself lusting after their collections. However, as Call Me Babs told me last year, I should be aware of the impression that I make by not wearing labels that others recognise and admire.

The other thing that I resent is the way that she drops the Stepford Wife routine when she's had a drink and goes from pious mother of three to wanton strumpet! Don't get me wrong, I have nothing against a little harmless flirting and have been known to engage in a little myself. But that's where it starts and ends – flirting. She flirts with anyone who seems to be eligible enough for her and loves the attention that she's paid. Most of our meetings end with Call Me Babs snogging furiously with someone who's been buying her drinks and saying the right things to massage her ego. Occasionally, the lucky object of her attentions has successfully lured her back to his room, although she strenuously denies it the next morning when she has sobered up and returned to virtuous mode. I guess that she is probably bored at home and I get that but don't claim to be a paragon of virtue when it's patently untrue.

Barbara's email has put me in somewhat of a quandary. Should I really wear what I used to wear when I was fifteen – exclusively black, lacy and usually strategically ripped? Or should I play the game and go for the expected mix of fluorescent brights, big hair and plastic jewellery? Do I feel the need to make a statement? Could I be comfortable in an outfit that I wouldn't usually be seen dead in? What's more, do I really want to splash on an outfit that I'll be wearing for four or five hours and will then hide at the back of my wardrobe until it goes to the charity shop? In the end, I decide upon a compromise. I go for a denim mini skirt with a black lace T-shirt., black stilettos and, in my homage to the 80s, a pair of fluorescent pink tights. I only manage to wear tights once before I rip them or put a huge hole in the crotch, so it's not a complete waste of money. Now I have to think about the hair. Given that I have relatively short, curly hair, I only have a certain range of options open to me. I decided to scrunch up my curls with mousse to make it as big as possible and wear a fluorescent pink scarf in a bow around my head.

It feels strange, so alien to what I wore at that time. While most other people were listening to Wham and Duran Duran, I was dancing to my own tune (quite literally) and listening to what, in one compilation CD, became known as the 'Dark Side of the 80s'. I loved The Damned and The Smiths and belittled more popular stuff by 80s pretty boys. I admit to a fleeting Duran Duran phase at the age of 12 but it soon passed. By the age of 14, I was borrowing tailcoats from the drama department of my school, buying black lace gloves and wearing T-shirts of my favourite bands, customised to demonstrate my rampant individuality. Still, I've been there and done all the goth stuff and now it's time to try something out of my comfort zone. After all, that which does not kill us makes us stronger and all that.

I'm trying on my outfit – clothes, shoes, hair, the lot – when Carl comes in from work. He's in a fantastic mood as he's just set a new record – three of his learners passed their driving tests on the same day. When he comes through the front door and shouts to me, I stay quiet and try to hide... I don't want him to see the 80s monstrosity that I've become. No such luck, though. He bounds upstairs, full of the joys of his majorly successful, cuddles the cat and then sets out to find me...

He opens the bedroom door and stops dead in his tracks for a moment, before bursting into howls of laughter. I was expecting him to whip his phone out, take a picture and post it straight to his Facebook page. What I didn't expect was what actually happened. My gorgeous, 42 year-old boyfriend regressed to horny teenager, reminded by the outfit of his earliest fumblings while safe in the knowledge that, this time, he could definitely be on a promise.

"Come here!" he said, pulling me onto the bed. I've never seen his clothes come off so quickly!

"Can you do something for me? he asked me urgently. "Yes?" "Could you keep the shoes and the bow in your hair on?" okay, so I'm about to indulge a long-held teenage fantasy. What better way to celebrate such a bumper day in the life of a driving instructor?

Have I really missed such a simple trick for all these years? Carl has never, ever disappointed in the bedroom (or the living room, or the bathroom or...) but this – this is something else. The passion of being so intimate with somebody that you love with all your heart, the skills of a lover gained over twenty five years and the urgency and stamina of a teenager who can't believe his luck! Afterwards, as I lay with his arm tightly around me and my head resting on his chest, all I could think of to say was "Wow, where did that come from?"

He laughed and replied, "The north Wales coastline, circa 1987".

We stayed in bed for a while, talking and making each other smile. After a while, he stroked my fringe off my face and asked, "So, how are you feeling about your trip to Birmingham tomorrow?"

Thanks, back to reality. "okay," I said, "Looking forward to seeing Alex but not sure about the rest of it".

"It's only one night, baby," Carl said soothingly. "I know, I just wish that it was over". Then my phone buzzed – a text from Alex.

"Hi hon. I'm SO sorry but I'm not going to be able to make it tomorrow night. Kids have chicken pox and I'm a single parent while he's in the US. Please don't hate me, I'm really sorry xxxxxxxxxx".

No! No Alex. My immediate reaction is to text Call Me Babs and tell her that I can't make it. That feels a bit churlish. There are other people there that I am genuinely looking forward to spending time and catch up with. Barbara is just one person and I can sit at the other side of the table from her, can't I? No, I'm going. The hotel is booked and non-refundable – as is the 80s thing. I specialise in communication skills and rapport building in my work so, if nothing else, I can use tomorrow night as a case study. That's one of the weird things. At work, I build the most amazing relationships with total strangers who say they leave feeling better about themselves and thinking very highly of me.

Yes, when I'm just Eve rather than Eve the trainer, it all seems to go to pot. My confidence and my belief in my skills abandon me and I become a self-conscious mess. When Carl and I have tried to analyse it, we came to the conclusion that, while I have strong belief in Eve the professional, I do not believe in plain old Eve without the trappings of my work.

While we're lying there, I start on a major rant about Call Me Babs and her superficial life, her superiority complex and her judgmental approach to people who are different than her. The language is choice and the dislike vehement.

Carl turns my face to his and says, "okay, trigger time. What's going on in that messed up head of yours?" I tell him how anxious I am and how I'm beating myself up about my abject failure to relax and enjoy myself like a normal person. He kisses me and tells me that his Evie can do anything she sets her mind to.

So here we are – or rather here I am – in a hotel room in Birmingham. My outfit is ready and I've had strict instructions from Carl to avoid any forty-something year-old men who look like they're going back into their own teenage fantasy. I think that the strength of his ardour rather took him by surprise and he's worried that the 80s get-up will have a similar effect upon the drunken sales reps who are bound to be there in abundance tonight. He has more faith in my ability to attract other males than I do. Besides, he's completely safe. I may have had my wanton moments in the past, but these days I am strictly a one-man woman. Seeing as we're on the 80s theme, wasn't that a hit for Sheena Easton?

It's about an hour before I'm due at the venue and I'm trying everything I know to make myself relax. Why am I so scared of being with a group of people that I've known for half of my life? They've seen me in various stages of inebriation and weirdness but they're still here. One member of the group, Gill, still talks about the time we went to a party and I ended the evening sliding down the road like a seal, resulting in a black eye and a completely scabbed nose for the next fortnight. That had been an emotional night, though. I had a HUGE crush on one of the guys, Dave, in the year above me on our course and, one night when we all went back, he invited me back to his flat and, well, I don't think I need to elaborate on what happened next. He was just my type – long hair, a rock fan and a bit rebellious. He was quite short but then so am I so it didn't really matter. I thought that I had it made, particularly when he told me that he'd really like to see me again.

The following week, we went to a party at the house Alex lived in. I'd made so much effort to look as alluring as it's possible to look on a student budget and had high hopes for a replay of the previous weekend. Dave was there - with his girlfriend of five years. Not only did they look completely loved-up but she was scarily huge, at least six foot and built like the side of a house.

He at least had the decency to appear a little sheepish when he saw me but broke my poor, tender heart about an hour later when he pulled me to one side and said to me "Forget last week happened, okay? I'll make life very difficult for you if you breathe a word of it to anyone. Understand?"

All I could do was to nod my head meekly then run off to find Alex and spend the next half-hour crying in the bathroom. When I emerged, make up redone courtesy of Alex, I resolved to be the life and soul of the party and make him realise what he was missing. I drank and drank, I danced and danced and I even had a very intimate girly 'getting to know you' chat with Dave's girlfriend. She confided in me that she thought that Dave was cheating on her but couldn't be sure. I gave her a hug and told her not to worry, that he seemed very into her. As I got out of the taxi later, I tripped on the door, slid in the frost that had formed on the pavement and kept sliding until I reached the end of the block. I was a complete mess and didn't leave the house for days afterwards – partly because of my scabby appearance and partly because of my broken heart.

That's the thing with people that you've known forever; these stories pass into folklore and become less real and less important than they seemed at the time. Gill teases me about it, but affectionately. She recognises the changes that we've all been through but still looks back with fondness at the people we were and the journey we've been on. I'll be pleased to meet up with her tonight and catch up on the latest news. Gill is now a highly respected pathologist who can be relied upon to have us in stitches with the goriest and most bizarre stories from her year. okay, thinking about that gives me confidence that tonight is going to be okay. Let's go and do this...

I've already said that I'm a coward and this cowardice extends to walking into new places on my own. We were meant to be meeting at 7.30 and I didn't like the idea of sitting on my own, surrounded by groups of people all intent on making merry. So, I arrived at 7.45 – fashionably late. There was a serious flaw to my strategy. I'd forgotten that my compatriots all share a congenital inability to be on time. All, that is, except one. When I walked in, there was Call Me Babs sitting alone, furtively looking around for suitable victims with whom to share her unique charms.

I thought about sneaking out and hiding in the ladies' for ten minutes until somebody more palatable appeared. I was too slow – she spotted me and called me over. Bugger! To her credit, the first thing that Barbara did was to offer me a drink. I'd come up with two strategies for the evening ahead: either drink nothing and stay in complete control or have a few and stay in relative control. The sight of Call Me Babs in hot pink spandex made the decision for me. "Vodka and slimline tonic please." "Large one?"

Pink spandex, pink spandex, pink spandex and no-one to rescue me anywhere to be found. "Why not? Thank you."

And this sets the agenda for the rest of the night. It seems as though we're onto strategy three – drink to forget your own insecurities and paranoia. When Barbara – sorry I just can't do the Babs thing unless it's prefaced with 'Call Me' – returns from the bar to the two of us. I ask her about her life and enquire about the husband and kids. Her husband she really doesn't want to discuss. Her kids, however, are a different matter. Little Timmy, the apple of her eye, has just been accepted into a prestigious public school, Jemima has passed her grade 6 piano exams and is excelling in both modern tap and ballet and baby Hugo (yes, really) is by far the brightest child in his reception class at primary school. How do we know this? Because his teacher has said that his painting is 'remarkable' and 'has unique style'. I'm wondering if the teacher is using the same approach to softening language as I've been working on with Carl.

I always play a game with Call Me Babs – to find out how much I learn about her world before she asks anything about mine. I almost make it a full house before anyone else arrives, though she does ask me which designer I'm wearing tonight. When I tell her that the skirt is by 'George' (said in a French accent to disguise its Asda heritage) and the rest is stuff I picked up in Debenhams, she wrinkles her nose in sheer disgust.

"Darling," she says, "You really should let me guide you when it comes to fashion. You obviously earn enough to afford better and it's beyond me why you stick to your silly principles and don't buy the best."

I'm talking myself out of smashing my glass against her perfectly botoxed face when, to my relief, Gill walks in.

"Eeeevieee," she screams as she sees me and wraps me up in the warmest, most welcome hug. Oh Gill, you are my saviour and I love you for being less late than the rest of our flaky crew. "Time for a big drink," she says, plonking herself down next to me and only then realising that she hasn't acknowledged Call Me Babs' simpering presence next to me.

"Barbara," she says, emphasising every syllable with absolute precision, "I see that you have gone to town with your outfit – damned good show". Barbara smiles her appreciation, completely missing the sarcasm and begins to reel off the list of designers that she's sporting for the occasion.

"And Gill," she says "Good for you, making such good use of the high street retailers. How remarkably thrifty."

Before Gill can respond, I take her by the arm and say, "So, about that big drink that you're obviously so ready for. Shall we go to the bar?"

Gill nods her appreciation and walks with me towards to packed and noisy bar. "Where does that woman get off?" she asks, as we push our way through the wobbling crowd towards the waiting barman. "Who the fuck does she think she is? Just because some of us have more to do than read inane magazines and spend all frigging day shopping".
The rant continues for the several minutes that we're waiting to be served. When she's finished and ordering a drink, I say, "I know, count yourself lucky that you weren't here with her on your own for 20 minutes".

"Yeah, sorry about that," she says, "I got waylaid by a call from the office with a particularly grisly murder case". Gill orders herself a double whisky and a gin and tonic. "I'm not drinking alone," she says, turning her head back towards me, "Give her whatever she's drinking."

The barman cocks his head to one side towards me by way of a question and I answer 'Vodka and slimline please." "Make it a large one," says Gill who has already downed the whisky and is half-way through the G&T, "And another one of these please," gesturing towards the now empty gin glass.

I'm pleased to say that, by the time we sashay back to the table, Call Me Babs has been joined by most of the other people we're expecting. We sit at the next table, ostensibly not wanting to interrupt the conversation about the best public schools in the West Midlands area but actually wanting to avoid Call Me Babs and her overbearing domination of any conversation of which she is a part. We park ourselves gratefully next to Liz and Dina and immerse ourselves in a conversation about their forthcoming civil ceremony and its tricky catering issues. I'm so happy for them. They are so obviously meant to be together. It makes my heart sing to know that they are going to declare their love for one another in the kind of ceremony they've always dreamed about.

I look around the table with a certain degree of affection. Here are the people with whom I grew up, worked hard and, ultimately, passed my degree. Here we are, 17 years later, dressed like a bunch of throwbacks to a bygone age, hungrily wanting information about what we've all been up to. I am most fond of Gill, Liz and Dina but there are others there with whom I share a past and many life-changing experiences. My nervousness and agitation reduce and I actually start to enjoy myself. So this is why I came. Yes, Call Me Babs has become a judgemental, superficial waste of space but there are other people her that I can still relate to and still want in my world.

Just as this dreamy feeling is still wafting its way around my being, we are summoned on the dot of 8.30 into the main hall for dinner. Gill and I place ourselves at the end of the table, with Liz and Dina acting as a buffer between us and Barbara. The food is as I expected – mass-produced pap masquerading as haute cuisine. However, with the two large vodkas and a big glass of wine swilling around my system, this doesn't seem to matter. I'm happy to be here and a little ashamed of myself for turning inwards and making the whole event into some huge black cloud to be endured. Now, I feel a little daft for making such a big deal out of everything. Gill regales us with stories of strange cadavers and murder mysteries and, at our end of the table, we laugh until we find tears pouring out of our eyes. All I have to do is surround myself with people who I can relate to, people who enrich who I am and I can be a fully functioning person; I can be enough for my situation and enough for the people I am with.

And so the evening unfolds. We eat our meal and then the 80s disco begins. First, there is a tribute band, two peroxided boys and two similarly bleached girls belting out such 80s classics as Wham and Kajagoogoo. Call Me Babs is in her element, dancing frenetically at the front of the stage and attracting the attention of the aforementioned sales reps who have more alcohol than judgement. Others in our group are dancing more tentatively at the back of the dance floor. Gill and I are still sat firmly in our seats, discussing those bands which contributed something different to the kids of the 80s. Pompous? Probably. Judgemental? Just as likely. Right and accurate? Definitely.

And then the disco starts. Gill is first up to the DJ, asking him for 'Heaven Knows I'm Miserable Now' by the Smiths. The irony, while not lost on either of us, goes completely over the DJ's head. Thankful that someone is talking to him and asking for requests that are actually from the 80s, he obliges and puts it on as the next record. The dance floor clears and there are only two people on the floor – one of them is Gill and the other is me. We dance in an over-emphatic way, displaying all of the teenage angst that we felt upon first listening to it. Gill 'does a Morrissey' and pretends to be sweeping her gladioli across the floor. We giggle as we dance and, for a few minutes, forget the contents of our heads and just enjoy the moment.

As the song finishes, so does our carefree mood. The next song goes right back into the cheese that defined the 80s – a good dose of Rick Astley. The dancefloor fills, minus its two previous incumbents as Gill and I sit down and fold our arms in disgust at the transient nature of good music and the rail against the pap. We continue to sulk for most of the evening, breaking our embargo for Nik Kershaw and then the Thompson Twins. Life is always better when you have someone else on your side. We had allies too in Liz and Dina, although they capitulated when the DJ got to the soppy part of the evening and they had a passionate clinch to 'Lady in Red' by Chris de Burgh. In our benevolence and gin- or vodka-soaked view of the world, we decided unanimously to give them that one. After all, they're in love and so they can be excused a little mush.

When the DJ announces a 10-minute break (a calculated attempt to get everyone to the bar and spending money?), we all flop back down onto our seats. Unfortunately, it's too late by the time that we notice that the seat next to us is free: Call Me Babs spies it and makes a beeline. It's pretty evident that she is plastered. The perfectly-applied make up is now slithering its way down her cheeks, she's flushed and her hair is sticking to her face.

When she starts to talk – or rather, to shout – her inebriated state becomes apparent in her slurred words and her inability to utter a coherent sentence. Gill and I smile indulgently at one another. Believe me, we are by no means sober but, by comparison, we're holding up quite nicely. Is it wrong to derive so much pleasure from Barbara's loss of control and poise? Probably, but what the hell.

"Have you seen that really fit bloke in the white shirt and Ray Bans at the next table?" she shouts so that said man with white shirt and Ray Bans looks round and smiles. The smile quickly disappeared when she followed it up with, "He's here with his wife but we had a quick snog while she was in the loo and he's going to try and get rid of her so we can go to his car for a bit". A bit of what, I wondered but didn't say. The next thing we knew, Mrs White Shirt and Ray Bans was at our table, looming menacingly over the seated Barbara. Oops! "Are you talking about my husband, you old slapper?" she asked, looming just a little closer. "Do you really think he'd go for you? Have you looked in a mirror lately?" Call Me Babs opened her mouth to say something and then seemed to think better of it.

"Just keep your nasty little paws off him," threatened Mrs White Shirt, "You hear me?" Barbara nodded meekly then turned to us. "Thanks for your help," she hissed. Us? What were we supposed to have done? She'd brought in on herself hadn't she?

After we'd watched Mr White Shirt being marched out of the room by an irate Mrs White Shirt, Gill and I tried to pick up the conversation we'd been having before the drama had unfolded. After all, it was an interesting and important subject – which music star from the 80s would you most like to be seduced by today? Gill went for her all-time hero, Stuart Adamson from Big Country. Good choice in his day I had to agree, but today? Given that he's been dead for over 10 years (a fact that still tugs at Gill and means that she marks the anniversary every year), I wondered if he'd still hold the same appeal.

"okay then," she challenged, "You name me someone from the 80s that you'd still be interested in today". Easy, David Bowie. That man has the ability to make me tingle, the combination of his talent, his incredible style and the sound of his voice. Gill loses me for a few moments into a state of Bowie-inspired reverie.

My daydreaming is rudely interrupted by Call Me Babs leaning over and prodding me in the shoulder. "Don't you fucking judge me!" she yells. "You try being married to that boring tossbag and you'd want to have a little bit of fun once in a while too!" Here we go...

"Barbara," I say, trying to stay calm and composed, "No-one is judging you. We didn't come to rescue because there was very little we could do and very little we could say to justify your position".

She tried to prod me again but missed and fell of her chair, onto the floor. As she pulled herself up, she spat out the immortal words, "You're all just jealous because I've made more of myself than you could ever hope to and you'd kill to be me, just for a day." okay.

I could sense that Gill was becoming a little agitated beside me so I leant over and asked Call Me Babs if she wanted us to call a cab to take her home.

"Go home? What, now?" she asked incredulously, "Not on your life. You boring lot do what you want; I'm off to talk to that bloke over there who's been giving me the eye all night". And so, with as much dignity as she could muster, she made her way over to a guy several tables away and promptly plonked herself down on his lap. Far from being offended by this, it seemed that he couldn't believe his luck. We watched with fascination for a couple of minutes before leaving her to it.

As the evening drew on, the grouped thinned out as people returned home or to their hotels. Once we'd said goodnight to Liz and Dina, Gill said to me, "So, now we're on our own, tell me how things are really going for you? Is that screwed up self-perception still clobbering you on a regular basis?"

I knew that the enquiry was meant with love, but I didn't really want to face that whole can of worms at this time of the night with more than a couple of drinks inside me. I knew that talking would make me maudlin and I'd been doing so well. I screwed up my face and asked if we really had to talk about it.

"Sweetheart," she said, "We hardly get to see each other these days and I'm worried about you. Talk to me."

And so I did. I found myself pouring out everything that had been on my mind, the alcohol in my system removing any of the usual inhibitions which cause me to censor my thoughts and keep the darkest parts to myself.

"On a day-today basis, I'm okay. I can work, I love being with Carl and I'm functioning," I say.

"But?" Gill asks.

"But it all feels like such an effort, carrying on. I'm struggling to find any joy in it. I've forgotten how to laugh, forgotten how to be playful, forgotten how to be me, really. Whatever I'm doing, it just doesn't feel like enough to make me feel worthwhile. I just can't find my place in the grand scheme of things. I'm aware that I'm becoming more and more anti-social, avoiding situations where I'll have to talk to people. It seems like such an effort to find anything to say and to keep conversations going. I'm so tired of it all; sometimes I really feel as though I've just had enough."

Gill takes my hands and looks me in the eye. "Oh Evie," she says, "What are we going to do with you? How is it that someone that has all the knowledge and all the skills that you have can help everyone else but yourself?"

I shake my head ruefully and reply, "I wish I knew. I know what I should do and how I should be thinking and I do try, honestly. It just never seems to be enough." I mean it as well. No matter what I try and whatever positive attitude I try to adopt, the critical voice inside my head, the one voice I can never get away from, erodes all positivity.

Breaking into my self-pitying thoughts, Gill asks, "Could it be time to go back onto the happy pills, honey? It's not an admission of failure you know? After all, if you had a physical injury, no-one would think twice about you seeking help."

I was just about to answer when Call Me Babs appeared and slurred, "What are you too miserable gits looking so sad about? This is a party remember! Come on, get with it!"

"Was there something you wanted, Barbara?" Gill snarled.

"Ooh yes," Call Me Babs replied. "Eve, can I borrow your room key? I want to go and change my tights. I fell over on the dancefloor and I've laddered them and I don't want to spoil my chances with Mr Sexy Football Manager."

"Football manager?" Gill and I ask in unison. It appears that either Call Me Babs is being spun a huge line or the guy whose knee she's been occupying is indeed the manager of a lower league football team, here with his coaching staff.

Gill and I look at each other – the same thought going through each of our brains: if ever there was somebody destined to be the archetypal footballer's wife…

She carries on prattling about how lovely his eyes are and what a lovely hairy chest he has. I realise that there is one way to stop the inane babble. I fish in my handbag, find my room key and hand it to her, asking her to bring it back to me once she's done.

That does the trick. Call Me Babs toddles off looking very happy and we can get back to our conversation.

"One more for the road?" Gill asks.

"Hmmm, not sure, I think I might have had my fill," I reply but it takes her all of ten seconds to convince me that it's only right for me to keep her company and so she heads to the bar. While she's away, I think about our conversation and keep playing the words over and over in my head. It really bugs me that I seem completely incapable of helping myself, of pulling myself back into a state of mind where I can enjoy life and bring enjoyment to those I care about. Even if I can't find a good enough incentive to do it for myself, surely I can do it for the sake of the people I love. I resolve to do something positive about it tomorrow, when my head is clearer and I'm in a position to take action.

When Gill returns from the bar, the mood changes and the conversation turns to happier thoughts. We talk about Carl and her recent experience of internet dating. She tells me about the man that seemed to be eligible and suitable but then bored the pants off her for the whole evening by talking about his love of fishing. Then there was the one guy who she actually went to bed with whose hair was obviously artfully coiffured until he was in the throes of passion.

"It was awful," she said. "As soon as he started thrusting on top of me, his hair sprung free from its moorings and this long strand of hair which must have been covering a massive bald spot started dangling down his face, way past his chin. I know it's appalling but it couldn't stop laughing. Totally ruined the mood and I never heard from him again!"

It's only after about an hour, when the crowds are really starting to dwindle, that we realise that we haven't seen Call Me Babs for ages. I'm getting tired and ready to sink into my bed and Gill is insisting on finding Barbara before she leaves me to find a cab home. We scour the hall for her, then try the ladies' loos, the reception area and the car park. No sign of her anywhere.

We try her mobile but there is no response. We think about calling her home number to check if she's left without returning the key but decide that it's too late to go disturbing her family unnecessarily. So, we go back to Reception, explain what's happened and ask them to make another key for my door.

With the new key safely in my hand, we make for my room, slide the key into the electronic lock and open the door. The sight that greets us will be etched for all time on my eyeballs. We walk into the room to find Call Me Babs, splayed legs akimbo on my bed and the spotty behind of the lusty football manager she's been seducing bobbing up and down on top of her.

And that's all I remember...

CHAPTER THREE

The Aftermath

"Good morning, oh sweary, explosive one".

I roll over onto my back and slowly open my eyes. There is Gill, standing at the side of my bed and placing a cup of tea down by the side of me. I groan and reluctantly relinquish those blissful few seconds when you wake up and forget that there's anything wrong. The problem is, I don't quite know what is wrong. I remember walking into my hotel room and finding Call Me Babs in flagrante with a nameless, faceless, pimple-arsed admirer and then it all goes black. The fact that Gill greeted me with the words 'sweary' and 'explosive' tells me that it's happened again and I've been in total melt down.

"okay then," I said. "Give it to my warts and all…"

"You sure? Warts and all?" Gill asked.

I nodded my assent before I could change my mind.

"Well, you remember walking into the room and finding Call Me Babs at it?" I nod, taking the first slurp of my cup of tea and mentally thanking Gill for remembering that I don't take milk.

"I looked over at you and it was like you were there in body but no more. The Eve I know wasn't in your eyes. It was just like you've described when you explode. For someone as articulate as you are, you certainly rely on expletives to get your point across. You walked over to the bed, tapped the poor guy on the back and asked him if was in the habit of using complete strangers' hotel rooms to fuck anybody who waggled their tits in his face. I know it wasn't funny but the look on his face was priceless – think he was almost at the point of ecstasy when a crazed woman with menace in her eyes and dodgy fluorescent pink tights interrupted him. His expression went from the pleasure of imminent release to annoyance that he was being interrupted to sheer panic when he saw your face!"

"You threw his trousers at him and told him to get the fuck out of your room before you phoned hotel security. Then you picked up his mobile which had fallen out of his pocket, scrolled through the numbers and found 'home'. You told him that this should be a lesson not to think he can get cheap thrills while his wife was at home.

He leapt across the room and tried to take the phone off you but he tripped up and went flying. You asked him to give you one good reason why you shouldn't make the call and he replied that you should think of the hurt it would cause to his wife and kids. You snorted (never heard you make that noise before) and told him that maybe it should be him thinking of the hurt he was causing by jumping into bed with a random married woman with no self-respect. My favourite bit was when you bundled up his clothes, threw them out of the room and shouted 'Fetch!', before kicking him out. It was a masterful performance."

"All this time, Call Me Babs was surreptitiously trying to gather her clothes and sidle towards the door. You shut the door and stood in front of it before telling her that she wasn't going anywhere, that it was time to hear a few home truths. And that's when you totally flipped."

I groaned and braced myself for what was coming next. Shouting at a man I'd never see again was one thing but what the hell had I said to Barbara and could we recover from it?

"You told her to put on her clothes then sit in the chair in the corner of the room. To my surprise, she did what she was told. When she's pulled on the few clothes that she could find, you began…"

"I'll clean this up a bit and paraphrase through the swearing. You asked her what the hell she thought gave her the right to use your room as a two-bit knocking shop with some random nobody who was obviously out to get his end away with anything with a pulse."

"Barbara interrupted you to say that he wasn't a 'nobody' – he was a Football Manager – and that she was flattered that he'd chosen her. You roared that he hadn't chosen her – that she'd not given the guy any choice with the way that she was slobbering all over him."

"And then you really let rip. You told her that she was the most self-absorbed, self-centred egotistical bitch that it had ever been your misfortune to meet; that she was so wrapped up in her own world and her own need that she didn't give a thought for anyone else. You described her as being completely devoid of empathy with not a single drop of humanity."

"My favourite line was when you said, 'If it isn't happening to you, it isn't real and you think that you can just ignore it; why the hell anyone would choose to spend a single moment in your conceited company is totally beyond me.' Then you told to get the fuck out of your room and never contact you again."

"And did she?" I asked.

"Not before telling you that you had no idea what it was like to be her, the pressure to stay glamorous and attractive and always be ahead of the trends. She said that it was alright for you, you wear what you like and do what you like without the constant social pressure to be what she had to be."

"okay, to which I replied?"

"Oh get over yourself, sweetheart. The monster that you are is the monster that you have created. Now piss off!"

"And then she did just that, mumbling that she was going to tell your sister exactly how you'd behaved and that if you thought you were going to get any more fashion tips from her, you had another think coming."

"I'm sorry that you had to be a part of this, Gill," I say. I hate it when other people are party to me losing control and I hate the fact that they see me completely lose it. It doesn't seem very dignified.

"Oh, Eve," Gill said. "Call Me Babs had it coming. She had no right to do what she did and you're right when you say that she's completely self-absorbed. You said what most people think and, after that stunt she pulled, you had more right than most to say it."

"So, you're telling me not to beat myself up too badly?" I ask.

"Not about that, no. However, I really do need to talk to you about what happened next: you scared the life out of me."

And that's when the chink of light I'd felt that maybe this wasn't too bad, completely deserted me and I felt a cold sweat on my back as I wondered what had happened. Please let me not have done anything to compromise my friendship with Gill. Please.

Gill sat herself down on the bed next to me and held my hand. "Evie, I'm so worried about you. When Barbara had left, you burst into tears and cried like your heart was going to break. You kept telling me how useless you were, how you'd had enough of everything and you hadn't got the energy to keep trying to make the world alright when it never could be because something inside you would always screw it up. You cried for hours and got yourself so worked up that I really didn't know what to do with you."

"I'm sorry I scared you," I said feeling totally ashamed and embarrassed.

"I don't want you to apologise," Gill said, "I just want my lovely friend to give herself a break, see the wonderful person that we all see and realise that you really are good enough and worthy of help. Please don't give up on yourself. You give so much to so many people and yet you never seem to think that it's enough. Please, let's find you some help."

I don't know what to say. I'm so grateful to Gill for caring, so grateful to all the people who care about me even though I'm not sure why. Because I can't find the words, I just hug her.

As tender as this moment is, I suddenly realise that my bladder is about to explode so I excuse myself and head to the bathroom. Looking in the mirror, it's clear that I have had a fairly serious explosion with lots and lots of tears. I look like a bug-eyed monster from hell. My hair is stuck up on end and my eyes are hardly visible through the puffed-up pink skin that surrounds them. I address myself in the mirror and say, "This really can't carry on, girl, you need to understand what is doing this to you and make it stop. If you can't do it for yourself, do it for the people who have to be there when this happens. Do it for the people whose lives you're affecting by freaking out". I nod to myself and say, "I will. I know I have to."

After finishing off my tea, I rouse myself enough to take a shower and get dressed, thankful that the tacky outfit from yesterday is a part of the past. To reaffirm this thought, I ball up the hideous fluorescent pink tights and throw them in the bin.

I'm packing up the last of my things when Gill says, "I need to go, hon. Please promise me that you'll find someone that can help you. You're too important not do, you hear?"

I nod. "I really do hear you and I will – I promise."

She hugs me and then leaves me to it. Five minutes after Gill's departure, I'm ready to go too. I check out of the hotel and set off on the journey home. I suddenly feel very alone, as though the bubble created by Gill's presence has been burst and now it's back to being just me. I decide to ring home, both because I want to reach out and hear Carl's voice and because I want to give him prior warning about what happened.

He answers the phone almost immediately and says, "Hi baby, I've been worried about you."

"Why worried?" I ask, wondering if I dragged him into the maelstrom of emotions last night.

"You left me a voicemail and you sounded upset. I'm sorry that I didn't pick up; I had an early night so my phone was off. Then I got a message from Gill telling me that you'd been upset but she was going to stay with you and make sure that you were okay. What happened?"

And so I recounted the whole saga to him, filling the gaps in my own knowledge with what Gill had told me. "I did it again," I tell him, "I exploded and then couldn't stop. I scared the living shit out of Gill by telling her that I'd had enough. Why do I keep doing this? Why is there this thing inside me that puts a big black fog over everything?"

"I don't know, baby, but we'll work it out together," he says soothingly and reassuringly. "When you get home, we can just snuggle up on the sofa with Jess and forget that the world exists. Just you, me and our baby girl – oh and the new box set of Walking Dead that came yesterday."

Despite the fact that I felt so wretched, I had to smile. Carl and his bloody zombies! At least The Walking Dead has a good story and the zombies are only part of the plot.

"Sounds good," I say. "I can't wait to see you."

"Drive safely, baby and there will be a big hug waiting for you when you get in."

And there was. I felt myself climb into his arms and welcome his warmth. We stayed cuddled up for most of the day, only moving to scavenge for supplies in the very bare kitchen. We shared a bottle of Pinotage, ordered a nice hot curry and let the day melt into the evening before finally moving upstairs to bed.

The Carl bubble was broken in the early hours of the morning. I woke to find my brain processing the previous day's events and questioning why I hadn't had the self-control to prevent the explosion from happening. Just in the middle of rampant self-criticism, I noticed that my phone was flashing. I picked it up to find a text message from Barbara. okay, here we go, I thought. For a moment, I considered ignoring it and waiting until morning but I knew that I'd just fret about its contents and make it into something bigger than it probably was. So I opened it.

"Eve, I think that we both said and did things that we might now regret and I hope that you are feeling ashamed of some of the things that you said to me. When you are ready to apologise, I will be ready to listen."

I can feel the bile starting to rise up in me again. The message started out with something approximating mutual wrongdoing but the way it ended made me want to scream. I decide that I'll wait until morning to respond as what I'm thinking right now would not be useful at all.

I eventually fall back to sleep, only to be woken what feels like five minutes later by Carl's alarm. He's on early duty this morning as one of his learners has their test at nine and has booked a final practice lesson before the test. I think about pulling the duvet over my head and going back to sleep but I know that would be fruitless. Nope, time to get up and face reality.

Two cups of tea into the morning I'm feeling a little stronger and able to face the day ahead. My phone flashes again. Surely not more patronising, blameless words from Barbara? No, instead it is the patronising words of my sister.

"Eve, Barbara has told me about the hurtful and insulting things that you said to her last night. When are you going to stop taking your problems out on other people? You are too old for ridiculous behaviour like this."

This time, I decide not to wait before responding. Actually, it was probably more of a reaction than a response but I did it anyway.

"Sarah, once again, you are taking half a story and making the judgement that I am in the wrong. If you knew the facts, not even you could think that this was all one-sided. Try asking a few questions before leaping to unwarranted conclusions. If you want to talk about it with me, feel free."

Before I could think twice, I press the send button. I knew that it was likely to provoke more outrage and judgement, but it needed to be said. Sarah needs to know that it isn't okay to assume that she knows more about my life than I do and it isn't okay to form her opinions based upon the information she wants to hear rather than the full information. I know that I probably haven't done our relationship too much good with the text I've just sent but I'm sick of her overbearing, know-it-all approach. Needless to say, she doesn't talk to me about it. In fact, she seems to stop talking to me altogether. I decide to leave Barbara's message unanswered as I can't find anything constructive to right. Coward's way out? Yes, potentially but there's no way to reason with such a blinkered outlook.

Once I've calmed down about the injustice of both Barbara's assertion that it's me who owes her an apology and Sarah's accusation that I must be in the wrong, I changed my focus to something more positive and start to think about how I could keep the promise I made to Gill. Firstly, I phone my doctors' surgery and try to make an appointment with the GP who has been really understanding of my mental difficulties in the past. I find out that she is on maternity leave for the next month but am offered an appointment with the practice's Senior Partner instead. He has a cancellation and I book in for the following day.

I also look up the number for a local mental health charity that's been recommended to me in the past. Somebody I know used their services when they were in crisis and received really useful one-to-one support services. I think about calling but decided to wait until I hear what the GP has to say the following day. I don't want to take valuable resources from the charity if I can access something on the NHS.

Knowing that I have done something constructive and found the courage to call the doctor, I ease up on some of the pressure I'm putting upon myself. I decide to do something useful to occupy my time and divert my focus away from the weekend. And so I settle down to write a training course that I'm due to run the following week. There are two courses that need my attention: one on Influential Communications and one on Emotional Intelligence. I decide that the Emotional Intelligence one is probably a tad too close to the bone for today's state of mind and so elect to work on Influential Communications. Despite the impression that Saturday night's performance might have given to an impartial bystander, it's a subject I know well and enjoy. Once I get my head around it, I progress quickly, enjoying the process and looking forward to delivering it.

I'm still hard at it when Carl comes home from work. His 9am test passed with flying colours but since then, he's had a couple of frustrating lessons, one of which was with a boy racer who, in Carl's words, "doesn't think that the rules around speed and safe driving apply to him – jumped up little shit." At the end of this lesson, he had a word with the lad's mother and told her that, if her son didn't start to abide by his rules when in his car, he wasn't prepared to work with him anymore.

Despite these frustrations, he's in a reasonable mood and suggests going out to see a film that evening. We are film junkies. We have these cinema passes where you pay monthly and can then devour as many films as you want over the month. It's ideal for us and Carl is always keen to try and make sure that we get our money's worth in the first week. He thinks that this means that we win as we then get the next three weeks free. I tell him that I'm happy to go to the cinema but I need to spend a couple more hours finishing off this course. He cocks his head to one side and asks me whether I think that obsession over work is one of the triggers that something's not right. I have to concede that he's right and we go to the film. I find it hard to concentrate and I keep thinking about the course that's waiting its final touches. I hate to admit it but I have to – Carl's right. I'm displaying one of my trigger signs and I should acknowledge and tackle this before it gets any worse. One explosion in a week is more than enough.

It's the following day and I'm waiting in the doctors' surgery for my appointment. I've brought my Kindle with me to while away the inevitable delay between my appointment time and time I get called but I just can't focus on it. I start to feel quite vulnerable at the thought of having to describe to someone new what happens to me. I find myself rehearsing what I'm going to say, how I'm going to explain myself and how I can help somebody who knows nothing about this to make sense of it all.

When I'm called into the consulting room, I am greeted by an imperious looking older man who gives me a brilliant but insincere smile. "And what can I do for you today, my dear?" he asks.

I ignore the 'my dear' and take a deep breath before starting to talk. I find all of the words I'd rehearsed disappear and my mind feels like an empty mush. "I'm sorry," I say, "I'm struggling to find the words to explain."

He smiles at me indulgently and seems to give me permission to take my time and order my thoughts. Again, I take a deep breath and this time the words start to tumble out.

"I've struggled with depression for many years but recently, something else has been happening. I seem to have almost an 'out of body experience' where I completely lose the plot and it's like I've left my body because my eyes are blank and I say and do things that are really out of character. I'm not sure if I'm making any sense but it really scares me and I really need help."

There seems to be an overly-long pause while the doctor processes what the babbling idiot in from of him is saying and tries to work out what to say next.

I feel as though I've given him a lot of myself in the few minutes that I've been talking and so I was expecting a little more from him than what he said next.

"It's probably just your periods, dear. They can do funny things, you know. Maybe you should just try to relax a bit more."

"I was thinking that maybe going back on the antidepressants might be the best option," I say.

"I think we're being a bit hasty there," he replied. "I don't want to put you back on something like that without trying other alternatives first. What I'd suggest is that you go home and try some relaxation techniques and come back in a month or so if it's not making any difference."

I think about arguing my case but when he asks me to shut the door on my way out, I realise that it's a battle I'm not going to win. I leave the surgery feeling quite inadequate – inadequate because I think that I completely failed to get my point across and explain how badly I needed some support and inadequate because the 'expert' seems to think that whatever is wrong with me is inconsequential and something that anybody with an ounce of gumption should be able to resolve. I also felt deflated because I'd found the courage to reach out and make myself vulnerable and had nothing in return.

By the time I've walked back from the doctor and had a little chat to myself, I'm more upbeat again. I've decided that Plan A – talk to the doctor – hadn't worked but I still had Plan B – talk to the mental health charity. And so I call as soon as I arrive home.

The lady that I speak to is lovely and explains that the first stage is for me to have a telephone consultation to understand what it troubling me. Then, if they think they could support me, I'd be invited in for a face-to-face session with one of their counsellors. From here, they'd talk me through the resources they have to help me and we'd make an action plan. It all sounded reasonable and so I arrange a telephone consultation for the following week.

I text Gill to let her know that I've been keeping my promise and she texts back to ask how it's going and tell me that she's proud of me. That makes me smile.

And so it's time for me to call the charity and have my telephone consultation. As I start to dial, the nerves hit me. Here I am, about to uncover my innermost craziness to a complete stranger. Admittedly, it is a stranger who has an interest and experience in dealing with mental health issues, but I still feel very vulnerable.

The phone is answered and I explain why I am calling. I am passed onto a lady called Emma. Emma explains that today's conversation is aimed at understanding what is going on for me and working out what they can do to help me. She asks me what made me call and I start talking.

I tell Emma about my general depressive tendencies. She asks me how long this has been going on for and I say that I remember feeling this way for a long time – way back into my teenage years and maybe even before that. I explain how, even as a young girl, I remember feeling different and self-conscious. I tell her how I used to be paranoid that people were criticising me and was convinced that people were making judgements about me, none of which were complimentary. I tell her that I used to feel disconnected from the world a lot of the time and not able to reconnect. Of course, these are the feelings of a much younger me, translated into the vocabulary of the me who's here today.

Emma brings me back to the present and asks me how the depression affects my life. I tell her that when I'm feeling down I isolate myself and so deprive myself of the love and affection that people have for me. After all, I feel unworthy of that love and don't deserve it. I can't understand why people would want to give me things that I don't want to give myself.

I explain how it is a progressive thing; I have a number of triggers that, I've come to learn, mean that I am on my way down. As well as cutting myself off from most of the world, I also have a very strange response. Although I hardly ever really watch TV, when I'm getting lower I obsessively start to watch old TV programmes, almost as if I'm immersing myself in a different world. Blake's 7 is my refuge of choice most of the time. Carl knows that the sight of the DVD boxes is an early sign of trouble.

I move on to tell her about my explosions and how much they scare me. I tell her how I completely lose the plot and become somebody I don't recognise – somebody cruel and mean – and I tell her that I have no recollection of these explosions afterwards, just a sinking black feeling that it's happened again. I tell her how much it scares me that I seem to lose all of the goodness in me and then, almost as a recognition of this, I turn on myself and become hopeless and question why I'm even here.

And then she asks me the question that I knew would come at some point in the conversation. She asks me whether I ever reach the stage where I feel like taking my own life – although she doesn't actually use those words.

I've noticed that, whenever this question comes up, it's never asked directly. People dance around the question and use language that makes it less direct. In my time, I've heard, 'Does it ever all feel too much?', 'Do you ever want to escape?' and 'Do you wish that you weren't here?' For me, none of these really get to the heart of the ultimate question. There is a big difference between not wanting to be here and wanting to escape and actually planning to do yourself in. I understand why the question is softened: to some people, it can be too stark. However, to me, being stark can be a very good thing. It can help to focus the mind and help the person to work out just how bad things really are.

When I was a volunteer for Samaritans – yes really, with all of my hang-ups – we always asked every caller whether they were feeling suicidal. Then we'd go on to ask if they wanted to be dead forever or just away from everything for a period of time. There is a real difference between wanting to be away from everything and wanting to be dead and it's important to differentiate between them.

I answer Emma as honestly as I can. I tell her that I do wish it would all go away and that I could escape from being me, escape from my own head. However, I also tell that I have no plans to take my life.

Emma thanks me for my honesty and invites me into the office to meet with a member of their team to talk through the options that might be available to me. We arrange an appointment for three weeks' time – the first time that they have a free slot for me. In some ways, it's a bit frustrating that, after I've started to confront all of this stuff, I now have to wait to do anything more about it. However, I understand the constraints and find the positives in having a couple of weeks to forget about it.

And so I go back to trying to get on with my life. I go to work, I do my very best to engage with the people I'm training and do something to help them to move forward. Carl and I go to the cinema and lose ourselves in different worlds for a few hours. I shop and cook and deal with the overflowing washing basket and spend precious time with both Anna and George. Life carries on and I try really hard to find the positives in it all. I even enjoy a few fleeting moments of it all. However, the dull, aching emptiness never quite goes away.

The three weeks pass and it's the day of my meeting with the charity. It's a little out of town in an area that I don't really know so I end up being ridiculously early. I sit in the car and try to amuse myself by playing the Sudoku game on my phone but I'm distracted and not really concentrating. I move my attention to cleaning up my car. I've been away a lot recently and there are far too many Diet Coke cans littering the floor. I find a carrier bag in the boot and collect all of the rubbish together, ready to throw it away when I get home. The distraction works and it's time to go for my appointment.

The nerves start to hit me the moment I reach for the door handle to let myself into the office. I take a deep breath and walk in. I'm met by a lady called

Lydia and taken into a private room just off the main office. She says that she has spoken to Emma and understands what has made me contact them and tells me that I don't need to go into all of the details unless it would be useful to me. She asks me how I have been over the past few weeks and I tell her that, although I haven't had another explosion, I've been struggling a bit to keep it all together. She asks me about the techniques that I use to manage the depression and I share a couple of these with her. For some reason, this feels more uncomfortable than talking about the depression, probably because I'm exposing the weird ways in which my mind works.

I tell her that I usually manage to hold things at bay during the day, keeping myself too busy for time to think. She asks me how I handle the night times and this is where it starts to feel a bit uncomfortable. I tell her about my two tricks that help me to take things out of my head and enable me to sleep.

The first is to trick my brain so that it thinks it's still thinking but is in fact not thinking about anything emotional or dangerous. I play what I call 'the A to Z game'. I think of a subject – Star Wars, The Tudors, anything that is outside my real life – and then challenge myself to think of something connected with that subject starting with every letter of the alphabet in turn. It keeps my brain active but stops me from thinking about anything that might bring about an emotional response.

The second is to take things out of my head and almost banning myself from thinking about them. I imagine that I am on a beach where the sun is going down but it's still warm. I imagine myself writing down whatever is bothering me on a slip of paper. While I'm writing, I see the words appearing on the paper, say them out loud, syllable by syllable, and feel the pen pressing onto the paper as I write. I finish the words with a full stop and then imagine myself rolling up the piece of paper, slipping it into a bottle, screwing the cap onto the bottle and tossing it into the sea. Then I watch the bottle float off on the tide towards the horizon. This only works for me and my environmental sensibilities by imagining that all of the bottles are biodegradable and melt into the sea after contact with the salt water. One less thing to worry about…

When I finish talking, I give Lydia a look that says 'please don't judge me for being a weirdo'. Lydia simply smiles and tells me that she thinks that I have well-developed coping mechanisms. However, she points out (as I already know and regularly beat myself up about) I am dealing with the symptoms rather than addressing the causes of my problems. I know. And I also know that, this time, I need to deal with the tough stuff.

Lydia tells me that the charity is there to help people just like me and that I've taken a big step by being here. She tells me that the bad news is that they have had their funding severely cut (not unusual in the current economic climate) and that they have had to reduce the services that they can offer. Many of the courses that they used to offer – mindfulness, meditation and so on – have been cut, as has the amount of one-to-one counselling that they could offer. There is a long waiting list for the counselling service but she will add me to it.

She suggests that the most immediate support that they can offer is the support group which meets every Thursday evening. She tells me that this group of people with mental health difficulties is facilitated by a member of the charity and addresses whatever's going on for the members at that time. She asks me if I think that this would help. My hesitation communicates my uncertainty.

"Don't worry," Lydia tells me. "Everybody gets nervous when they join the group, but everyone is welcoming and you'll soon feel at home. It's a good opportunity to meet people who've had similar experiences to you and share ideas about how to help yourself. Why not give it a go?"

I can't think of a good reason not to and so I agree to go along the following week.

The following Thursday evening, I don't have time to go home and change out of my work clothes and so I head straight there. Early again, I sit in the car trying to entertain myself. Nothing distracts from the thoughts whizzing around my head. What kind of people will be there? Am I creating the right impression, turning up all suited and booted? Will there be anybody who can relate to what's going on for me?

As I'm parked just down from the charity's office, I can watch people going in. I don't want to be the first in but I don't want to be the last. I wait until I've seen a few people go in and then I get out of the car and head for the door. I'm pleased to see Lydia there – one friendly face at least. She smiles and waves then, ending her conversation, she comes over to me.

"You came! "she exclaimed. "Please come in and meet everyone." She leads me over to the group that is assembling around the table at the back of the room. "Everybody," she says to the group, "We have a new member joining us tonight. This is Eve."

A man with crazy grey hair and kind eyes comes over to me. "Hello, I'm Patrick," he says, shaking my hand. "And this is my girlfriend, Jane."

I smile at Jane but she shoots me a funny look and turns away. Oops, not a good start. The threat of another woman in the group? Something that she doesn't like the look of about me? I'm not too sure. Do I go over and talk to her or do I just let her get on with it? The decision is made for me when another man comes over, a man with homemade tattoos of 'Mum' and 'Dad' on his arms and another one of 'MUFC' on his wrist. "I'm just going to make a cup of coffee," he says, "Want me to show you where everything is?"

And so I follow Phil into the kitchen area and make myself a cup of tea. We talk a little over the boiling kettle, small talk about where we live and what we do. Phil tells me that he is a cleaner for the Council and lives in the flats over the road from where we are now. He asked me what I do and I tell him that I run training courses for businesses. I ask him how long he has been coming to the group and he tells me proudly that as the longest-serving member of the group he's been coming along for the last eight years. I ask him what he likes about the group and he says that he lives on his own and Thursday nights give him a night away from the pub, with people who are happy for him to be himself.

When we come out of the kitchen, more people have come in and are talking away quite happily. I am struck by the friendly atmosphere and the fact that everyone seems happy to be here. The session starts with Lydia welcoming everybody and then asking the question, "What's on your mind today?"

I've decided that I want to sit back and listen to start with until I get a feel for what's going on. Patrick tells us that he and Jane have just booked tickets to see *The Lion King* next year and are both really looking forward to it. Jane pipes up that he didn't get the right tickets and they are going to be sitting up in the roof but she's looking forward to it all the same.

Another woman tells us that she's had trouble paying her gas bill. She tried to talk to someone on the phone but they said that she owes them money and needs to pay it or she might get cut off. This leads to a long discussion about how much easier it was when you could just take the money into a shop and pay them that way. The group drifts off to talking about the shops they used to go to – to pay gas bills, electricity bills and phone bills – and what happened to them all.

After what felt like an age, during which time I had to assemble my face into an interested, open pose even though the conversation was long-winded and frustrating, Lydia brought some focus back to the conversation. She brought out what she called the 'issue tree' — a pâpier maché tree with labels hanging from the branches, a discussion topic written on each one. She held the tree out to me and said, 'Eve, as our newest member, would you like to choose a topic?'

I leant forward and looked at the labels before choosing the one which said 'Communication'. Maybe this would help me to explore some of the things in my head and find out how other people dealt with communicating with the people around them.

"Communication," read Lydia. "And what made you choose this one?"

"Probably because there are some people I really struggle to communicate with and I'd love to be better at talking to them. I'd like to know how other people handle it and get some advice on how to communicate with the people I find really difficult."

There was a pause while everyone stopped to assemble their thoughts and work out what to say. I was ready to learn and share some of my own experiences, and waited for somebody to kick off the conversation.

It was Phil who spoke first. "I don't like using the phone," he said. "I get my words mixed up and then get angry when they don't understand me."

There are nods of agreement around the room. Lydia picks up the thread and asks Phil how he deals with getting angry. "I shout at them and let them know that they've pissed me off." And that's where that line of discussion ends. The conversation moves onto the internet and the latest YouTube sensation of a dog playing the piano. I haven't seen it so can't really contribute.

And so the evening goes on with well-meaning but not very useful conversation. As the session breaks up and we're all saying goodbye, Lydia catches me by the door.

"How was it?" she asks.

I don't want to say that it was great but, on the other hand, I don't want to dismiss that whole thing. "I was very welcomed," I said, "Although I'm not sure that I really learnt anything."

"It wasn't a usual session," Lydia tells me. "I wasn't very good at controlling the conversation. We usually make sure that we go a little bit deeper than we did tonight. It's not always gas bills and YouTube."

She smiles and so do I. "I'm not ready to duck out quite yet," I say. "See you next week?"

And then we say our goodbyes and I head home. Carl is out with friends and so I curl up on the sofa with Jess the cat and try to process what has just happened. I feel quite angry: I just can't work out who with. Maybe it's because I was hoping for an experience which left me feeling better than I did. As it was, if anything, I feel slightly worse. Maybe I'm angry with myself for not leading the conversation in a way that led to something useful. But could I really have done that? Is it what anyone else would have wanted? They all seemed quite happy with the whole thing. Maybe it's just me being out of step – again.

I have a text from Gill which simply says, "So?"

How to respond? I want to find the positives. I want to find a way in which it's going to be helpful. In the end, I respond with, "It was an interesting start, find out more next week, I hope".

By the time Carl returns home, slightly worse for wear and in a giggly, charming and outrageously flirtatious mood, I have resolved to treat the evening as the first step on a journey and return the following week to try again. Carl suggests that we go upstairs and 'end the night with a bang'. When he finishes laughing at his own jokes, he winks at me seductively as says, "Come on, my little strumpet, upstairs now!"

Seems that, on this occasion, my lovely boyfriend was all mouth and no trousers for, when I go into the bedroom five minutes later, he is fast asleep, sprawled across the bed wearing nothing but his pants and socks. The last of the great lovers…

And so, the following week, I head back to the support group. This week, it is Emma – the first person I spoke to at the charity –leading the session. There are different people around the table this evening and I hope this means a new dimension to the conversation.

Emma says, "Tonight, I thought we'd talk about how you manage it when you get a bit down."

okay, this is a bit more like it. Should I talk first? That would mean that I could set the pace of the conversation, but will people think that I'm muscling in and taking over? When nobody else offers an opinion, I decide to go for it.

"I find that walking helps me," I say. "The fresh air and the exercise, as well as being out in the natural world just makes me feel better. I quite often listen to music too while I'm walking. Does that work for anyone else?"

"I just go to the pub," says Phil. "There's nothing that seven or eight pints can't deal with."

And so then we embark upon a long conversation about the pubs in the area and where to go for the cheapest pint. Eventually, Emma wades in and says, "okay, let's get back to what we were talking about. What else can we do to make you feel better when you're feeling down?"

Patrick digs Jane in the ribs and says, "I can tell you what she does – she sticks the telly on."

"What do you watch, Jane?" I venture. She's still been wary of me this evening but I did get a 'hello' and so I want to build on this.

"I love the soaps," she says, "Watch them all. *Corrie, Eastenders, Emmerdale, Hollyoaks* and some of the Australian and American ones too."

This time, I have a suspicion that the diversion might have been my fault. Jane talking about the soaps that she watches leads to a discussion about what's happening in them all. Once again, I can't contribute. I only used to watch *Eastenders* in the Dirty Den era because my Dad told the teenage me that I wasn't allowed to.

And so I leave again feeling as though I've learnt nothing and contributed nothing.

The following night, I'm having dinner with Anna and I tell her about it. I tell her how confused I am about it all and how I feel as though I'm missing something. I feel as though I should be able to do something to make the whole experience more worthwhile.

"Is it really judgemental of me to say that I have nothing in common with pretty much everyone who goes there? I can't relate to them and I don't think that they relate to me. We just live in completely different worlds and, to be honest, their world isn't one that I really want to visit." I feel guilty, snobbish and too superior just saying these things. I don't think that it puts me in a very good light and I'm not proud of myself.

"Evie," says Anna, "Will you bloody stop it! It's okay to say that you don't relate to them, it's even okay to say that they are people who can't give you anything."

"But they have given me something," I say. "They have given me welcome and acceptance. And what have I done? Just dismiss that because I find the conversation not of my world. Not very grateful is it?"

We talk about it over our plates of noodles, using our chopsticks to emphasise our points and spilling food all over the paper table cloth in the process. Anna tries to convince me that it's okay to admit that this isn't the right environment for me and to move on. To me, this feels as though I haven't really committed to it and that I've given up without really trying. In other words, I've failed.

"Is it not more of a failure to keep on going, getting nothing out of it and becoming more and more frustrated in the process? Evie, it's not up to you to save the world single-handed. If it's not right, it's not right. Give yourself a break, woman!"

We come to the conclusion that the best course of action is to go once more and then make a decision. I resolve to arrive early at the next session to talk to the facilitator and explain my position.

And so I do. I arrive at the office fifteen minutes before the session starts and ask if I can talk to either Emma or Lydia – they are both there this week. Lydia comes to talk to me while Emma awaits the rest of the group. I explain my misgivings and my guilt at the way I feel about the whole situation. I feel guilty even saying the words. Lydia seems to understand. I tell her that I don't expect the group to change just because it isn't right for me but I'm not sure how it's going to help me. Before we can talk any more, the noise in the next room tells us that the session is about to begin, so we head next door to join the group.

I try really hard in the discussion to contribute and explore useful subjects. I fail miserably. Tonight, we cover Wetherspoons pubs, Status Quo's latest tour, Peter Kay and the new tax on pasties. At the end of the session, I hang around to talk to Lydia.

"I know what you're going to say," she says, "And I understand why. You're still on the list for some personal sessions so maybe we just need to wait for that, eh?"

I nod and thank both her and Emma for their time and their support. When I get home, Carl has a cup of tea waiting and pats the sofa next to him, an invitation to sit next to him. He asks me how it went and I tell him the whole sorry tale.

He strokes my hair and says, "Well you gave it a good go and you tried, baby."

Yes, I tried. And I failed.

Chapter Four

The Respite

It takes me a couple of weeks to forgive myself for giving up on the mental health support group. Even now, I still turn it round and around in my head and wonder if there isn't something I could have done to make it more beneficial. I mention it to Carl and he strokes my hair and tells me to give myself a break.

I had a text from Rosie this morning. I'm pleased as I haven't seen her for a few weeks while I've been hiding myself away.

"U missed a meeting of the witches' coven last nite. Barbara came over to see Mum. Ur not very popular ru? Sounds like a load of old bollocks to me. Uokay? Fancy a coffee over the weekend? Luv u xxx"

I think about my reply before I send it. However naffed off I am with the pair of them, Sarah is Rosie's Mum. It doesn't surprise me that they've been talking: Call Me Babs is still probably trying to justify herself and probably a bit worried that they story might get out. In some ways, I wish I could have been a fly on the wall to hear how she explained the situation and which sordid details she left out. It's probably just as well that I didn't hear the conversation when it turned to how dreadful a human being I am.

Having processed all of these thoughts, I compose my response to Rosie:

"Hi sweetheart. Good to hear from you. Yeah, I'm not their favourite person just now and for once, it's really not deserved! Love to meet up, just let me know where and when. Love you too xxx"

And so, on Saturday, I arrive in the coffee shop to find Rosie waving furiously at me and a big, steaming cup of Earl Grey tea waiting for me. Actually, it's more like a bucket of tea but very welcome. We hug each other warmly and settle down to catch up. I ask about her studies and she tells me how much she's learning and how she's been researching social work courses at University.

"And how's that going down at home?" I ask.

"Hmm, I haven't mentioned it," she says, slightly shame-faced. "I know that I have to tell them at some point but I just can't stomach the histrionics from Mum and the emotional blackmail that'll come my way about how I'm letting them both down and how they hoped for better. Why can't they just accept that I want to do something worthwhile with my life and not just conform to their success stereotypes? Just because she wants to hold her daughter up as the Queen of Suburban Success. Does she really know so little about me? Does she not care about what's going to make me happy?"

I look at her fondly and cover her hand with mine. I want to tell her that I agree with her and that I admire her for knowing what she wants to do. I want to tell her how proud I am of her for wanting to do something positive with her life. I want to tell her to tell her mother to get over herself and support her fabulous daughter. I want to but I can't. Regardless of my mixed feelings for my sister, I respect that she is Rosie's mother and I have no right to interfere and cause problems.

"Given that they're going to be paying your university fees, I guess that conversation has to come," I say, feeling completely inadequate and disloyal as the words come out of my mouth. "Have you thought about how you're going to broach the subject and convert them to your way of thinking?"

And so we start planning the best way of tackling this and how to work through Sarah's inevitable line of persuasion to bring her daughter into her plans for her offspring. We think about the best way to explain why this is all so important to Rosie. As we talk, I have this sinking feeling that, however passionately, reasonably and articulately Rosie makes her case, Sarah really won't want to hear it.

When we have exhausted our thoughts and come up with what, in most non-Sarah-related cases would have to be a winning strategy, Rosie changes the subject.

"So, come on then," she wheedles, "What was that witches' coven all about? What's happened to leave my mother so outraged and Barbara so humble?"

Humble? I'd liked to have seen that. Not sure I can actually believe it.

"Hmmm, I think your mother might kill me if I told you the whole truth. Actually, I'm not sure she would believe it, given the crap that Barbara has probably been feeding her. Given what actually happened, I'm not sure that Barbara's version of events to your mum could have included much of the truth."

"Now you really HAVE to tell me!" she said, excitedly, as though she was about to uncover a huge scandal. "Go on, I'll buy you another cup of tea as a bribe."

Could I tell her? Should I tell her? Probably not, but the fact that I'd undoubtedly been so maligned in Call Me Babs' retelling of the story made me crack and decide to spill the lot. I'm still not sure that it's the best idea and I'm sure that it'll come back and bite me on the bum at some point, but...

"okay, I give in!" I say, smiling. "I'll go and buy the drinks and I think that you're going to need something sweet and naughty to stomach what I'm going to tell you so it's time for a cake. You let your imagination run riot for a few minutes while I go and order."

I seem to have picked the wrong moment and have to join a long queue, reappearing almost ten minutes later with drinks for us both and two great slabs of caramel shortbread, which has been Rosie's favourite since Carl introduced her to it years ago.

I put the tray down on the table and Rosie looks at me expectantly. When she's taken her first triumphant bite of the gooey loveliness and cleared the mass of crumbs from around her mouth, she says, "Go on then, spill!"

And so I do just that, still feeling more than a tiny twinge of guilty but, if I'm honest, enjoying the hilarity the story causes in my niece. I tell her about the hideous outfits and Call Me Babs' drunken behaviour, how she attached herself to the supposed Football Manager and then how I found them in my room.

Giggling, she has so many questions. Who was he? What did he look like? How did Barbara react when she was caught out? To the first, I tell her that I'm not sure but apparently he was the Manager of some lower league football club. To the second, I have to confess that, apart from him being quite tall with dark hair, I have no idea because I spent more time looking at his arse than his face and then he couldn't look me in the eye when I was ejecting him and his clothes from the room. This makes her spit out a mouthful of her cake and scream with laughter. To the third, I tell her that Barbara couldn't really offer any defence, just told me that I'd do the same if I was married to someone as boring as she was.

When her laughter had finally subsided, Rosie asks me how her mother became embroiled in all this. I shrug and tell her that I can only assume that Call Me Babs called her in an attempt to recruit allies. After all, I do vaguely remember her hissing at me that she'd tell Sarah. Risky strategy, given what had happened and the damage it could do. As it was, I had absolutely no intention of breaking the story to anyone else.

We chat happily for another twenty minutes, then Rosie says, "Right, time to make a move. Got a hot date tonight and I need to dye my hair before I go."

I wish her luck, tell her to let me know how it goes, we hug and then go our separate ways. I smile to myself and am thankful for a happy hour with Rosie. I'm worried about the drama which will most probably unfold when she's honest with her parents about her life's ambitions but I have faith in her to handle it in the right way.

When I arrive home, Carl is avidly watching *Football Focus*, having heard on one of the many Leeds United fan sites that there is a feature about the club on the programme. I sit down next to him to watch and yelp in surprise. "Who the hell is that?" I ask in amazement, pointing to the tracksuited man on the screen.

"John Parkin," he replies, "His team are the first team for years to get into the quarter finals of the FA Cup and they're playing Chelsea tomorrow. Why the surprise?"

I look at the man who is talking away, using all the usual football clichés about it being a game of two halves and having everything to play for and realise that, the last time I saw his face, he was scrabbling around the floor of my hotel room, searching for his pants and begging me not to tell his wife that he'd been caught with the lovely Call Me Babs.

Carl bursts into fits of laughter. "John Parkin?" he asks incredulously, "Barbara's great conquest was the dirtiest dog in the history of football? Has that woman got no shame?"

So it's true, she did bag herself a Football Manager. Just a shame that she bagged the one with the worst reputation and the spottiest bottom known to man. I resist the temptation to text Call Me Babs and suggest that she turns over to BBC1. I wonder what Sarah would make of it...

Once *Football Focus* is over, the Leeds United article thoroughly analysed and the various fans' forums have been scoured for comment and insight, we have lunch and then plan what to do with the rest of our day. Neither of us is feeling particularly active, so we decided to do a double feature at the cinema, with an Indian feast in the middle, courtesy of the Spice Valley restaurant next to the cinema. It's one of those places that only has to be mentioned for my taste buds to start tingling. The food is incredible.

The first film is okay, but not earth-shattering. It was one of the new genre of zombie and vampire stories aimed at teenagers after the success of the *Twilight* series. The food was incredible as always. They go way beyond the usual repertoire of your average curry house and have a particularly unusual vegetarian selection. The second film is much better, with a good story and believable characters that you could empathise with. When we get home, we round a thoroughly good day off by opening a bottle of sparkling Saumur wine and putting on some music.

As we snuggle up to one another, Carl tells me that he needs me to consult my diary. I bring it up and ask him what he needs to know. He tells me not to make any plans for the following Saturday night – my birthday – and to block out the week in two three weeks' time as I'm not going to be available. I ask him about the work I have booked in and he tells me not to worry, he has it covered. Then we go into our usual dance that happens whenever Carl has a secret. I like surprises and don't want to know anything to spoil the surprise. When he's feeling pleased with himself, Carl wants to share the secret and bursts with the pressure of keeping it to himself. He asks if I want a hint and I disappoint him by telling him that I'm more than happy to keep it as a surprise.

We keep dancing for most of the following week, Carl desperate to share his plans and me wanting to wait until Saturday. When Saturday comes, it's time for Carl to spill his plans. And boy, had he made some AMAZING plans. Over a cup of tea in bed, he tells me about the evening ahead. He's arranged a private wine tasting for us and some friends at the wonderful wine shop up the road. He'd invited George, Guy, Anna and her boyfriend, Gill and the chap she was currently dating, Liz and Dina. Everybody had been asked to assemble at our house at seven that evening for a glass of something bubbly and a few Indian snacks from the deli up the road. He really had thought of everything. I kiss him and thank him and he points out that, so far I only know about one of the two surprises that he has planned.

"And when do I get to hear about the other one?" I ask playfully, wondering what else it could be, given that he'd already so thoughtful.

"After you've taken off all your clothes and shown me just how grateful you are to have such a lovely boyfriend." And so I do…

Afterwards, I'm still lying under the duvet, basking in the afterglow, while Carl is up straight away and obviously on a mission. He races downstairs, reappearing five minutes later with my laptop. He looks like a kid at Christmas, obviously very pleased with himself for what was to come next.

"Log onto your emails," he instructs, passing the laptop to me. I comply and find an email waiting in my inbox from him, simply entitled, 'Open Me'. I follow these instructions and open it to find a link with the instruction 'Click On Me xxx'. I click on the link and the screen opens up to show a holiday site with details of a lovely-looking hotel in my favourite place in the world – Marsa

Alam in Egypt. Could he really have done this? As I am looking at the hotel and the description of the coral reef that it sits next to, my laptop alerts me that I have a new email from Carl.

"Pack your snorkel – we leave in 10 days xxx"

I'm lost for words. When he hears my squeal of delight, Carl comes back into the room and grins at me. "You like?" he asks.

"Like?" I reply, still not quite sure how to express the absolute pleasure that it coursing through me veins. "No," I say. "I don't like, I LOVE! You incredible, generous, wonderful man!" And with that, I throw my arms around him. He tells me about the booking and how he researched the hotel to find the one with the best coral and marine life. He tells me about the different places to eat in the all-inclusive paradise we're going to be inhabiting and the things that we can do while we're there. To my amazement, he tells me that he's decided to try diving. Whenever we've been to the Red Sea before, Carl has always been much more confident that me in snorkelling but has never quite built up the courage to do a proper dive. This time, the thought that he's going to be diving with me and marvelling at the life in the coral with me is music to my ears.

I spend most of the rest of the day grinning. I open my other cards, including a lovely card and present from Mum and Dad, a funny one from Rosie and Harvey, one from Gill telling me that she's looking forward to sampling the wine with me tonight, one from Alex saying that she's sorry that she can't be there tonight but she hopes that we have a lovely time, one from Liz and Dina which also includes our official invitation to their civil ceremony in the summer and one from Sarah which is lovingly signed, 'Best wishes from Sarah, Ronald and family'.

And so it's time for the evening's festivities to begin. Around seven, people start to arrive. George is first, carrying a spectacular birthday cake. His culinary skills are beyond compare and, every year without fail, he brings a cake. This year he's excelled himself: he's made a scale model of Jess the cat with liquorice bootlace whiskers and a Smartie for her little pink nose. Guy follows closely behind him, regaling us with stories of the football match he's been filming that day where the two managers had fisticuffs on the touchline. Given that his camera was positioned on the half-way line of the same side as the managers' dugouts, he heard the whole thing and said that the only thing missing was handbags.

By the time that Anna and Jon, Liz and Dina and Gill and her new man, James arrive, Guy and George have already started on the Cava they found in the fridge and cut into the Jess cake. They are deep in conversation about the outrageous way that Salford City Council are treating local landlords and both threaten to stand as Councillors in the next elections. The thing is, I could imagine George as Prime Minister one day. He has it all planned out, with me as his chief spin doctor. I'd vote for him but I'm definitely not the right choice for spin doctor. I couldn't cope with the nastiness and back-biting: even if it's a tad naïve, I'd rather cling onto my belief in peoples' basic goodness.

We gently coax George and Guy back into the room and remind them that there are other people in their space. They reluctantly put aside their political aspirations, promising that they'll talk soon to plan how to take the political world by storm. As we chomp our way through a mountain of Indian nibbles and then demolish the rest of the Jess cake, the conversation starts to grow in volume and a group of people who only really come together when I'm around start to reconnect and remember the easy company that they all share so naturally .

When the food and drink has been decimated as if by a plague of locusts, the assembled crowd walks to the wine shop and arrives on the dot of eight, ready to be wowed by the waiting selection of South African wines. We start with a glass of sparkling white and then move onto three different whites – a Chenin Blanc, a Sauvignon Blanc (not really to my taste) and one I'd never heard of before called Bukketraube. It was delicious.

As the wine flowed, so did the conversation. We got to know a little more about Gill's new man, James, and we liked him. He and Carl really bonded over a love of all things zombie and a deep hatred of Manchester United. They were talking away so happily that, in the end, I (being stuck in the middle of the pair of them and being caught in conversations which went way over my head) swapped places with James so that they could continue their bromance in private.

It must have been quite daunting to meet a whole new group of old friends so early in a relationship. All credit to him, he held his own and was charming, interesting and interested. It's really good to see Gill happy and with somebody who obviously thinks a great deal about her.

After the three white wines, the cheese and biscuits came out. James uses the opportunity to nip outside for a quick smoke and meets Guy out there, already half-way through a crafty spliff. I'm no great lover of cheese but I satisfy myself by pinching all of the baby plum tomatoes and grapes which garnish the plates. Carl makes up for my lack of interest eating his share, mine and pretty much everyone else's too.

And then come the reds. The final one is quite probably the most orgasmically delicious wine I have ever had – the Estate Blend from the Rust en Vrede winery. If you ever get the chance, grab it with both hands and try it.

As we sit there, sampling the most delicious wines I have a self-indulgent moment where I look around me, listen to the hum of conversation and absorb the warmth that I feel surrounded by. Despite the fact that I spend most of my time feeling like a total screw up, I feel completely blessed for the people that are in my world.

It strikes me that I spend a lot of my time fretting about the relationships that cause me problems. It's a disproportionate amount of time given the grief that they give me – time that I could spend thinking about the positive influences around me. Why is it that, over the past couple of months, I have spent so much time worrying about my inability to connect with Sarah and my frustration with Call Me Babs? Why have I wasted so much time on things that have very little chance of changing? There and then, I pledge to change my focus.

After the formal tasting, our guide for the evening puts all the half-opened bottles onto the counter and invites us to take what we fancied by shouting, "Right then, you lovely, squiffy people – fill your boots!" Without standing on ceremony, there is a swell of movement towards the counter. Liz and Dina get there first and snaffle the rest of the Rust en Vrede…Damn! Carl comes back to the table with three quarters of a bottle of Pinotage and two glasses. Just as I'm about to thank him, he pours the two glasses, takes a sip out of one and hands the other to James. My face obviously displays my surprise because Carl smiles and says, "Sorry, baby but you know what they say – bros before hos!"

I throw a napkin at him in mock displeasure before spotting the half-bottle of sparking white that's still on the counter and I take it over to where Gill and Anna are deep in conversation. As I come close to them, I realise that I'm the current topic of conversation. I hang back for a minute and listen. For a moment, I feel paranoid and exposed but I know that they are both on my side. This is confirmed by what I hear.

"She's always so hard on herself," says Gill. "Never gives herself a break and accepts that she's only human. And that bloody sister of hers, such a judgemental old cow."

"I know," Anna agrees. "I wish that Sarah would accept that Eve's living the life that she wants, even if it doesn't fit Sarah's idea of what's good and proper."

I'm starting to feel like a bit of a voyeur and so it's time to announce my presence. "If you can find a way of making my sister understand me, I'd be eternally grateful. In the meantime, there's a bottle of bubbly with our names on it so let's drink it and toast Sarah's narrow view of the world."

And so we fill our glasses and raise them in toast. Almost in unison, the three of us make the ultimate toast. "Bollocks to her!" the three of us cry. "And all who sail in her," Gill adds. We all stop to consider this final addition and, after a minute, start giggling at the thought of anybody trying to sail, or in anyway, steer, my sister.

Just after midnight, it's time to shut up shop and go our separate ways. We say our goodbyes as the taxis arrive and all promise to meet up again soon. Gill and James are staying with us and so we walk somewhat gingerly home, all of us a bit wobbly and not quite as nimble as usual. When we arrive home, Carl takes James straight into the dining room to look at our collection of DVDs and Blu-rays. They are quickly comparing and contrasting their collections and one another's top ten films of all time. They agree about *Star Wars* and *Heat* but then start to negotiate what else should be allowed in.

"Sweet, isn't it?" Gill asked sardonically. "A match made in heaven. Am I going to have to ask permission before I make any decisions about where things are going between James and me?"

"I'm not sure you have an option now. There are three of you in this relationship now." I smile and add, "It's what's right for you, honey. Do you like him?"

She grins and nods and admits, "I'm potty about him. Feel like a fifteen-year old, thinking about him all the time and worrying about what to wear and what to say every time I see him. I even found myself doodling his name the other day. It's a good job that I don't have a pencil case anymore or it would be covered with his name and soppy lovehearts. Problem is, I have no idea what he thinks about me. I don't want to throw myself into this if it's a one-way thing."

"Want me to interview him and find out what his intentions are? I still have the hat my nan wore when she interviewed my Dad, so I'm fully equipped."

"Kind offer but I'll pass," Gill says, laughing. "I know it's soft but I really don't want to jinx anything."

"Well, he's put himself in the position of being here tonight when he didn't know a soul. He's been charming and made the effort to get to know your friends. That doesn't sound like the actions of a man who's going to disappear tomorrow. Anyway, maybe he realises that he's very lucky to be with you."

"Hmmm," Gill replies, "There is a chance that you might just be a bit biased."

"Just because I'm biased doesn't mean that I'm not right. Maybe the answer is to try and enjoy it without worrying about every little thing. And yes, I do recognise the hypocritical elements of what I'm saying."

By three o'clock, Gill and I are dead on our feet and ready for bed. The boys are still going strong. In fact, Carl has just got out his smoke gun, conical flasks and expensive whisky and is planning to make them both his signature cocktail, a Smokey Old Fashioned made from bourbon, maple syrup, bitters and oak smoke from the smoke gun. We kiss our respective men folk goodnight, tell them to play nicely together and then head upstairs to bed. It's been a lovely evening and, for a nice change, I'm thankful to be me.

Gill and James have to leave earlyish the next morning. Whenever there are people in the house with us, I'm awake far too early and find myself showered and emptying the dishwasher by eight. I settle down with a cup of Earl Grey and switch on my laptop to do a few nerdy puzzles while I wait for life to stir upstairs.

At about nine, I hear Gill trying to coax James out of bed and then hear the agonised groan in reply. "But my head hurts," he moans plaintively. "Please give me another hour at least."

"Sorry, hon," comes the reply, "You know I need to be back by midday. I know you've got a poorly head, so how about we bundle you up and put you in the car then you can sleep while I drive home?"

I didn't hear the reply, but ten minutes later, Gill is downstairs, followed by a very sleepy looking James. He isn't looking at his best.

"Cup of tea before you set off?" I ask.

"No thanks, hon. I'd better get him in the car so he can go back to sleep. We'll stop on the way if I get any signs of life before Birmingham. Thanks for a lovely evening though: I really enjoyed it."

As Gill is gently manoeuvring the very delicate James into the car, and he is rubbing his head where he banged it on the doorframe on the way in, James lifts his head and says, "Top bloke, that man of yours. Tell him I said goodbye and I'll be in touch. Great night, bloody brilliant night!"

And so, with a final wave, Gill and James head off home to Birmingham. Jess and I have a cuddle on the sofa and then I go upstairs to inspect the damage. Carl is splayed on the bed, dribbling. I sit down and stroke his hair. He murmurs in appreciation but there is no other response. I leave him to it. He deserves a good lie-in after all he's done to make it such a special birthday.

The good lie-in lasts until the early afternoon. In the meantime, I've managed to get the house back into semblance of order, finished off three killer Sudoku puzzles and drunk more cups of tea than I usually have in a week. Just after two, I hear the first stirrings from upstairs and go up to say hello.

I'm greeted with a pained grunt and what I think was "What time is it?" As Carl manages to open his eyes, his first question is, "Is James still here?"

He seems disappointed and turns over as if to go back to sleep. "Baby, it's gone two o'clock," I tell him. Just tell me what you want to do and then I'll leave you alone, okay?"

"Need sleep, head hurts." And so I find him a couple of ibuprofen and a glass of water. He swallows them dutifully then snuggles back under the covers.

"I think I'll go into town to get the last bits for our holiday. okay with you?" Carl nods, I kiss him on the forehead and go out to buy all of those girly things you can't possibly do without when you're going somewhere hot.

When I get back, Carl has risen from his pit and is sat on the sofa, draped in his dressing gown and my woollen wrap. He's turning on his laptop and looking determined.

"Hello, Mr Poorly Head," I say. "To what do we owe the pleasure of your company?"

"Had a message from James," he tells me without taking his eyes from the computer screen. "The season finale of *Walking Dead* is available to download. Got to see it so we can talk about it later."

How can a mere woman even try and compete with a new bromance and a zombie-filled season finale? I leave him to it and go for a nice long bath and a good book. When I emerge a couple of hours later, he is talking animatedly to James, discussing the nuances of the plot and speculating on what will happen in the next series. Carl isn't always that easy to get to know (I still wonder what led him to let me in so quickly and so completely) and so I'm happy that he's found somebody he connects with.

The rest of the evening is spent on the sofa in front of the TV, happily catching up on the stuff that Carl has downloaded.

The final days before we go away are spent frantically trying to make sure that I've tied up all the loose ends both at work and at home. By the time it's time for bed the night before our flight, I'm happy that everything has been taken care of. It's funny, usually I'm a definite 'fly by the seat of my pants' kind of girl. However, before a big adventure like this, I can't rest until I have everything sorted and I know that I've thought of everything. I guess that it's because I want to be able to glide effortlessly into the holiday with no potential hassles. Having said that, serenity isn't something that comes naturally to me and I've usually forgotten something.

But this time we seem to have remembered pretty much everything. When we get up the following morning, the cases are packed, passports are safely stowed in my handbag, the neighbours are all geared up to look after Jess while we're away and the airport taxi is on its way. Even though it's still early when we've checked in, we decide to treat ourselves at the champagne bar. Just one glass, but it felt like the right thing to do to start the holiday off in style.

Our good mood even manages to transcend some of the less amenable types crammed with us onto the budget flight to Marsa Alam. I thought that we were decadent having one glass at that time in the morning but some of our fellow travellers are well and truly trolleyed. I avert my eyes and just pray that they are not going to be in the same hotel as us. Carl and I are a bit antisocial at the best of times, but on holiday I really like to keep myself to myself. To drown out the drunken conversations behind us, I plug in my earphones and listen to music for most of the flight, pausing for a little snooze as we head across the Alps.

The push for visas and luggage at Marsa Alam airport is as chaotic as usual, but it isn't long before we are safely in our taxi and starting the 50km journey from the airport to our hotel near the coral reefs of Hamata. From what I can see, there is only one decent road from the airport to the area's hotels, a very long road which goes from the airport and then up and down the coast. The scenery isn't too inspiring –mainly sand and rocks with the odd half-finished building to punctuate the desert – but I'm just happy to be back in Egypt and within hours of my first snorkel.

Since Carl and I met, we've developed a real passion for the coral reefs and myriad life forms of the amazing underwater world. We've travelled along most of the Egyptian coastal areas, finding Sharm el Sheikh too commercialised for our tastes and then settling on Marsa Alam for its unspoilt beauty, wonderful people and truly inspiring underwater life. This is our third visit to the area and we're feeling brave this time: we're going about as far south as it is possible to go and staying near the corals around Hamata. From all the research that Carl has undertaken, it seems as though we're in for something truly spectacular.

After a little more daydreaming, the taxi arrives at the hotel. First impressions are that it's beautiful: smart and quiet and relaxed. After we have checked in, we are taken to our room and are delighted to find that the view from the single-storey room looks straight out over the water. We're about as close to the shoreline as we could be.

"Come on then, out with it!" Carl says, knowing exactly what's going on in my head. "I can see you getting impatient, woman."

Without needing any more encouragement, I say, "Let's go for a snorkel! SO excited. Can we go now? Can we, can we, can we?"

Carl had anticipated exactly what I was going to say and was busy packing a beach bag with our snorkels and underwater camera. We both wriggle out of our clothes which felt a bit grimy after the flight and threw on our swimming gear ready to plunge into the reef. I feel like a kid at Christmas and bound down the steps to the beach. I'm halfway to the water's edge when Carl reminds me that we need towels. We pick up the towels, find a place to set up camp, check the snorkels and then make our way along the pier to the water. The sun is so hot that the wooden pier is scorching: I'm glad I decided to wear my flipflops. Carl hadn't made the same choice and was dancing along the pier, trying to avoid searing the flesh on the soles of his feet.

As we walk along, I get a sense of just how good the reef is likely to be. Even in the shallow water, I spot a pair of butterfly fish, a blue spotted ray and a lion fish skulking behind one of the pier supports. When I arrive at the end of the pier, Carl has been there for a while, soothing his poor feet in the pools of water left by other people getting out of the water.

"okay, so first big decision," he says. "Do we go off the left side or the right side?"

"You choose," I say, not minding which side we went as long as I was in the stunning turquoise water. He chooses left.

We climb down the metal ladder, check the depth of the sea beneath us and then plunge into the water. Immediately, we are transported to another world – a world which thrives and flourishes despite our humans attempts at its destruction. A few little black and white sergeant major fish swim up to check us out. Then we see what we have half expected, several sohal surgeonfish – or 'bastard fish' as they're sometimes known. According to all the guides, they are not particularly dangerous but they look evil, as if they're always spoiling for a fight. They are usually found patrolling the edge of the coral, protecting their young. They quickly see off any other fish who wander into their patch and seem more than content to do the same to any stupid human who gets too close.

Just the sight of them makes me nervous and it takes me a few seconds to regain my confidence. We swim past them and find ourselves in a lagoon of coral. The water is only about three metres deep and so we can see the bottom clearly. There is a family of blue-spotted rays wobbling along the bottom towards the wall of coral and then we spot a turtle swimming away from us over the top of the reef.

For the next hour we are in absolute heaven, getting to know the reef and marvelling at the teeming marine life that around us. When we eventually need to get out of the water for the sake of the water-tight seal on the underwater camera, I realise that, between us, we have taken over one hundred photos already. The beauty of the digital camera, of course, is that we can review them and delete the rubbish. I reckon that about seven in every hundred are worth keeping.

We go back to the room about five o'clock, shower and then flop back on the huge bed. I cuddle up to Carl and we go over what we've just seen and review the photos we've taken. We obviously haven't quite got our eye in yet, as only three out of all of the photos are worth keeping. Then we both drift off to sleep.

The next thing I know, I'm aware of the sun peeking through the gaps in the curtains. At first, I think that we are about to see our first sunset of the trip. However, having watched the sun for a few minutes, I realise that it is going up, not down. We have slept through the night. I check the time and it is just after six. I suddenly realise how hungry I am and then realise that breakfast doesn't start for another hour.

The sea is perfectly calm and the sun's rays dance over the horizon. The only sound is the whisper of the waves as they meet the shore and then a dragging as they're pulled away from the beach. I hear the sounds of conversation and see two guys removing the cordons from the pier's ladders. The reef seems to be open for business. I turn around to find Carl standing behind me, watching the water.

"So, what do you reckon?" he asks. "Shall we be first into the water today?" Without further hesitation, we grab our stuff and go. This time, we choose the right-hand side of the pier, which seems to be better given a total absence of bastard fish. We follow the coral ridge until we find a shallow area where the coral rises up in small islands and the fish congregate around them.

The early morning sunlight makes the water clearer and even more beautiful than ever. The fish are all up and about. We hear the purple and green parrot fish crunching at the coral. Carl spots a huge moray eel slithering between the islands of coral. He takes the camera and dives down to take a closer look. He surfaces after what seems like an eternity, grinning because he thinks he's caught it on video before it disappeared through a gap in the coral.

When we emerge from the water, it's clear that the hotel has woken up. The first sun worshippers have staked their claim on the sunbeds which line the shore and behind them, there is a man with a camel prowling along the sand, looking for his first tourists of the day.

After we've showered and changed, we set out to find breakfast. We're both very happy with what we find. Fresh fruit and creamy white yoghurt for me, followed by fresh pancakes and syrup. For Carl, it's a huge omelette packed with tomatoes, onions and peppers with a side order of beef sausages. Carl looks at the video he has taken of the moray and is pleased with himself. "Not a bad start," he says.

One of the waiters comes over as we're checking out the video and asks to take a look. "Did you see turtles?" he asks.

"We saw one in the reef yesterday," I answer, "But he was swimming away from us so we didn't get too good a look at him. Are there a lot of turtles around here?"

"Not a lot in the reef," he says "But there is special place with family of very big turtles. You want to know where?"

The answer to this is a big fat yes, and the waiter describes the place to us. After breakfast, we head straight there. We walk down the beach for almost a mile until we reach a secluded bay. The place is deserted with a half-built hotel near the shore. There is a small reef of coral to one side, but the rest of the bay is sandy and covered in the sea grass so loved by the turtles.

After leaving our stuff on a rock on the beach, we wade into the water and start our search. We swim for about fifteen minutes, looking for the shadows that suggest the turtles' presence, and then we see our first signs of turtle life. We swim closer and, to our delight, find three turtles together, happily chomping away at the sea grass. We approach them slowly, not wanting to disturb or distress the family. They are giant green turtles. Two are about a metre across and the other about half the size.

They look up and register our presence and return to their chomping. Carl and I hang in the water, watching and marvelling at how these beautiful creatures are allowing us into their space. I think that we both have a bit of a moment at the same time because, just as I'm getting very soppy about the sheer beauty of what we are experiencing, Carl reaches across and holds my hand. After about half an hour, the turtles obviously decide that it's time for the next part of their daily routine. They leave the patch of sea grass and start to swim away from the shore. We leave them to their day, thankful for the fact that they have let us into their world.

As we walk back along the shore towards the hotel, we can't stop talking about what we've just witnessed and the privilege of it all. Back to the hotel, we shower off the dried sea salt and grab a beer. We settle onto a couple of sun beds and start to plan our next adventure. If it wasn't for the fact that our camera needs to be out of the water for about twenty minutes every hour, I think we'd be in the water all day.

By the time we head back to our room that night, we've been on five little adventures around the reef and taken about four hundred pictures that'll some serious editing. As I'm getting ready for my final shower of the day, Carl comes into the bathroom and shrieks with laughter.

"Haha! Snorkeller's bum!"he laughs.

I reach down to feel the skin on the back of my legs where my thigh meets my bum. It's quite tender. I look in the mirror and see that it's bright pink.

It's an occupational hazard, snorkeller's bum. It happens to me every time. When you're face down in the water all day, your bikini bottoms have a habit of riding up. The sun hits these bits of unexposed flesh and burns them. Blissfully unaware in the water, you don't notice until the damage is done.

After I've showered, Carl has just about finished laughing at me and he plasters after sun on the offending areas.

After a brief siesta we head for dinner in the hotel restaurant. Because the area is so remote and life is really restricted to the hotels, there isn't really a lot of choice – or, indeed, any choice – about where to go to eat. It's not going to be a problem, though as the food is fantastic and there's so much variety on offer that there's no chance of getting bored.

Once we've eaten our fill and I've managed to drag Carl away from the incredible array of deserts and pastries, we have a drink on the terrace. By now, the moon is out and the sky is full of bright stars. Given that we're in Egypt, we order a shisha pipe and puff away on the apple-flavoured tobacco until all of the coals are burnt out. Despite the enthusiastic cajoling of the " animation team"

we manage to avoid the evening's show. As we walk back to the room we can hear it in full flow, the thump, thump, thump of some instantly forgettable Euro pop tune and the regular 'whoa!' shouts of the performers.

As we get into the room, the white sheets of the big bed are enticing. The sensuous feeling of the crisp bed linen soothing our still-hot skin is too much of a temptation. I reach over to Carl and he responds instantly, touching my skin and kissing me deeply. Feeling him so close to me, on top of me, inside me, is the perfect end to a perfect day.

We drift off to sleep. Despite feeling calm and relaxed, my dreams are nothing of the sort. I dream that I'm trying to reach the water's edge to go snorkelling but I keep being diverted from the shore. I try to get back to the water but the harder I try, the further away from the water I seem to be.

Over the course of the night, the dream repeats endlessly. The only thing that changes is the person directing me away from the water. First, it's Sarah. Then, it's Call Me Babs. Then it's me: I'm leading myself away from the place I want to be. I wake up while it's still dark and find myself drenched in sweat. I try to get back to sleep but the dream keeps coming back. Just before dawn, I give up, sit on the terrace and watch the sun come up.

We quickly fall into a routine, an early morning swim, breakfast, visiting the turtle family and spending the rest of the day exploring the reef. In the evenings, we have dinner followed by a drink and some shisha under the stars. I feel peaceful and about as far away from the real world as it's possible to be. Although it's tempting at times, I don't switch on my phone. Anna, Gill, Alex and George have all said that they won't contact me so there's no point switching it on. I know when I'm being told off and I comply with their instructions. After all, if there's an emergency, I've left the hotel number with several people, so it's not like we're completely incommunicado.

The only thing that bothers me is the recurring dream. Night after night, I'm trying to get to the water. Night after night, people – usually me – stop me from getting there. I talk about the dream to Carl and he thinks that I'm frustrated about something and feel as if I'm preventing myself from moving forward in some way. I think that he's probably right but I'm not sure what it is that I'm being prevented from doing.

On the fourth day, Carl makes an announcement. He wants to try diving. I'm delighted: I've always wanted us to be able to dive together. We head to the dive school and ask to book in for a trial dive. There's a free slot that afternoon. We sign up before Carl can change his mind.

I can tell that Carl's becoming a bit nervous. At lunchtime, he forgoes his usual couple of beers and eats salad instead of the usual pizza. I know better than to tease him, wanting to make sure that he feels as comfortable as he can do. I know it's a big deal for him.

Carl's nerves are temporarily forgotten when I emerge from the changing rooms in the wetsuit that I have been given. It is about a foot too long for me and I need turn-ups to stop me tripping over. We sit through the briefing and then make our way to the pier with our instructor. We climb down the ladder and then the instructor goes through the final safety drill. Carl looks uncertain when the instructor tells him to remove his mask underwater, but he does it. The sense of achievement is written all over his face. Despite a few problems with his breathing and controlling whether he goes up or down in the water, Carl quickly takes it in his stride and we are ready to explore.

The next hour goes by in a flash. I love watching Carl discover a whole new world. He's much braver than me when it comes to diving down with his snorkel. I'm much more of a surface girl and leave the acrobatics to him, but I can see him marvelling at the different perspective that diving gives him. We follow turtles and spot an eagle ray flapping majestically through the water. For a while, we follow a shoal of squid with their huge eyes and strange backwards swimming motion, and then Carl's attention is caught by an outcrop of coral which is used by the bigger fish as a cleaning station. We watch the tiny, brilliantly coloured clearer wrasse as they tend to their heavyweight customers, cleaning their gills and making them pristine again. Carl spots a barracuda waiting its turn to be cleaned and goes to investigate. They scare me so I hang back. Just the sight of their sharp teeth is enough to have me swimming in the opposite direction.

When we surface onto the pier, Carl is elated and bursting with energy. He wants to talk about every second of the experience and to know why I've never told him how amazing diving really is. I have told him, or tried to tell him, but I guess that it's one of those things that everybody has to find out for themselves.

On the afternoon of our last day, I start to feel an unexpected wave of sadness crash over me. When we come out of the water for the final time, I know that it'll be a while before I feel this free and alive again. We talk about this when we are having our final shisha pipe under another perfectly clear, starlit sky.

"So, what can you take back with you from the past week to help you in real life?" Carl asks. A very good question. What is it about being here that makes everything so much better?

"I feel like the best version of me right now," I reply after a while. "I feel as though it's okay to be me and that I'm appreciated for being who I am."

"And you don't feel like that at home?"

"When I'm with you, I do. And when I'm with my friends, the people who really know me. But when I feel as though I'm being scrutinised for who I am and the way I choose to be, I don't. I just want to be myself but I often feel as though that's not enough."

"Believe me, Evie," Carl says, taking a lungful of shisha and blowing it out like his best Puff the Magic Dragon impersonation, "Being you is enough and the only person who seems to think otherwise is you."

"The only person apart from my sister or Barbara," I say ruefully.

"Fair point, but what do they matter in the grand scheme of things?"

I wish they didn't matter and I wish that I didn't let them matter quite so much.

We are up very early the next morning to take the long trip back to catch our plane home. The inbound plane is about an hour late arriving, which means that we are later still leaving. As we wait in the uncomfortable airport seats, scanning for news of our departure time and finding nothing, I give in. I check my phone. I've taken my emails off the Blackberry and so don't know what's been going on at work, but that's okay until tomorrow.

Two texts come through. The first is from the dentist reminding me about the appointment the following week. The second is from Rosie.

"When u talk 2 Mum, don't believe her when she says it's your fault. I've made my own decisions and she's going have 2 get used 2 it. Luv u xxx"

Oh great, what am I going back to? I tell Carl and he takes the phone off me and turns it off.

"Whatever has happened has happened and there's nothing that you can do about it now. Sarah's always gunning for you for some reason and it's about time that she realised her daughter has a mind of her own."

"Maybe I could reply to Rosie to find out what's happening?" I suggest.

"You could, but you're not going to because I have your phone. We're still on holiday until we wake up in our own bed tomorrow morning and I want to spend those last few hours with my Marsa Alam Evie. okay?"

I nod. It is okay and I want to hold onto that version of me for as long as I can. Carl keeps the phone until we're back at home and I do my best to put it out of my mind.

It's just a shame that real life can't wait just a little bit longer.

CHAPTER FIVE

The Explosion: Part Two

Waking up in our own bed, without the sounds of the sea or the promise of a day exploring the underwater paradise, feels strange. As I'm slowly coming to, Jess comes into the bedroom, squawking for food. When we arrived home the previous evening, she followed her usual routine of punishing us for leaving her: five minutes of love and cuddles, then ignoring us for the rest of the night.

This morning, feline pragmatism has obviously kicked in again as she is hungry and knows she needs us. I can't resist those beautiful big green eyes or the way she rubs her face against mine and so I get out of bed, put on my dressing gown and go downstairs to feed her. One of the things we realised very quickly about Jess is that she likes conversation. She likes to be talked to. So, as I open a tin of tuna for her – an unashamed guilt offering for the fact that we've been away and, in her eyes, a big step up from usual cat food – I tell her all about the fishes we've seen and the adventures we've had. As soon as the plate of tuna is on the floor, she loses interest in my stories and concentrates instead on wolfing down the food.

Neither Carl nor I are working today and so we can ease ourselves back into normal life. With a cup of tea in hand, I settle down to catch up on emails.

There's the usual crap which seems to come through daily – offers for teeth whitening and penis extensions – but also some good news. A piece of work we tendered for before I went away has been successful. Not a huge contract but enough to keep us gainfully employed for the next month or so. So far, so good.

Then I see that I've two emails from Sarah. She never gives her messages a title so I have no idea what to expect. I take a deep breath and open the first one, sent the day after we left for Egypt. It's an invitation to her and Ronald's 25th wedding anniversary lunch in about three weeks' time. I look at the distribution list and it's as expected – Mum and Dad, Carl and me, their friends Val and Tony – except that she's also invited Barbara and her husband Peter. Deep joy. As well as the formal invitation, there is a message from Sarah:

"Eve, please remember that we are meeting at the golf club where our membership is very important to both Ronald and me. Please ensure that you both dress appropriately and uphold the club's standards."

I show the email to Carl and he snorts derisively. "If she thinks I'm going out to buy a nasty Pringle sweater for the occasion, she has another think coming. Does she really believe we can't work out how to behave? Honestly, Eve, I know she's your sister and everything but sometimes she really does need to climb out of her own backside and join the real world."

I might have chosen different words, but I really can't argue with the sentiment. I plough on and open the second email, wondering if it's a copy of the golf club's rules and procedures. Given that neither of us plans to wear shorts, I can't see that the rule about knee-length socks is going to be applied. When I read it, I wish that it had been about something so trivial.

"Eve, thank you once again for meddling in my family. Thanks to you, Rosie is determined to pursue a career which Ronald and I believe is beneath both her and the social standing that her father and I have worked so hard to build up. In future, when you're having your little rebellions, please do so away from me and my family."

What? I'm guessing that Rosie has broken the news about her dream to have a career in social work. I'm also guessing that she has told her mother, probably in the heat of an argument, that Auntie Eve thinks it's a great idea.

While I'm pondering this and the next move to make, another email pops up – from my Dad. It's simply entitled 'Good Hols?' I open it straight away and feel a flood of warmth.

"Hello, Eve.

Are you back safely? Hope you've had a lovely time and been able to relax properly. Mum and I are around all day if you have chance to give us a ring.

Lots of love, Dad xxx"

I pick up the phone straight away and call my folks. My Dad answers. "Hello, sweetheart. I was hoping it would be you. How are you? Did you both have a good time?"

We chat for ages about the holiday and about their life. My Mum and Dad are both in their sixties but very active and not 'of their age'. Dad tells me that he's already been swimming that morning and that they're having some friends round for lunch. Then we talk about music. He's been downloading music from my Amazon Cloud account and both of them have got really into Matchbox Twenty, one of my all-time favourite bands. This is good to hear as I have secretly bought them both tickets to go to see them with me in about six months' time.

Matchbox Twenty have this uncanny ability to express in their lyrics so many of the things that I feel. The lyric that dominates most of my life is from the song, 'Unwell':

"I'm not crazy, I'm just a little unwell. I know, right now you can't tell, but stay a while and maybe then you'll see a different side of me. I'm not crazy, I'm just a little impaired. I know, right now you don't care, but soon enough, you're gonna think of me and how I used to be."

And then, there was the lyric from 'Rest Stop' which made me realise that the relationship with the guy I was with before Carl was doomed:

"While you were sleeping, I was listening to the radio and wondering what you're dreaming, when it came to mind that I didn't care. And I thought, hell if it's over, I had better end it quick or I could lose my nerve."

I guess that they just speak to me and make me feel that I'm not on my own. After fifteen minutes of pleasant conversation with Dad, I feel I can't put it off any longer and I ask about Rosie and Sarah.

"Oh I don't know really," Dad says. "Rosie seems to be dead set on this social work thing and your sister has decided that it's not good enough for her."

"And what do you think, Dad?" I ask.

"I think that Rosie should do what makes her happy, but I'm not sure that Sarah sees it the same way. She's a bright girl and she wants to do something useful. Where's the harm in that?"

"I agree. She knows what she wants and that's a rare thing for people of her age. I've had an email from Sarah implying that it's all my fault. Any idea why?"

"I don't know, love. I guess she needs to blame somebody and she's chosen you."

We carry on talking for another five minutes, mainly about the steam train trip that he has planned for the following weekend, and then my Mum comes into the room and asks Dad if there's any chance that she could talk to me too. Dad says his goodbyes and hands over the phone.

"Hi Mum! How are you?"

"Hello, love. I'm very well, thank you. Keeping busy in the herb garden at the moment. Everything's just starting to come into bloom so it's time to start harvesting."

I'm convinced that my Mum was a white witch in a previous life. She is so in tune with nature and concocts all kinds of lotions and potions to cure a whole range of ailments. When we were growing up, we had to be careful whenever we raided the fridge as we might well end up with comfrey ointment on our toast instead of lemon curd. Her herb garden is her pride and joy and the source of many new inventions. It's left me with a working knowledge of medicinal plants and the firm belief that the application of comfrey can cure just about anything.

We talk about her plans for the plants that she harvests and about her new Yotam Ottolenghi cook book which has introduced her and Dad to the wonders of tofu with black peppercorns… It's not surprising that I've developed a love of different types of food, given my role models. Sometimes, I think that I was born British by mistake and my love of chilli and garlic is from another place. What does surprise me is that Sarah has such conservative tastes, a serious meat and two veg girl.

"I heard you talking to Dad about Rosie," Mum says in a swift change in direction.

"Yes, I had a text from Rosie while I was away and then an email waiting for me from Sarah. I still don't really know what's going on, but I think that a conversation with Sarah is on the cards."

"I think you're right. I'm not sure why she is blaming you, but she has taken it very badly."

"Taken what badly? What exactly happened?"

"There was a careers day at the school to help the students decide about their university choices. Rosie spent a lot of time talking to the social worker there and wanted to know about the best places to study. She came home and told Sarah and Ronald that she wanted to go to Sheffield to study. I think that Sarah had high hopes for her going to Oxford or Cambridge. They started arguing and Rosie walked out, telling Sarah that she'd do what she wanted and that Sarah should accept the fact that she was a real person, not somebody who was there to fulfil all the things that Sarah never managed to do. She disappeared for the night, went to stay with a friend and that's as much as I know. I just hope that they manage to sort it all out for everybody's sake."

"Yeah, it's not going to be too much fun at their anniversary do if that big black cloud is hanging over us all."

"I know, love and I know that you want to support Rosie. But Sarah is really struggling with this. She's feeling as if Rosie is rebelling for the sake of it. She just wants the best for her children."

"I know that, Mum, but the best for them isn't always what Sarah thinks it is. I think I need to talk to her, don't I? I want to help both of them."

"Yes, give her a call. We'd both be pleased if you do. Now, about this anniversary party. Would you and Carl like to stay over here to save you having to drive back?"

"That would be lovely," I say. "Thank you. I'm going shopping next week for a twinset and pearls so that I blend into the golf club crowd."

"Oh Eve, there's no need to be like that. Sarah just wants everything to go well."

"okay, I'm sorry. I just don't like being told that I'm not capable of rising to the occasion and being appropriate for the situation."

Then the conversation changes back to our time in Egypt. Mum is pleased to know that Carl enjoyed his dive and she really wants to see our videos of the turtle family. I tell her I'll post them on Facebook when I get off the phone. We say our goodbyes and I promise to keep her posted about conversations with Sarah.

I put off calling Sarah, convincing myself that I've promised to post up our best underwater videos and I'm therefore honour-bound to do this first. Rubbish delaying tactics, but they work for half an hour or so.

Carl comes in when I'm looking at the phone and willing myself to dial Sarah's number.

"What's up?" he asks breezily.

"I need to call Sarah but I keep putting it off," I reply, grimly.
"No time like the present, I guess. What are you going to say?"

"I haven't really thought about it. I'm hoping that the inspiration will find me when I open my mouth."

"Well, just remember that she can't hurt you unless you let her."

"Wise words indeed. Could you maybe repeat them to me when I get off the phone?"

And so, with no further ado, I dial the number. Sarah answers in her sing-song tone which I've always liked. However, when she found out that it was me, the tone changed.

"And what can I do for you?" she asked stiffly.

"I've read your email and I want to talk to you. I especially want to know what I can do to help."

"I think that you've done more than enough already, thank you very much," Sarah said. I could hear the pout in her voice.

I have to have a little chat to myself at this point and persuade myself that being defensive wasn't a good ploy. From the sound of Sarah's voice, there was no way that I was going to be able to justify my actions – whatever my actions were.

"Sarah, I called so that I can understand what's happening and do what I can to resolve things. I'm not your enemy. I just want to know what's happened and then work with you to figure out if I can do anything to help. Please, talk to me."

"Well, I suppose you already know all about it anyway from your pal, my daughter. What's the point in going through it all again?" That pout is still in evidence in every syllable.

"Sarah, I don't know anything. I only arrived back in the country late last night and I wanted to talk to you before anybody else." I guess that bit isn't strictly true, given the conversation I've just had with Mum and Dad, but I did want to talk to her before I contact Rosie. "Please, Sarah?"

"After having her head filled with nonsense by both you and the social worker she met at school, Rosie is now hell-bent upon being a social worker."

"What makes you think that I've been filling her head with anything? She's a headstrong girl and I'm not sure that I or anyone else could persuade her to do anything that she didn't want to. She's told me about wanting to do social work and she explained why. She wants to do something that makes a difference."

I can hear Sarah wanting to interject and so I stop talking. There seems little point when she has stopped listening.

"Make a difference?" Sarah snaps. "She could make a difference by being a doctor or a lawyer, a profession with some kind of credibility. I don't want my daughter walking around those grubby council estates and talking to undesirables. What would people think?"

"Maybe people would think that Rosie is doing something worthwhile and something to help others."

"The kind of people you know, maybe," she said. "But it's hardly fitting for someone who moves in our social circles, is it?"

I really don't know what to say to this. Actually, I really do know what to say but every option I can think of would only inflame the situation, something that I want to avoid. And so, I elect that the best option is to turn the focus back onto Sarah rather than share my opinions.

"I can tell that you're very upset by what's going on and I'm sorry if you think it's my fault. What is upsetting you the most about it all?"

"What isn't upsetting me about it? My daughter wants to choose a career that is beneath her, I'm being painted as the big bad witch whereas darling Auntie Eve is the heroine because she understands and encourages. It's bloody easy to understand from where you're sitting, isn't it? You can give your opinion and then disappear into the night. It's Ronald and me who have to deal with the reality of all of this and with the disappointment, and of course, Ronald and I who are expected to pay for university so that she can spend three years studying for a job with few prospects and not much money."

okay, now we're getting somewhere. She's feeling as though I have usurped her role. Have I done that? If I have, I need to do something to restore the balance. All I want to do is to support Rosie. However, I understand what it must be like from Sarah's perspective.

"Sarah, have you and Rosie been able to talk about this without getting angry? Have you heard about why she wants to go into social work? She talks about it with such passion that it's actually really moving. She genuinely cares about people and wants to make life better for them. Isn't that something that we should listen to?"

The tut in Sarah's voices alerts me to the fact that I appear to have crossed another line.

"You can say what you like, but no daughter of mine is going to give up all the opportunities she has been given just to waste her life. And, in future, I'd like you to keep your nose out of things that don't concern you. Understand?"

Again the options of what to say next come flooding into my head, but all seem inappropriate. I don't want to give Sarah the satisfaction of being able to complain about anything that I said to her. I know she'll probably complain anyway, but I don't want to give her any reasonable cause to.

"Sarah, I'm sorry that you think that members of my family are not my concern as I care deeply about what happens to all of you. I was hoping that I could help and listen when Rosie needs someone to bounce ideas off. I won't court Rosie's attention and encourage her to be disloyal, but neither will I turn her away if she needs me. I really hope that you can find a way to talk things through with her; I know that she wants to share her ideas and her dreams with you."

"When she decides to find some dreams that better fit the person we have brought her up to be, I will listen with pleasure. The thing is, Eve, neither Ronald nor I want her to turn out like you and we will do our damnedest to make sure that that doesn't happen. Now I'm late for my hair appointment, so goodbye!"

And with that, the phone went dead.

Even after Sarah has hung up, I stare at the phone in disbelief. Does my own sister really think so badly about me? Am I one of the 'undesirables' that she was describing? I really don't know what to say, or what to think.

I go upstairs to find Carl: I need someone to help me to work this one through. I remember Carl's words about Sarah only being able to hurt me if I let her, but she has hurt me.

I recount the conversation to Carl, remembering it almost word for word. That's one of the things that really annoys him about me when we argue... I remember words and I quote them back when they support my point. When they don't, I forget them.

When I finish, he asks me how I'm feeling now. How am I feeling now? Shocked that my sister has such a low opinion of me, frustrated that I can't find a way to persuade Sarah to listen to her daughter and torn between wanting Rosie to know that she has someone to depend upon and not wanting to get in the way of mother and daughter.

"What do I do now?" I ask Carl.

"How about absolutely nothing?" he suggests. "Whatever you do, you're not going to win so maybe it's time to go into self-preservation mode."

"But what about Rosie?" I must sound like a petulant child but I really don't know where to turn.

"So, you said to Sarah that you wouldn't go out of your way to talk to Rosie but that you wouldn't turn her away, right?" he asks.

I nod and he says, "So, wait and see if Rosie contacts you and then decide what to do. That way, you're keeping your promise to Sarah but you're also there if Rosie needs you. In the meantime, put those hateful things out of your head. Far from being ashamed, Sarah should be proud if Rosie turns out to be like you."

"I love you, Carl," I say and I mean it. It's the only thing I can say in that moment.

I'm hoping that Carl's masterplan will give me a little respite and time to think about other things. However, less than an hour later, a text comes through from Rosie.

"Spoken to Mum then? I heard her talking to Dad about it. U okay?"

okay, so I did say that I wouldn't turn her away if she needed me and so I'm not about to ignore her text.

"Yeah, I'm okay. I know I'm not going to win this one. I'm more worried about you. How are you? Sounds like the social work idea isn't popular. Big hugs xxx"

Rosie replies almost straight away.

"Had enough. Can't she understand that I'm not like her and I don't want to be? Stupid bloody woman!"

So how do I respond to this? If I don't pull her up about what she said about her Mum, am I doing exactly what Sarah is accusing me of? On the other hand, if I do, will Rosie stop talking to me? I decide to go for the half-way, humorous approach.

"Hey, that's my sister you're talking about (!) Am worried about you, honey. Is there any way that you can make her listen and understand? Don't give up but be kind to her – she's worried about you too. Want to talk about it? xxx"

Rosie picks up the phone and calls me. She tells me how she came home after the careers day buzzing with ideas but was met with a stone wall. She says that Sarah left the room and told her that she didn't want to discuss it because it wasn't going to happen.

"So what did you do?" I ask.

"I packed a bag and went to stay with a friend. I couldn't stay there with that attitude. She won't listen to me. It's all about what she wants for me, not what I want for myself. Why won't she just stop and listen to me? It's all about what the neighbours will say and what she can boast about at the golf course. I'm not going to be a puppet that helps her to live the life that she wants for herself."

I'm sure that she has more than a fair point, but I don't really want to go there. So, instead, I ask, "What happened when you went home?"

"She asked me if I had come to my senses and was ready to be reasonable. I told her that I'd already been reasonable but she was too caught up in herself to actually hear that. I told her that if she wouldn't listen to me, I'd talk to someone that would. I told her that you understood what I wanted to do and why I wanted to do it. I asked her why she couldn't be more encouraging like you are."

"I bet that went down well…"

"Nope. She told me that you were probably just trying to stir up trouble and be controversial by supporting me. I told her that you were supporting me because you listened to me and thought about what was best for me because you actually understand who I am and what I'm all about. She hasn't really spoken to me since then."

okay, so I guess that explains why this has all become my fault.

"And what has happened since?"

"Mum hasn't mentioned it.She hasn't really said anything to me but I've heard her talking to Dad about it and on the phone to Barbara."

I can just imagine that conversation.

"okay, so what do we do next?" I ask. "It seems to me that you need to find a way through it. You want to follow your dreams but you're kinda reliant upon your folks because they're going to be the ones footing the bill for your studies. How can we find a way to help them to understand how important it is to you?"

"I was hoping that you could tell me that," Rosie answered.

"When it comes to influencing your mother and getting her onside, I'm not sure I should be your role model. I can't seem to get it right, however hard I plan it and try to do the right thing."

"So you understand what I'm up against?"

"Yes, I do, I really do, but I feel so torn. I want you to be able to be the person that you want to be but I don't want to alienate Sarah in the process. I wish I had a winning formula for both of us. To be honest, I constantly feel as though I've failed because I can never find a way through."

Wow, that was honest and revealing. It's true though. I wish I could find a way to build a relationship with Sarah. She's my sister and I wish that I could be close to her.

"This is a completely inadequate thing to say," I admit, "But I wish I could give you a great big hug now. I know how important this is to you and I know that you know it's right for you. Maybe she thinks it's a dead end job. Do you know anything about career progression opportunities in social work? Do you know where you could end up in the role?"

"I'd never thought about that. If she thinks that I can rise up the ranks and do something that she would think of as 'important', maybe she'd buy into it a bit more. I knew that you've have the answer, Auntie Evie. You're a star. I'm going to go and research that right now. Thank you, love you, bye!"

And with that, Rosie was gone. I just hope that I haven't fanned the flames and led her on a wild goose chase that gets her nowhere. I really still haven't worked out how to play these situations, when to offer my opinion and when to keep quiet. I wasn't very good at corporate politics when I worked for organisations and I'm no better at family politics. I think I'm destined to put my foot in it with someone. My old mentor once told me that the most important thing was to be true to yourself and make decisions that you could live with. The problem is, although I can live with a lot of the decisions I make, other people don't seem to be able to. So what's the answer?

Over the two weeks leading up to Sarah and Ronald's anniversary lunch, I can feel the tension rising within me. What should be a nice family event feels more like a trip to the dentist for something nasty. Lying in bed at night, I can't stop rolling it all around in my head, thinking about Sarah and Rosie and Call Me Babs. I start to feel guilty that I told Rosie about Barbara's escapades with the football manager: I really shouldn't have done that. I imagine the conversations that Sarah and Barbara have been having and think about all of the things that they've been saying about me. Of course, in my head, it's never complimentary and I always come out as the villain.

When I talk to Carl about it, he asks me how much their opinion matters to me. He tells me that I shouldn't focus on what they think because they're not going to agree with my view of the world. Objectively, I know he's right and I know I shouldn't let it get to me. In reality, though, it becomes an obsession. I play out imaginary conversations where I have to justify everything I've said and done. Their opinion becomes central in my thoughts and I know that it's affecting my mood.

I feel myself becoming brittle, distant and over-critical. I go through my wardrobe and can't find anything that seems suitable for the lunch. I go on at Carl to make sure he's had a shave (his least favourite thing in the world) and tell him that he needs to make sure he has a decent shirt ready to wear. I warn him off certain controversial topics such as football managers with spotty bottoms and Rosie's career plans, topics that I know that he would naturally avoid without me having to tell him. In short, I become a control freak. If I were to analyse it, I'd say that I feel that I had no control over what would happen and so I'm clinging onto the parts I can control. Whatever I was doing, I am damned sure that I'm being impossible to live with.

I make a couple of decisions. The first is that I am not going to drink. Alcohol would only heighten the tension I'm feeling. I also decide that I'm going to find the perfect anniversary gift for Sarah and Ronald. I opt for a pair of silver-plated wine goblets. They like their wine and the goblets will be something that they can keep. I'm probably over-compensating but it feels really important for me to do this.

The night before the anniversary lunch, I'm going through my wardrobe once again, trying to find something sufficiently conservative but still with an essence of me in there. I decide upon a red dress with boots and a scarf, something I usually wear for work but I know is smart. It seems apt really, because the lunch feels like work to me and I have also decided that I need to be 'work me' for the occasion – considered, thoughtful, listening more that I speak and the social lubricant that keeps the conversation flowing. It feels as if I need to be the more socially acceptable version of me.

This plan is all very well, but it felt like I was going to have to hold my breath from start to finish. It's almost as though I don't trust myself to behave appropriately so I have to check everything I say and do. Is this what everybody else expects of me or simply what I expect of myself? Am I assuming that everybody else has the same expectations as me? Whether they do or not, I seem to have an iron grip on myself and I can't relinquish a single iota of control. This tight control means that I feel completely on edge and unable to relax.

In the car on the way to my Mum and Dad's, the tension is evident. As I'm driving later in the day, Carl offers to drive and I gratefully accept. However, within five minutes of leaving home, our favourite in-car argument starts. Carl has this habit of relentlessly criticising other people's driving. Usually, I tell him playfully to stop moaning and the world is alright again. Not today, though. In the first five minutes, he's condemned six other drivers and all I've heard about is every other road user's stupidity. I feel myself tighten and I stop talking. After several minutes of silence, he asks me what the problem is and I launch into it.

"Why is it that everything you say when you're driving is bad?" Carl opens his mouth to reply but I don't give him the chance to. "Do you know how negative you sound? Do you think that what you say has any impact on those you're criticising? No, it doesn't; the only impact is on me and believe me, it's not a good one."

"Here we go," says Carl, "You're all wound up about today and I cop for it on the way there. Just relax, will you? Neither of us is looking forward to this but we're going to do it. Alienating me isn't going to help, is it?"

I know he's right and I know that he needs my support to get through this as much as I need his. Carl and Ronald have very little in common and so conversation is awkward to say the least. Sarah doesn't like him at all and isn't very good at hiding that fact. So, given all this, I should have used the opportunity to calm down and let Carl know that we're on the same side. I didn't really achieve that.

"You might be driving, mate, but that doesn't give you the right to fill the car with all your negative crap. I don't want to listen to it, okay?"

Mate? That's not a good sign. I know that I only use that word when I'm trying to put distance between myself and the other person, to signify that I'm not close to them. Why am I trying to put distance between me and the one person that I'd always want beside me and on my side? This is worse than I thought.

After ten minutes of huffy silence, I get over myself and try building bridges.

"You're right. I'm sorry, I completely overreacted. I'm just so tense about this thing today. I haven't seen Sarah since everything blew up with Rosie and I know that she's putting a lot of the blame on me. I haven't seen Barbara since the hotel room and I'm still angry with her. None of it's your fault though, and I'm sorry."

By the time we reach Mum and Dad's we are friends again. Carl knows me too well and he recognises the signs when I am tense. I'm grateful that he is so forgiving. Could the day come when his patience runs out? Could he come to the conclusion that he's had enough and all the rubbish he gets from me really isn't worth the hassle?

We're early arriving at my folks' house and we have a time for a cup of tea before we set out. Their warm company helps me to relax a little and I actually manage a smile when my Dad describes his steam train adventure. From his account, I can almost smell the coal and hear the hoot of the whistle. My Dad's always been a steam train nut and we were brought up loving them too. In fact, when I was about four, I won a badge for knowing the difference between two famous engines. As I recall, it was something to do with the number of chimneys. My Dad's not your average train spotter: he replaces the obligatory cagoule with Jasper Conran and has the kind of camera that most of his fellow spotters would kill for. I could listen to him talking about the engines and his travels for ages. It makes me feel so close to him and takes me back to the times we used to share together.

Actually, it was my Dad who gave me my enduring affection for Blake's 7. We used to watch it together while my Mum was out and about. He had the hots for the female arch villain, Servalan. I think I lost my first tooth while we were watching it. If I was very lucky, he'd also make us he ultimate feast to accompany our viewing – a Vesta beef curry. Simple pleasures inspire the fondest memories.

Even though I'm interested in the conversation, I do realise that a part of me is prolonging it and asking questions to put off the inevitable. However, I notice that my Mum is starting to get twitchy which means that it's time to be on our way to the golf club. As much as I don't want to go, I also don't want to make my Mum late.

As we pull into the golf club car park, I start to feel uncomfortable, as though I'm arriving at an alien place where I'll struggle to fit in. This is partly due to my apprehension about seeing Sarah and Barbara, and partly the place itself. I've always thought of golf clubs asplaces where I really don't belong and will stick out like a sore thumb. An ex of mine was a keen golfer and loved the whole golf club culture. After we'd split up, he was made Captain of his club and called to tell me so.

"Just think," he gloated, "If you hadn't left me, you'd now be the Captain's girlfriend."

He meant it as a way of demonstrating the wrongness of my decision to split up. Maybe he never really knew me because it had the exact opposite effect and made me even more certain that it was one of the best decisions I've ever made!

I park the car and we all get out – all of us in our Saturday afternoon finery. My Mum, as usual, looks stunning and my Dad can only be described as elegant with a touch of funky. Carl comes over to me, holds my hand as we're walking, and winks.

"You're going to be fine, baby, and I'll be with you all the way."And with that, we walk into the clubhouse and Sarah and Ronald's anniversary lunch party. I can feel my nerves jangling. I feel myself wanting to scoff at the place's pomposity and take the mickey out of the whole thing. Classic uncomfortable Eve – I'm being critical for no reason to mask some of my discomfort.

The rest of the assembly are already in the bar – Sarah resplendent in powder pink frills, Ronald in his best sports blazer, Rosie and Harvey talking animatedly to one another and ignoring the others, their friends Val and Tony and, of course, Barbara and Peter. I feel my hand tighten around Carl's when I catch sight of Barbara.

Mum and Dad walk straight into the group and say their hellos. Carl and I hang back until they have done so.

"Come on then," Carl whispers, "Let's get this show on the road. Deep breath, most dazzling smile and in we go. Ready?"

I nod and we move into the group. Rosie and Harvey leap up to hug us both and we receive polite yet not unfriendly kisses on the cheek from both Val and Tony. Ronald moves in to say hello, shaking us both by the hand and thanking us for coming. So, time for Sarah. I readjust my smile and take her by the hand.

"Thank you for inviting us to such a happy occasion," I say to her. I go to kiss her but she subtly moves her head away. Message received and understood.

"Well, you are a part of the family," she says, warm as ever. "Carl, I really thought that you would be wearing a tie. You'll notice that all the other men are and it is expected here."

Rather than being fazed by this, Carl grins and fishes in his trouser pocket, producing a tie. He puts it on with a flourish and says, "Problem solved! Is that more acceptable, dear sister-in-law?"

I know that he chooses his words carefully as it is still a bone of contention with Sarah that we have never married. Sarah gives him a withering look and moves on to talk to someone else. Ah well, at least we have the first encounter out of the way. The only people that we haven't said hello to are Barbara and Peter. It feels churlish and immature but I cannot think of a thing to say to her. Luckily, Carl steps in.

"Peter! Good to see you, mate. How's it going?" He shakes Peter by the hand and then moves to Barbara. Today, she seems to be very much Barbara, rather than Babs. "Looking as expensive as ever, Barbara. How do you do it?"

Barbara smiles at what she perceives to be a compliment. Now is the time for me to do my bit.

"Hello, Barbara. How are you?

"Oh, you know, busy as ever. There's never enough time is there?"
Time for what exactly? Not work – she doesn't do that; not housework – she has a woman to do all of that. Stop it, woman, bitchy really doesn't suit you.

"Seemingly not. It's good of you both to be here to celebrate with Sarah and Ronald. Peter, how's business going?"

Tough times at the moment, Eve, but we're struggling through," he answers. "Sales are down but we've managed to make efficiency savings. I'll tell you about them over lunch if you like?"

"Sounds interesting, I'd like to hear more," I say. That's not strictly true but I feel sorry for Peter; he always seems to be overlooked and nobody appears to listen to him. I also feel a strange guilt for what happened in my hotel room in Birmingham.

"And what about Leeds this year, Carl?" Peter asks, steering the conversation onto comfortable ground for them both. "Time to start looking for a new manager, eh? A bit disappointing after such a promising start?"

"Yeah, damned right," Carl replies, "Not really what I was hoping for. At least we beat Spurs, eh, Evie?" he teases, digging me in the ribs.

I roll my eyes and stick my tongue out at him, but I know that it's all in good humour.

Before I can respond, Carl picks up the thread and says to Peter, "Your lot are having a better time of it with Chelsea. Shame about the FA Cup though, eh?"

I start to piece things together but need to ask a question to make sure. "You lost?" I ask him.

"Yes, unfortunately. Not only that, we lost to a second division team… total humiliation! You've got to give it to that John Parkin, though, he's had a great run. Just a shame they didn't make it to the final."

So, not only did Call Me Babs shag a football manager but then, to add insult to injury, her conquest's team beat her husband's team. Oh, it just gets better…

After another couple of minutes of football chat which has obviously completely switched off Barbara as she's gone to inspect the wooden plaques cataloguing previous Club Captains, Carl says, "Right, time for another drink I think. What can I get everyone?"

Between us, we take everyone's orders and I go to the bar to give Carl a hand. While we're waiting to be served, Rosie sidles up to Carl and links her arm into his. "Uncle Carl," she wheedles, "Have I ever told you that you're my very favourite uncle? You're so clever and handsome and ever so funny."

"Overlooking the fact that I'm you're only uncle and your mother would dispute that I am actually your uncle, given that we're still living in sin, thank you, Rosie. Now, what is it you're after?"
Rosie gives a feigned look of hurt, then grins and asks, "Any chance of a cheeky Malibu and Coke?"

"Hmmm, I'm not sure that I should be leading you astray, young lady. What do you think, Auntie Eve?"

They both turn to look at me. "Well, I'm tempted to say no, not on the grounds that you want alcohol but more because you want Malibu."

"Ooh, hark at Miss Judgemental!" Carl responds. "Just for that, Rosie, my love, I will buy you a Malibu and Coke with pleasure."

And he does, knowing that I would have done exactly the same. We rejoin the group, hand out the drinks and I go to sit next to Harvey. I haven't seen him for a while and I'm keen to know what he's up to.

"Harvey, my favourite nephew, how's your world at the moment? Any luck with the ladies?"

"Yeah, not bad. I've got a few girls chasing after me and I can't decide which I like best."

Carl butts into the conversation. "Why choose, mate?" he asks. "At your age, you're not exactly ready for marriage and kids so why restrict yourself to just one if you've got a queue of them after you?"

"I hadn't thought of that," Harvey replies thoughtfully. "You mean like take a couple of them out and see who I like best?"

"Precisely. Play the field, work out what you like, work out who's the best kisser." Now he's just being controversial.

"Is that what you did, Uncle Carl?" Harvey asks, obviously relishing the opportunity to enjoy the laddish banter that he probably doesn't get very often at home.

"Certainly did, only I wasn't as devilishly handsome as you so I usually had to take what I could get." He shot a glance at me and dared me to respond.

"And it that what you're still doing, darling?" I ask.

"Ah, well, you see," he starts, trying to get himself out of the hole that he had inadvertently dug for himself. "I was a late developer. Had to wait until I was in my thirties to meet someone worth keeping."

Reasonable rescue I suppose. I leave the boys to do the boys' talk and go and talk to my Mum who is sat nursing a Jack Daniels and ice.

"Everything seems to going well, don't you think?"
"Yes, Mum. We all want Sarah and Ronald to have a nice day."

"Your Dad gave in to Rosie and bought her a Malibu and Coke; we didn't think that one would hurt her."

"No, she's just about old enough to go into pubs anyway." I say, not wanting to tell Mum that Rosie had managed to con both of us into buying her a drink. At least it's not the strongest drink that she could have ordered.

We are all ushered into the dining room for lunch. Carl and I have already agreed that we are going to sit as far away from Barbara as we can manage so we wait for her to sit at one end of the table and then make our way to the opposite end. Again, I feel a little churlish, but I can't imagine being stuck next to her for the whole meal with so much anger still coursing around my veins. We are joined by Harvey and Rosie. Harvey makes a beeline for Carl and I'm pleased to be able to spend some time with Rosie.

I don't want to focus on her recent troubles with her parents but I do want to know how she is. I decide that I'll wait for her to introduce the subject if she wants to. I chase around for a question to ask which won't lead us straight to her future studies and settle on the least controversial that I can find.

"So, Harvey's discovered girls then?"

"Like you wouldn't believe. Carl's not going to be able to get away from him now. He can't talk to Dad about it so having Carl there is just heaven for him. You know, neither of us were ever given the 'birds and the bees' talk by either of them. I had to pick up everything I know from the girls at school."

"And does Harvey know everything he needs to know?" I ask, wondering if Uncle Carl might be called upon for a man-to-man chat.

"Well, he's certainly got a fair idea. The cleaning lady found a stack of porn magazines under his bed. That was an interesting evening, I can tell you. Mum just shouted about how disgusting it all was and how she was banning 'that filth' from her home and Dad disappeared until it was all over."

"So, your brother now thinks that all women should have massive boobs and be up for it at a moment's notice?" I ask. "Good luck to him with that one when he realises that there is a distinct line between fantasy and reality."

"Yeah, he'll learn soon enough. He does seem to be very popular with the girls at school though. Can't understand it myself."

"I'm sure that Carl will set him straight. It's just good that he's found someone that he can talk to."

We both look over at the two of them, talking ten to the dozen and Harvey hanging on Carl's every word. I was pleased that Harvey had found someone he could talk to. I'm not sure that his Dad disappearing at such a pivotal moment was the right thing to do, but I accept that I'm not exactly a leading expert on parenting.

Rosie seems to be echoing my thoughts. She asks me, "Why is it that we can both talk to you and Carl but our own parents don't want to know?"

"I don't think it's that they don't want to know, I think it's more like they don't know how to talk about certain things. It's easier for Carl and me: we're not as involved and we can take a step back rather than being completely immersed in what's going on."

At this point, the waiter brings bottles of red and white wine and puts them on the table. Rosie asks her Dad if she can have a glass and he nods. She pours herself a large glass of white and asks if I want one. I'm only going to have one and so would rather have red. I pour myself half a glass of red.

"Take it easy, kiddo," I say to Rosie. It doesn't feel comfortable to be giving her advice, but I know that there are so many things going around in her head that I don't want the alcohol to bring them all too close to the surface.

"Don't worry, they're not looking," she says gesturing towards her parents. "Not that they'd care anyway; as long as I stay quiet and act like a good little girl, they'll be happy."

"If you find out how to act like a good girl, can you teach me?" I ask. "I think that would make your Mum happy with me too."

Oops, wrong thing to say. That's not going to help me to swerve the stuff that's going on for Rosie. Why can I not learn to engage brain before mouth?

"Let's face it," Rosie says, "Neither of us are ever going to be able to make her happy. She's so bound up in how things should be and what everybody has to do her way, that she'll never accept some people think differently. She'll certainly never accept that it's okay to think differently. Oh no, my Mum will only accept one way of being and that's her own."

How should I respond? I want her to know that she can talk to me but I want to avoid her feeling that it's me against Sarah. I want to be honest but I know I can't.

"Did you manage to talk to her about the career progression in social work?" I ask. I know I've changed my tack to deal with the situation head-on but it feels like the right thing to do, given the direction we're heading. Is it the right thing to do? I'm still not convinced but Rosie's anger is obviously getting the better of her.

"What do you think?"
"Tell me about it," I suggest.

"I did loads of research and sat them both down to talk it through. I told them I'd been researching careers in social work and what I could aim for. I'd thought about what to say to try and be as reasonable as possible. I started to tell them about the potential careers for people who have studied social work, but before I could finish the first sentence, Mum stood up to leave the room and told me that she thought she had made it clear that the discussion was over."

"I'm sorry that the idea didn't work," I say, immediately kicking myself for such a feeble response.

"It would have been a great idea for any reasonable person who'd take the time to listen and try to understand. My mistake was forgetting that my mother is rarely reasonable."

"You're angry," I say, making a statement of the bleeding obvious. "I'm just worried that because you're so angry, your emotions get in the way when you talk about it. Being cynical, it might be that your folks use the emotion as a reason not to take you seriously. Let's get together in the week when there's no-one else who might listen in, and we'll think about what to do next."

I'm not even sure that this is the right thing to do. It could make the gulf between Sarah and Rosie as well as Sarah and me even wider, but I really don't want everything to erupt now, at such a public occasion.

Rosie nods and covers my hand with hers. "Thank you, Eve," she says. "I feel as though I'm going out of my mind at the moment and I don't know what I'd do if I couldn't talk to you about it."

I kiss her on the cheek and excuse myself so I can nip to the ladies. There's only so much sparkling water a girl can take before her bladder starts to rebel.

When I come back, the wine glasses have been refilled and the tension at our end of the table is a little less palpable. We all dig into the food that's been served. Very meat and two veg, apart from my vegetarian option which is a plate of broccoli, cauliflower and carrots. I guess that a request for a bottle of Tabasco would not be the done thing.

Halfway through our main course, Rosie reaches for the wine bottle again. I put my hard on her arm, trying to give the message that it's probably not a good idea. I'm about a millisecond too late as Sarah has spotted what Rosie is doing. She stands up and moves to our side of the table until she is standing over Rosie.

"Young lady, you have had more than enough," she hisses at her daughter. "And you," she says turning to me, "You should stop encouraging her. Have a little respect for where we are and who you are with."

"As a matter of fact, Mother," Rosie says loud enough for the rest of the table and the surrounding tables to hear, "Eve wasn't encouraging me, she was telling me to stop. Check your facts before you start coming over here with your ridiculous judgements. Just leave me alone and go back to your golf club chums."

"Rosie..." I start to say, not really knowing what was coming next.

"Don't bother, Eve, the damage has been done. I should have known that I couldn't trust you to behave properly in decent company."

The injustice of that statement stings and I'm considering my response but my thoughts are interrupted by Rosie.

"If you want to talk about behaving properly, go and talk to your dear friend Barbara and ask her about she got up to in Birmingham. Go on, Mother, ask her!"

Oh no, I knew that telling Rosie about Barbara and her football manager conquest was not the right thing to do, but I had the feeling that the next few minutes were going to prove to me just what a mistake I had made in my judgement.

Rosie stood up and shouted across the table, "Time to fess up, Babs. Tell us all what these respectable friends that my Mother thinks she has are really like!"

"Come on, you," I say taking Rosie by the hand, "Time for some fresh air."

We walk around the car park for a while and then go to sit in the car. Rosie is evidently upset and still very angry.

"It's just all so fucking unfair!" she shouts. "What the hell gives her the right to talk to you like that?"

'Hey,' I say as soothingly as I can muster, 'I can fight my battles, but not today.' As I say this, I think that I have two almighty battles coming my way, one with Sarah and one with Barbara. It strikes me that both battles demand a little nugget of honesty - honesty that unravels the façade of respectability and proves there are some things that don't go away by simply pretending they don't exist.

However, both of those battles are for another time; my immediate concern is Rosie's state of mind. She is obviously in pieces about what is happening with her parents and scared that she's not going to be able to live the life that she chooses for herself. The problem is, I don't know what to do.

We sit for a while, sometimes talking and sometimes not until Rosie starts to cry.

"Why can't I make them understand how important this is to me?" she sobs."Why can't they understand that this isn't just some stupid teenage whim? I know what I want to do and I know why I want to do it. How can that be a bad thing? It's not like I've decided to become a drug dealer. It's a good choice isn't it? "Rosie looks at me with her tear-stained face and my heart breaks for her.

I hold her to me and stroke her hair. I don't want her to feel so alone with all of this. I want her to know that somebody understands and that someone is on her side. I know that it's not going to sit well with Sarah, but I decide that, given the circumstances, I can live with that.

"Okay, I'm going to be completely honest with you," I say, wondering what kind of mess it would get me into. "I want you to be able to follow your dreams and live the life that you chose. I feel that I should be trying to find some middle ground between you and your parents, and I feel I ought to support my sister. However, I don't understand what is happening and why it's not okay for you to be who you want to be."

"That said, I desperately want to find a way for you all to come out of this feeling okay about it. I don't want to take sides against my sister. It just breaks my heart that you are in this situation and I've decided that my first priority is to offer you my support because you really need it."

Rosie listens to all of this and then flings her arms around my neck. Sometimes, because she is so wise and clever, I forget that she is still trying to find her own way in the world and still learning.

I dry her tears and use a tissue to rescue the carefully applied make up.

"So then, what happens now?" I ask her.

We agree a plan of action and walk back into the golf club. As we walk towards the dining room, I see Rosie falter a little. I squeeze her hand. "As your Uncle Carl would say, the sooner we start this, the sooner we finish it."

By the time we reach the table, everybody is tucking into dessert. I take my seat while Rosie stays standing.

She clears her throat and then says, "Everybody, I'm very sorry about my outburst before. I have a lot on my mind, but it really shouldn't have come out the way it did and I'm sorry. Mum, Dad, I didn't mean to spoil your big day but I need you to understand how important this is to me. I need to be able to talk to you about it and for you to listen to me. I hope that we can find a time soon."

I'm so proud of her that I want to cheer at the end of the speech. After saying her piece, Rosie retakes her seat and pours herself a glass of water. After a minute or two of stunned silence, the buzz of conversation begins again.

"I don't think I've ever been more proud of you," I whisper to Rosie.

Carl leans over and says, "Good one! Very dignified and remarkably assertive, young lady."

She smiles and thanks Carl and then clearly wants the whole subject to go away, so we change topic and go back to Harvey's strategy for picking up the ladies. I wonder what on earth Carl has been feeding him. Whatever it is, it seems to have done the job.

After dessert comes coffee and little pieces of fudge that send Harvey into a state of rapture. He works his way around the table, scavenging for pieces that the other guests don't want. My Mum, who I happen to know is a big fan of fudge, gives in to her grandson and gives him her bit.

During coffee, it's time for presents. Hopefully, I have at least got this bit right. When we hand over our gift, Ronald thanks us and Sarah manages a nod.

As we say our farewells, Peter comes over to us, slaps Carl on the back and wishes Leeds luck for the last few matches of the season. He looks at me. "Well done with Rosie," he says. "Think we managed to avert a major crisis there. Good job!" I give him a hug, feeling more warmth for him that I had before and wondering what would happen between him and Barbara.

"Happy anniversary, Ronald," I say, following the usual convention of shaking his hand.

"Thank you, Eve and thank you for the wine goblets, excellent present."

I want to say something to him about Rosie but the moment is lost.

Sarah is studiously avoiding me but I can't let this moment pass as I had done with Ronald. I move over to her. I know better than to kiss her, but I take her hand.

"Thanks for lunch, Sarah. I hope that everything is okay with Rosie. She's pretty messed up but I'm sure that you can talk it through. She seems a lot calmer now and ready to talk to you and Ronald. Let me know if I can do anything to help."

"I think that you've done more than enough for today and I'd thank you to keep out of our family business from here on."

"I was doing what I thought would help. I'm sorry if that's not how it came across. I want to help you all if you'd just let me in. Please, Sarah."

Sarah left to say goodbye to someone else and I was left not knowing how things stood between us. It was obvious that things weren't great, but I was unclear about whether I'd left things in a better or worse state. Please let it be better. Please let them find a way to hear each other and work something out.

We got back into the car, all feeling a little subdued. My Dad broke the tension by telling us how much he liked the wine goblets that we'd given to Sarah and Ronald. Carl picked up the conversation by talking to Mum and Dad about the wine we'd had over lunch. They came to the conclusion that the white was passable but the red was exceptional. Carl told them about the wines we had had when we went to the wine tasting for my birthday. He kept the conversation going almost all the way home and I was thankful to him for that.

When we arrived home, Mum went into the kitchen to put the kettle on and I followed her.

"Please tell me honestly, Mum. Was I to blame for what happened over lunch? I'm really trying to make sense of it and work out what I could have done differently."

Mum looked at me and cocked her head to one side, the way that she always does when she's thinking.

"No, darling, you weren't to blame. Rosie and Sarah have some stuff to work out and I think that Sarah finds it really difficult that Rosie turns to you rather than her."

"I know and I don't know what to do about it. I don't want Sarah to think that I'm taking sides against her, but equally I don't want Rosie feeling like she's on her own, not when there's something so major going on for her. I really don't know what to do for the best."

"Maybe just try being there for both of them?" Mum offered. I know that Sarah doesn't always make it easy but please don't shut the door on her. I think she might need you in the coming months."

"I won't shut the door," I promise, "But most of the time I feel as though I can't do anything right for her: whatever I try it's just not enough."

Carl and I are staying overnight with Mum and Dad and it's good to spend some time with them, despite what has happened during the day. They've been recording the new David Attenborough programme about Africa and ask if we'd like to watch it. Yes we would! During a scene with a young male elephant in musk (ie feeling very horny) who finds his first female conquest, Carl starts giggling like a small boy at the sight of the elephant's enormous penis. Once he starts, he can't stop.

The evening passes pleasantly and we all manage to forget about the drama of the day. We drink tea, watch TV and chat amiably to one another. It may sound ridiculous, but I'm reassured that Mum and Dad haven't taken against me for what they could have perceived as my wrongdoings during the day. I'm always convinced that people will assume I'm in the wrong and make judgements about me and how I have made wrong decisions.

There are, however, judgements to come: judgements that send me into a deep, black place. Before we go to bed, I switch on my phone. There are three text messages waiting for me. I feel a quiver of trepidation as I press the button to see the first message. I let out my breath in relief as I see it is from Rosie.

"Thank u for being there 4 me today when no-one else was. I luv u xxx"

It pleases me that she sounds calmer and more in control than earlier. It also pleases me that she's taken the time to get in touch, despite everything else that's going on for her.

The second message isn't quite so warm. It's from Barbara.

"How dare you spread such malicious lies about me? Are you trying to ruin my marriage?"

Ooh, that's rich. Malicious lies? In what way was any of it untrue? And putting the responsibility on me for her marriage? Although I think that she's out of order for blaming me, I do feel very guilty for letting Rosie in on the Barbara story. It was irresponsible and I regret it.

I start to slip down into a place in which I question everything about myself. I feel completely incapable of doing what's right and doubt my decision making on even the simplest things. The third message sends me rocketing further downwards... It's a message from Sarah.

"Stop meddling in my family. You're enjoying causing trouble aren't you? Stay away from me and stay away from my family. Understand?"

Can she really think so badly about me? Can she really believe that my intentions are so divisive?

I hear myself wailing and feel the tears streaming down my face and then my memory fails me.

CHAPTER SIX

The Spiral

I wake up in Mum and Dad's spare room. The sun is streaming through the gap in the curtains so I'm guessing it's not that early. Carl isn't there. I'm usually awake before him so this strikes me as a bad sign. I trawl my memory for clues about what happened last night but draw a blank. I remember crying. I recall winding myself up into a frenzy... but no details to reassure me. I just have the overriding feeling that all is not well.

Downstairs, I hear voices. Although I can't make out what is being said, I can hear that Carl is there, talking to Mum and Dad. A wave of paranoia hits me. They must be talking about me and all the awful things I said and did last night. They must be reaching the end of their tether and deciding that there's nothing else they can do to help me. They're all going to leave me, just as I always knew they would -leave me in the knowledge that they've tried everything but can't get through to me. This time, I'm going to be completely and utterly on my own.

I try to decide what to do for the best: do I hide up here and buy myself more time or go down and face whatever music is waiting for me? If I stay up here, I'll just torture myself by worrying about what might have happened and what might be waiting. There is only one option: I need to go downstairs. I look at myself in the mirror and it's not a pleasant sight. My eyes are swollen and I look like the bug-eyed monster from hell. My hair is stuck up on end in some places and plastered against my scalp in others. I do what I can to make myself look slightly less scary, throw on some clothes and head down the stairs.

Before I walk into the kitchen, I stop and I listen. I want to understand what I'm dealing with and what's being said about me. Yes, my paranoia is still definitely with me, persuading me that even the people who love me most in the world are against me. But just as my paranoia is definitely present, so my sense of perspective has completely deserted me. I feel sneaky and underhand for hanging around the door and listening but I do it anyway, hoping that I might learn something.

"The fact is," says my Mum, "That Eve really needs some help. I thought that we might be able to give it ourselves but I don't think that any of us is equipped to give her the kind of support she needs."

So, they are still thinking about wanting to help me, that's the good bit but it's pretty clear that I did something bad enough to rattle them all.

"This is the worst it's ever been," Carl replies. "Usually, I can talk her round and make her feel safe but there was no chance of that last night. I don't recognise her when she's like that: it's like a completely different version of my Evie. It's like she's not even in there, as if someone else is driving her. Where does she go? I knew that she was worried about Sarah and Rosie and about seeing Barbara again, but I really wasn't expecting what happened last night. I don't know what to do."

"None of us do, Carl. The thing is that we all want to but maybe first we need Eve to face up to the fact that she really does have a problem and make it her decision to find help. She needs to do it for herself, not for any of us."

This is my Dad's voice. I can't stay out here any longer, it just doesn't feel right. I know that there's probably a long discussion to come but at least they don't seem to be actively angry with me.

"Good morning," I say, walking into the kitchen. I hang back, feeling as if I should wait to be invited to sit down.

"Good morning, darling," Mum says and smiles at me. "You look as if you've been in the wars. Sit down and we'll get you a cup of tea."

"Yes, please," I say somewhat sheepishly. "I don't know what happened last night but I know it wasn't good. I just want to say that I'm really sorry for upsetting you all and making you a part of it. I really don't remember."

My Dad takes my hand. "You gave us all a real scare, Evie. We thought we were going to have to call the doctor out. You were absolutely manic and we couldn't say anything to calm you down."

"I'm sorry. It scares me so much and I hate myself for dragging you all into it. Looking at you all I'm guessing that I've hurt you, and I'm so sorry. You three are the people I love most in the world and I hate the fact that you're on the receiving end of all of this. I don't know what to say. I wish I could remember so that at least I could apologise for actual things rather than just give a useless general apology that you've every right not to accept."

I notice that Carl hasn't said anything yet and that worries me. Usually he is the first person to leap to my defence and reassure me that the world is okay. Does that mean that the world of him and me isn't okay?

"Please tell me," I implore them all, "Tell me what happened and how you feel about it."

Now, Carl speaks.

"You really don't remember what happened?" he asks.

"No, I really don't but I want to know so that I can start to put things right."

"You were okay until we went to bed," Carl tells me, "And then you completely lost the plot."

"How?" I ask, not wanting to know but knowing that I have to know.

"You asked me what I thought about what had happened and whether it really was your fault." he says. "I told you that you had done the best for your niece and tried to do the best for your sister, but you seemed to have ended up in the middle of it. You asked me whether you could have done anything differently and I said that maybe it wasn't a good idea to tell Rosie about what had happened with Barbara. That's when you flipped.

You told me that I was judging you just like everybody else, and that I should be trying to understand you and be on your side. When I said that I was on your side, you screamed that I wasn't and that, just like everybody else, I thought you were a complete waste of space and a disgrace to everybody around you. You started crying hysterically and telling me that you'd had enough. You just kept saying, 'I've had enough, I've had enough, I've had enough'. You kept saying it over again. I really didn't know what to do with you. That's when your Mum and Dad came into the room."

"And what happened then?" I asked, not really sure that I wanted to know. Dad took over the story.

"You were in floods of tears, and kept telling us all that you weren't worth the effort and we should just leave you. Then you got it into your head that *you* should leave. You packed your bag and made for the front door. Thank goodness it was locked and you couldn't find a way out. You told us that you couldn't inflict your poisonous company upon us for another minute and that you had to be alone where you couldn't do anybody else any harm.

When you couldn't get out of the door, you slumped onto the floor, crying and crying and telling us all not to feel any sympathy for you because you didn't deserve it. You told us that we'd all be better off if you just walked under a bus and put an end to it all. That really hurt, Eve, the fact that you thought we'd prefer it if you were dead. Do you really think that any of us believe that? We don't, you know. We want you to be happy – happy in yourself and happy to be around those who love you. I don't understand what's going on in your head but you need help, sweetheart, you really do."

At this point, I break down in tears and cry as if my heart was well and truly broken. How can I put the people I love so much through this? How can I just expect them to pick up where they left off as if nothing had happened? I'd said that I wanted to throw myself under a bus. Is this what I was really thinking? Did I want to be dead in that moment? Did I want to be out of this, escape from the torture in my head and not have to deal with it anymore?

As I am crying, Mum comes over and puts her arms around me. Then Carl puts his hand on my shoulder and my Dad puts his on the other. All three of them are reaching out to me and I have absolutely no idea what to do. I raise my head and look at them all in turn, trying to smile despite the tears still streaming down my face. I want them to know how grateful I am that they still care enough to be here for me. I don't feel I deserve any of their love or care. I have hurt them all deeply and worried them silly. Why should they still want to talk to me?

My Mum breaks the silence. "Eve, darling, please know that we all love you and we can't stand to see you like this. We want to help you but we don't know how to. Please find some help… find someone who can help you to understand and deal with all of this. You're a successful woman, living a good life but you're still our little girl and you always will be. Please, please get help."

The compassion in her voice and the concern in all of their eyes make me cry again. How can I continue to do harm to these people? How can I put them in the position of more hurt and more worry? I am really ashamed of myself for being the cause of such distress.

Dad adds, "If you need to go privately to find the right help, don't worry about the cost. Your Mum and I will pay for it if it means that you're happy again."

"I will do, Dad, Mum, Carl. I promise. I hate the fact that I do this to you and I hate myself for doing it. I don't know why it happens but I promise that I'll find out and I'll do something to stop it."

Carl moves over to me and says, "Baby, we're all here for you. We want our happy Eve back and we want to find a way to make that happen. Talk to us, help us to understand and tell us what you need from us."

This is what I most needed to hear, that I haven't lost Carl and that he is still with me.

"Do you want us to talk to Sarah for you?" Mum asks.

"Talk to her about what? I'm not sure why she blames me for everything. I want to understand but I really don't." I say.

"Let us talk to her. We know that she's angry but I don't think that we really understand why." Mum says.

"I thought I was doing the right thing," I tell them. "I feel so torn between doing right by Sarah and making sure that Rosie has the support that she needs. Rosie needs to know that someone is there to listen to her."

"Yes, Eve," Dad reassures me. "We know that you're trying to do what's right, but maybe the best thing to do is to put some distance between you for a while. Let us talk to Sarah, eh?"

I nod in agreement. There's no point in me trying to talk to Sarah at the moment.

We have breakfast together and all try to lighten the mood. After breakfast, we go for a walk for half an hour to blow away the cobwebs and it's time for Carl and me to leave. I don't want to go when things are so up in the air, but I know that there will be little merit in hanging around when none of us know what'll happen next.

In the car on the way home, I pluck up the courage to ask Carl something important.

"Carl?" I ask.

"Yes, Baby?" he asks in return.

"Yesterday, when I was teasing Rosie about drinking Malibu, you called me judgemental. Is that true? Do I make too many judgements about people?"

He thinks about this for a minute or two before responding. "That's a funny one," he says. "Over the stuff that most people are judgemental about – race, sexuality, background, life choices – you don't have a judgemental bone in your body."

"But?"

"But you do make judgements about some things. You judge the music that people listen to and judge them harshly if they don't listen to 'proper' music and like manufactured, X Factor stuff. You judge people who can't use language well and can't spell or punctuate properly."

I have to concede both of these because he's absolutely right. I never thought of it as being judgemental, but of course it is.

"The biggest one," he continues, "Is that you make judgements about people who are doing normal things that don't figure in your world. People who choose to get married, people who want kids, people who talk about their kids. It's almost as if you resent them for showing that you're the one who is out of step with most of the world."

Wow, that's insightful. It pains me to accept the truth but I know that's what it is. So, I deal with the fact that I feel out of step by condemning the choices that other people make. Again it's Uncomfortable Eve coming to the surface and dealing with that discomfort through criticism. I don't like it but I agree with Carl's assessment.

"Thank you for being so honest with me. I don't like the things that you've pointed out but I do agree that you're right. I try to be so inclusive but only about the stuff that doesn't threaten my life choices. I'm really not proud of that. In fact, I feel thoroughly ashamed of myself."

"Evie, I said what I just said to be honest with you. Please don't use it as a weapon to beat yourself up, please don't."

I'm not sure that I can give Carl what he wants here. I have discovered something particularly unpalatable about myself and, at the moment, it's just another piece of evidence to add to the pile to prove that I am an unworthy person.

"I'm glad that you were honest with me," I say and mean it. "It's just come as a bit of a shock to realise that I do such horrible things."

We are both quiet for most of the journey home. When we arrive, I'm suddenly overcome with tiredness and I crawl into bed. Bed is like a sanctuary and I pull the duvet around me as a shield against all the outside sources of attack. Of course, the duvet shield is powerless against the things attacking from the inside: I can't switch off the inner voices that repeat all the things I've said and done and wish I hadn't. The duvet shield just seems to amplify them so that my head swims with accusation and criticism.

Eventually I drift off to sleep, but it asleep fraught with bad dreams and people telling me about all the things I do wrong. When I wake up, Carl is lying on the bed, reading.

He says, "Hello, sleepy."

I smile and reach for his hand. "Hello, I'm glad you're here. Thank you for staying with me, even though I really don't deserve it."

"Evie, if you want to continue to beat yourself up, there's nothing I can do about it, but please don't assume I'm doing the same thing. I'm here and I'm staying. I love you and I like you: I just wish you could feel the same about yourself."

At these impassioned words, I feel tears springing to my eyes again and I reach out for Carl. My Carl shield is more powerful than the duvet shield. It even has the power to drown out some of the critical voices.

We spend our evening together, me glued to Carl's side, my anxiety growing whenever he leaves the room. I feel safe when I'm with him and, right now, I really want to feel safe.

The next morning, Carl is up early for a driving lesson before the first test of the day. He checks how I'm feeling. I smile and tell him I'm okay. What I actually want to do is to beg him not to go, to stay with me so my Carl shield remains intact. But I know better than to do this: it would only worry him and distract him from what he needs to do. And so, the watery smile and the 'I'm okay' is what I do.

I hear the door slam and feel utterly bereft. Now that Carl is gone, there's no-one to protect me from the nagging voices and no-one to dispel the images that remind me what a dreadful person I am. Even though it's still early, staying in bed is futile. My duvet shield is powerless this morning.

And so I get up. I take a bath and switch on my computer to try and distract myself with Killer Sudoku puzzles. It works up to a point. My strategies for carrying on (even when I don't want to) are well-honed and keep me functioning. I know there are things that I really need to think about – most importantly, the fact that I told my folks and Carl I wanted to walk under a bus and have done with it all – but I don't feel strong enough to face up to them yet. I'm just going to get on with my day as planned and brush the tough stuff under the carpet until the bulge gets so big that I need to tackle it. High functioning fuck up indeed…

When the surgery opens for the day, I call and try to book an appointment. My lovely doctor is back from maternity leave now and I really need to speak to her. I know that I need her help. When the receptionist tells me that she is fully booked all week, I panic. I tell her that it is an emergency and that I am very worried about my mental health and please could she try to fit me in. She offers me appointments with other doctors but that's not what I want. I need to be comfortable and open with someone I trust. In the end, she tells me the only thing I can do is to join the end of the queue after evening surgery, but she doesn't know how long I'll have to wait. I take it. I don't care about the wait.

Doctor's appointment sorted, I turn my attention to the day ahead. I have a couple of proposals to write for new work that I'm hoping to win and I've arranged to see George over lunchtime. One of my customers needs some help with some technical stuff which is way beyond my knowledge so I've drafted in George, the IT whizz, to help them. To be honest, as much as I adore George, I really don't feel up to it today. I can never hide the truth from him and I don't want to have to relive the events of yesterday.

When I arrive at George's, he knows that things are not good. He's perceptive at the best of times, but today, I'm giving away strong clues. The bug eyes and the lack of make-up are revealing, so is the fact that I can't meet his gaze when he asks how I am.

"Let's get you inside," he says, "There's a cup of Earl Grey waiting for you."

I smile my gratitude and follow him in. We sit on the sofa and he says, "Right then, out with it!"

"Oh, are you sure that you want all of this? There's a good chance that you'll regret asking."

"This is me you're talking to: of course I want to know."

And so the whole sorry saga tumbles out of my mouth; what happened yesterday and the day before, how useless I feel and how I don't know what to do next.

"Firstly," George says, "We all know that Call Me Babs is a sanctimonious bitch who conveniently forgets the wrongs she commits but has the perceived wrongs of others hard-wired into her memory."

I know that there is no love lost between the two of them: they live in completely different worlds. George always has an eye for a bargain and is resourceful in everything that he does; Barbara considers this to be 'cheap and nasty'. I silently thank him for not saying anything about Sarah. Although I don't understand her animosity, I know that I would feel duty-bound to jump to her defence had he said anything unkind.

"And secondly," George says, breaking me out of my self-pitying thoughts, "I think it's high time for us to try the cinema trick, don't you?"

The 'cinema trick' (not its official title) is something I taught George when he was studying Neuro-Linguistic Programming with me. It's a way of programming your brain to scramble unpleasant memories so that they lose their negative impact. You disassociate yourself from the memory, imagining you're looking at the memory on a cinema screen rather than being a part of it, then changing the people in the memory so that they lose their power in your mind.

I smile because it feels like one of those moments when, to use a Star Wars reference, the Padawan becomes the master. I smile as well because this is the perfect tool for the occasion and I'm pleased he brought it to mind so easily.

"Okay, then," I say. "Work your magic, oh wise NLP guru!"

And so he does. George asks me to focus in upon the memory that troubles me most and I pinpoint the texts from Sarah and Barbara and the injustice they made me feel.

He asks me to close my eyes and imagine that I'm sat in a cinema, watching Sarah and Barbara composing their texts to me and hitting the 'send' button – the first level of disassociation. Then he asks me to imagine that I am the projectionist in my cinema booth, watching Eve watching the images on the screen – the second level of disassociation.

Then he tells me that I need to change what Sarah and Barbara are wearing to make it as comical as I can. Sarah, I put in head-to-toe biker gear: black, fringed leather with a red and white bandana covering her perfectly coiffured hair. Barbara, I put in a cheap orange nylon ensemble with Primark logos all over it. George asks me what outfits I've chosen and hoots with laughter when I describe Barbara. "I think you've just condemned Call Me Babs to her own personal hell!"

Now he asks me to imagine that I am back in the projectionist's booth, watching Eve watching the screen where the scenario plays out with the new costumes on full display. I can't help but smile.

"And now," George says, "We are going to think about their voices. I want you to think about the daftest voice you could give both of them as they are writing these texts."

The voice for Barbara comes first – Sylvester from the Tweety Pie cartoons. I have to think slightly harder about Sarah, but decide upon Mr T, to go with the tough-guy leathers.

I share my choices with George and he asks me to play the scenario again – me in the projectionist booth, watching Eve watching the scenes on the screen, complete with silly costumes and daft voices.

I do as instructed, hearing both Sarah and Barbara reading out the texts as they compose them in their new voices. It really is ridiculous, but it's working.

"Now, the final step," George says. "Imagine that the projectionist has managed to put the film in the wrong way round so that the images play backwards."

I do it, struggling to imagine the words in the wrong order but making the scene play out from the moment the send button is hit back to picking up their phones to compose the text.

"So how does the memory feel to you now?" George asks me, pleased with himself for being able to use his skills in an appropriate way.

"It doesn't have the same negative impact, that's for sure," I tell him and mean it.

"Good! So keep those images in your mind. You've had texts from Mr T and Sylvester dressed in orange nylon. Can you really take what they say seriously?"

I hug him. It does actually work; maybe I'm not the charlatan that I think I am.

"So, is madam now ready to move onto the next order of business for the day?" George asks.

"Yes, I think that madam is. Before we move on, can she just say how proud she is of her clever student?"

And so we start to talk about work and George puts together a plan for what he needs to do to help my customer. To be honest, a lot of it goes right over my head, but I'm confident that he knows what he's talking about. I arrange for him to come with me to see the customer later in the week.

Before long, it's time for me to leave so that I can make my appointment with the doctor. I want to arrive early so that, if anyone else has been told to wait until the end of surgery, I am first in the queue. Unfortunately, the others have had the same idea and I find myself third in line. I take out my Kindle and try to read while I'm waiting but I can't settle. My mind is racing as I try to make sense of what I want to say and how I can make anybody who isn't in my head understand what's going on.

I wait for about forty five minutes, but finally my name is called. Helen has been my doctor for a while and has helped me through a number of mental crises. I trust her to listen without judging me. When I walk into the consulting room, we greet each other warmly and I ask after her new daughter. We talk for a minute or so and then Helen asks me what's brought me in to see her today.

"I'm in a bad way, mentally," I start, suddenly feeling tongue-tied and unable to articulate even the simplest of concepts. "I've had a couple of really bad episodes over the past few months and I feel completely wretched. I don't know what to do and I'm scared that my head is getting worse and worse. I really need some help."

"I'm glad you came to see me when you're feeling so low," Helen said and I felt reassured that I have done the right thing in being here. "There's one thing I do need to ask you. Has it got so bad that you've thought of harming yourself?"

The inevitable question, but phrased in a really good way. I think for a minute before giving my answer.

"My initial reaction would be to say no, but I'm not sure. Both times I've got really upset recently, I've talked about not wanting to be here. It's not something that I consciously think about but it seems to be there, lurking at the back of my mind and coming out when I'm having one of my explosions."

"So, would it be fair to say that you do have some suicidal thoughts, but no specific plan to do anything about it?" Helen asks.

"That sums it up very well," I reply. "It scares me that these thoughts are locked away somewhere at the back of my mind and they're obviously in there somewhere, because I express them when I'm feeling desperate and out of control."

"Okay, so we need to get you some help, don't we? Given your previous experiences, what do you think you need?"

"On a day to day basis, I need some help to cope. As much as I've tried to avoid it, I think it's time to go back on the happy pills. There's something else though, too. I need to understand what's happening in my head and what's driving me to the point where I lose the plot and explode. It really scares me and I'm sick of causing the people I care about so much hurt. I hate myself for it and I need to find a way to make it stop."

Helen considers this for a moment and looks back through my notes. "So you had CBT a couple of years ago. Was that helpful?"

I screw my face up a little and say, "The CBT was useful for some of my general depressive feelings, but this feels different. The general depression, I sort of understand and can manage it. These explosions are different and I want to understand them. I might be wrong, but I don't think that CBT will help in this case."

"So what I think we'll do," Helen offers, "Is to write you a prescription for the anti-depressants and refer you to the Mental Health team for assessment by one of their clinical psychologists. How does that sound?"

"Thank you," I say.

"You're welcome. I'm just sorry that you're feeling so rubbish. We'll get to the bottom of this: just remember that I'm here to help you."

I believe that she is. I leave the surgery with a prescription for anti-depressants, a referral to the Mental Health team and the reassurance that somebody in the medical profession is taking me seriously and wants to support me out of this blackness.

I'm pleased that my appointment with the Mental Health team comes through quickly – just under three weeks after my appointment with Helen. I've been struggling. I'm isolating myself from pretty much everyone in my life, not returning phone calls or answering emails, and even doing my best to isolate myself from Carl. I know that I've been distant and I can't find any pleasure in the things we do together. We've been to see several films, but I just can't get in the mood. He's been patient, but I know it must be getting him down. I don't want to do anything, I don't want to see anyone and I don't want to talk to anyone.

One night over the weekend, I got drunk on wine and went into a fit of despair. I tried to push Carl away, telling him I was no good for him and he should find someone else who could treat him the way he deserves. I insisted upon sleeping in the spare room so that he didn't have to be near me. When he tried to talk to me, all I kept saying was, "You must have had enough of me; I've suddenly had enough of me."

He was so upset the next morning and kept asking me if I was trying to tell him that I wanted to split up. I think he thought that I was trying to goad him into leaving me so that he was the bad guy. I did my best to explain that splitting up was the last thing that I wanted, that I didn't know how I'd carry on if he wasn't around.

"So why do you keep pushing me away?" he asked, trying to make sense of it all.

"I don't know, I don't know, I DON'T KNOW. I love you so much but I feel I'm such a burden on you. I'm such a miserable cow at the moment and that must be bringing you down too. I feel so guilty for inflicting myself on you and I'm so sorry. I've just had enough. Not of you but of being trapped in my own head. I'm scared that I'm going to explode again and I can't put any of you through that, not again."

I'm still trying to persuade Carl that I don't want to leave him and I don't want him to leave me. I can understand why he thinks otherwise and I wish I could find a way of making him feel more secure. If I screw up this relationship, I really have screwed up everything. I resolve to be more positive around Carl and more attentive.

Talking about pushing people away, I've really had to be careful about my communication with Rosie. I've had strict instructions from Sarah to leave her family alone, but I can't bear the thought of leaving Rosie to deal with things on her own. I don't contact her but she does contact me. She texts me and says:

"Hi. How r u? I know ur not meant 2 talk 2 me but I miss u and I need u in my life. R u still there?"

I reply straight away; I can't bear not to.

"Hi sweetheart. I know it's difficult but please know that I'll ALWAYS be there, whenever and wherever you need me."

"That's all I needed 2 know. I luv u xxx"
"I love you too, my darling. Stay strong xxx"

It's all too much. She really shouldn't have to deal with this on her own. I'm just glad she has Mum and Dad there for support, as they're probably going to be more use to her than I can be.

Last week, I was running an Emotional Intelligence course in Liverpool. I felt such a fraud. Who am I to teach anybody anything about self-awareness of self-management? I managed to keep it together while I was facilitating the group, but on both days, I fell apart on the way home. How is it that I can be professional and perky in front of an audience yet so inadequate when I'm on my own? I believe in everything I teach and in its ability to make a real difference to people and how they feel about themselves. I just can't make it work for me.

I want to be authentic in what I do and what I teach, but how can I be authentic if I am completely incapable of using my own principles? I start to avoid thinking about work too because I'm ashamed of my inabilities and my fraudulent advice to other people.

One of the other things that's been scaring me is the dreaming... Each night, I dream I'm locked in a cell, waiting for a court appearance which will convict me of a crime. The crime is slightly different every time – from neglecting a penguin (yes, a penguin) to stealing a coconut – but the pattern is the same, I'm waiting in a cell and then get taken to the court room to the sound of jeers from the gallery. Each night, the star witness for the prosecution is somebody I love, yet their evidence convicts me of the crime. I'm at the point where I dread going to sleep because the dreams are so vivid and real that I wake up feeling awful. Worse still, I wake up absolutely bathed in sweat.

So, I start my day feeling awful and, when the nightly negative thoughts kick in, I end my day feeling awful too. Something's got to give.

For this and myriad other reasons, I am grateful that my Mental Health appointment is today. On the way to the Health Centre, I agree with myself that I am going to be open and, if necessary, vulnerable, in order to get to where I need to be. Vulnerable is a state that I've had a lot of problems with over the years. I think I've always believed that I need to be capable and allow no chinks to show in my armour. Eve is always the person who can, the one who's resourceful enough to find the resolution for even the trickiest problems. I pride myself upon my ability to help others and provide solutions. So, choosing to be vulnerable is a new experience for me and one with which I'm still not altogether comfortable.

I am early for the appointment and so spend twenty minutes in the waiting room. It's fairly busy and so I have little choice but to stay sitting behind the man who is picking his nose with such diligence that he might well be hoping to find gold in there. When my appointment time has been and gone, I start to become irritated. It's only about five minutes before I am called, only about seven minutes late for my appointment, but I feel ready to kick off and make a scene. I don't because I recognise that my irritation is just my nervousness at work.

The psychologist who sees me is called Jackie. She introduces herself and shows me into a room with comfortable chairs and a huge clock on the wall. Jackie tells me that the purpose of the session is to understand my needs and work out the best way to help me. She runs through my past mental health history – on anti-depressants on three separate occasions over the past five years, referred to Mental Health two years ago and had a number of sessions over a three-month period with a Cognitive Behavioural Therapist.

"And so what makes you ask to be referred to us again?" Jackie asks.

Was I just imagining the criticism in her voice? Was she really making a judgement about the fact that I obviously failed after the last round of CBT? I push the thoughts to the back of my mind and try to explain why I'm here again.

"I'm very worried about my mental state and about the effect it's having on those who are important to me. I've been having these difficult episodes that I don't remember afterwards. I want to understand why they're happening so I can make them stop." I tell her, trying to make her understand something that I don't really understand myself."

"Let's go back to when you went through CBT two years ago. Did that help you?"

"No!" I screamed in my head, "Let's NOT go back to the CBT. I don't want to talk about CBT, I want to talk about what's happening now, I want to talk about the explosions that I can't control."

"Just a second," says the calmer, more rational side of my subconscious, "Let's just go with the conversation for a while. It might get you where you need to be."

I listen to the calmer voice in my head and decide to play ball for a while longer.

"To some extent, the CBT was useful. It helped me to address some issues in my life and find different coping strategies. So it was useful to a point."

"And what do you think it preventing you from using the techniques you learnt in CBT and applying them to your current situation?" Jackie asks.

I think for a minute, trying to drown out the voice in my head which keeps calling Jackie a patronising cow. I want to give an informed answer which contains some semblance of intelligent thought.

"As I said, CBT helped me to deal with some of the issues in my life at that time, but it felt as though it was trying to deal with the outcomes of my problems rather than addressing the root causes. I don't need a strategy to deal with the day-to-day, I need to understand the things going on in my head so I can control them before they reach explosion point."

Despite what I said, we seem to be on a CBT track now and I'm not sure how to divert us to somewhere more useful.

"Tell me what you learnt through the CBT and what it enabled you to achieve," Jackie asks me, either unaware of my feelings towards the topic or stubbornly determined to keep on down that CBT track.

I reel off a number of things that I did as a result of the CBT – none of them major but they felt like little victories at the time. Jackie seemed pleased that the CBT had had some value for me and nodded every time I cited an example of how I'd used it.

"So, I'll go back to my previous question. What do you think stops you from using your CBT techniques now?"

Okay, I get it we're going for the John Humphries technique of asking the same question until you get a decent answer, are we? Well, you can try, honey...

"As I thought I'd explained," I said, not masking my irritation very well, "I'm not sure that CBT can help me in this situation, but I'm willing to listen if you think that I'm wrong."
"Well," says Jackie, "Explain to me what it is you want to achieve and why you think that CBT is not the answer."

Is it me, or are we starting to go around in circles now? Come on, girl, take a deep breath and just go with it.

"I want to understand why I have these scary and destructive explosions, as I call them, and I want to be able to recognise when I'm building up to one so that I can prevent it. As for why I don't think CBT can help, well I'm no expert, but this feels quite different and I think I need to delve deeper to really understand it."

"Maybe the CBT isn't working for you because you're not really trying to use it?" Jackie offers.

And maybe you should be very careful with that pencil you're holding as I'm very tempted to jab it up your nose.

"Believe me, Jackie, I've tried everything that I know," I reply. "I've tried the CBT techniques and I all of the NLP skills that I teach to other people."

"I don't know what NLP is," Jackie says dismissively.

"Neuro-Linguistic Programming," I tell her. "I thought that, in your profession, you might have been aware of it."

So now I'm starting to be sniffy and condescending. Not good: she's obviously got me riled.

Jackie seems to ignore me and press on.

"And what would you say if I suggested a further course of CBT for you?"

What would I say? I'm not sure that you really want to know.

Another deep breath to give me time to formulate a more polite response.

"I would be disappointed because I'd feel like I hadn't really been listened to. I'm here, being completely honest with you and I'm trying to express how scared I am about what's happening to me and, having experienced it before I really do not believe that CBT is what I need."

I think that there may be a chance that I have managed to get through a little bit. The conversation changes direction a little bit, away from CBT.

"What is it that scares you?" Jackie asks.

"I'm scared because my outbursts hurt other people and I worry them because I express suicidal thoughts when I'm in the grip of the explosion."

"And do you feel suicidal at other times?"

"Not really. There are times when I want to be able to step off the planet, but that's different from wanting to die." This feels very honest and about as open as I can be.

"Do you know what you'd do if you were feeling suicidal?" Jackie inquires. Yes I do and you're not going to like it.

"I fundamentally believe that, if people choose to take their own life, they have the right to do so. Because health professionals like you have a responsibility to report people who are planning to harm themselves, I wouldn't come to you. I'd talk to my family and friends first and, if I still needed support, I'd go to Samaritans."

I get the distinct impression that this wasn't the answer I was expected to give. However, I wasn't just trying to be controversial, I meant it. Don't get me wrong, I don't think that anyone should be encouraged to die, but I know from my experience with Samaritans that some people genuinely think that they would be better off dead. If somebody wants to die, the last thing that they want is people telling them that are wrong. Again, I don't think that we should just say, 'okay then, off you go!' but we should talk to the person and understand what is going on for them.

By the end of the session, we've agreed that Jackie will refer me to see a clinical psychologist to explore my explosions and try to get to the bottom of them. So I achieved my outcome but it didn't feel easy. I was left feeling frustrated and un-listened to, and it felt like I had to fight to get my voice heard.

When I arrive home, I call Mum and Dad to tell them about my experience with Jackie. I explain my frustrations and irritations and also tell them that I've achieved what I wanted as I refused more CBT and now have a referral to a clinical psychologist.

Mum is pleased to hear that I'll get some support and glad that I held out for what I believe I need. I ask her if they have spoken to Sarah and she goes quiet.

"Yes we have, but we're not making a lot of headway in bringing the two of you any closer together. She is still furious and we don't think Rosie's helping; she's angry too because she's not being listened to, and she's using every opportunity to needle Sarah."

That evening, I'm grateful when Carl arrives home so that I can tell him about the day. We've texted each other during the day, but it's hard to get all the emotions into just a few words. He seems surprised and pleased that I actually want to communicate. I guess I've been very distant and uncommunicative over the past few weeks and I'm glad I can make him smile again.

We are just settling down to a good film and a good bottle of wine when there is a rap at the door. We look at each other, neither of us expecting any visitors at this time.

Carl goes to the door and says a surprised 'hello' to the person standing there. "What are you doing here?" he asks, but I can't hear the reply. My curiosity gets the better of me and I wander out from the living room towards the front door. I'm very surprised to see Rosie, still waiting for Carl to invite her in. She has a large sports bag with her and is bedraggled from the rain and wind. It's a horrible night.

"Come in, sweetheart," I say, amazed that Carl hasn't thought to get the poor girl inside and out of the rain. "You're soaked to the skin, come upstairs and let's get you dry."

"Thanks, Auntie Eve," she says gratefully, pushing past Carl who is still standing in the door, looking completely bemused. She hugs me, covering me with the rain which had soaked through her flimsy coat.

"Thanks for that," I say, "Just what I needed – to share your raindrops."

"Oops, sorry. I hadn't realised that I was so soaked." Rosie apologises.

"You look as though you could do with a nice warm bath and a change of clothes," I suggest, not wanting her to catch her death of cold.

"That would be lovely," Rosie enthuses.

"Want a glass of wine while you're soaking?" Carl offers.

"Yes please!" she replies.

"So, a bath and a glass of wine and then we talk, eh?" I tell her. "There are towels in your room and a dressing gown and slippers; I'm guessing that you'd like to stay over?"

"Yes please," she says, looking imploringly at us. "I'll explain, I promise. I just had to get out of there."

I go upstairs and run her a bath, slipping a bit of my precious Jo Malone bath foam in there. She looks as though she needs a treat.

Half an hour later, Rosie appears downstairs wrapped up in an oversized dressing gown and carrying her empty wine glass.

I pat the seat next to me and Carl refills her glass. "Feeling better?" he asks.

"Yes thanks," Rosie replies, "Much better. It's been a long journey."

"You should have said you were coming," Carl says, "We'd have come to pick you up."

"I thought it was better if I just turned up," Rosie admits. "This way, it was more difficult for you to turn me away. I'm sorry if I'm putting you out: I just really needed to be here with you."

How could we possibly turn her away?

"Well, if that's the case, I'm really pleased that you're here. " I say in all honesty. "And just for future reference, we won't ever turn you away if you need us. One thing I really have to ask though, does your Mum know that you're here?"

"Erm, no, she doesn't. Do we have to tell her?" Rosie asks.

"I'm sorry, love, but we do need to tell her. You're very welcome her, but I need your Mum to know that you're safe and well. Okay?"

"Okay, I guess," Rosie says, "But will you talk to her because I can't?"

"Sure. Maybe you should tell us what happened before I call her so I know what I'm letting myself in for."

"Fair point," she concedes and starts to talk.

Rosie tells us that she and Sarah have had an almighty row over her plans for university and Sarah's refusal to accept her daughter's life choices. This led to Rosie packing a bag and leaving a note to say she was out of there.

"And so here I am," she tells us, "Back in the land of the living, where I can talk to people who actually let me have my own opinions and can be who I want to be."

"Let me talk to your Mum, then we can all relax and catch up," I suggest.

I sound braver than I feel. I'd really rather not be doing this. I doubt that I'm going to get a warm response and, somehow, the fact that Rosie is here is bound to be my fault.

The phone rings and Harvey answers. "Alright, Eve," he says, buoyantly, "How you doing and how's my main man?"

"Your main man is good thanks and I'm okay too. Just need to talk to your Mum. Is she there?"

"Sure, hang on a sec." The next thing I hear is Harvey shouting 'Muuuum, phone!' at the top of his voice. I guess that I should be grateful that he doesn't tell Sarah that it's me: that increases the chances of her actually picking the phone up exponentially.

"Good evening, Sarah speaking," says the voice at the other end of the phone.

"Hello, Sarah, it's Eve," I say, "I need to talk to you."

"What can you need to talk to me about?" she asks, haughtily.

"Your daughter," I reply, "She's here with us and I thought that should know. She's quite safe but obviously quite upset. I just wanted you to know." I'm aware that I'm rushing my words out while I have Sarah's silence.

"So, she hasn't killed herself like she threatened?" Sarah sneers.

"Killed herself? No. She's here and she's safe and we're taking care of her. What makes you ask that?"

"That's what she threatened to do on the note she left us, told us that we'd driven her to suicide and she was going to end it all. Manipulative little madam. She makes those threats but is actually travelling to see you. Put her on the phone."

"I'm sorry, Sarah but she doesn't want to talk just now. Do you want me to pass on a message?"

"Don't trouble yourself. Just take good care of my daughter and don't go filling her head with that liberalist rubbish that you and that boyfriend of yours spout. She's been brought up to know the value of things."

Well, that told me, didn't it?

"Do you want to know when she's likely to be home?" I ask.

"I'm sure that the two of you will work it out between you," she chides me.

I give up, I don't have the energy to fight this one.

"Okay, Sarah, I'll stay in touch." I tell her and hang up after she has already put the phone down.

"Alright?" Rosie asks me.

"Yep, sorted but I do have a question." I tell her.

"What's that?"

"Your Mum is concerned that you threatened to kill yourself. Want to fill me in about that one?"

Rosie looks a little shame-faced and says, "Yeah, I left her a note telling her that I was going to kill myself. I just wanted her to feel as crap as I've been feeling. I thought that saying that might make her think."

"I understand what you were trying to do, but threatening suicide is a huge deal, Rosie. Believe me, I know. It's not something to say lightly because people remember. I know because I've said it and I know the hurt and worry that it's caused people."

"I didn't think, I just wanted to cause her the same kind of hurt she's been causing me. She has no idea how I'm feeling and no interest in listening to me. Surely that's not what a mother should be like?"

I do understand but I can't condone her behaviour. I know first-hand how upset people become when suicide is mentioned and, regardless of what Sarah has or has not done, she doesn't deserve that.

"Welcome to the house of Jessie," Carl quips, "Just remember that the first rule is that Jess expects her needs to be catered for before the rest of us get a thing! Remember that and you'll be fine and dandy. It's good to have you here, kiddo."

And it is good to have her here. I love Rosie's company and, I have to admit, I enjoy having the opportunity to look after her for a while.

Rosie stays with us for the next three days. On two of the days, she comes to work with me and develops a fascination for all things NLP when she sits in on an NLP in Leadership course that I'm running. As we're driving home, she's waxing lyrical about her experiences and making insightful, intelligent links to what she wants to do in social work.

"Just think if all social workers knew this stuff!" she enthuses. "What an awesome difference it would make to the way that we could help and inspire people."

The fact that she's saying 'we' before she even starts studying tells me that her heart is set.

When Saturday comes and Rosie has been with us for the start of her fourth day, the time has come to broach the subject of her going home. If it were just up to me, she could stay for as long as she likes, but I know that this isn't the best thing for either her or for her family. I've been texting Sarah every day to let her know that Rosie is okay, but have yet to receive a reply. Today, I know that it's time for action.

"Rosie," I say to her while we're eating breakfast together, "I love having you here and you're always welcome when you need us."

"But?" she asks perceptively.

"But I'm worried about the impact it's having on your Mum. I know that she's not been very communicative but I bet she's missing you."

"Missing me? She's probably pleased that she doesn't have to be near me. I think that she has you and me in the same neat little box in her head – the one marked 'trouble'."

I can't help but smile: there's probably a lot of truth in that statement.

"Even so, I think we should ring her. Apart from anything else, you're missing school and that's not great when you're so close to exams."

When did I become so grown up in my thinking?

"So what do we do?" Rosie asks.

"I'm thinking that we give her a call and maybe suggest that we meet at your Nan and Granddad's tomorrow. What do you think?"

"I'd rather not, but I think we probably should. Just promise me that if she's completely vile I can come back with you?"

Reasonable I guess, but it probably won't be popular. Where is my loyalty? With my sister or with my niece? I know where it should be, but I can't help but be on Team Rosie for this one.

"Okay, if we really can't find a resolution and you really feel that you can't go back, you can come back with us. Fair?"

"Very fair, thank you."

"Just promise me that you will try and sort it out. If you need to come back with us, we've all failed really, haven't we?"

I guess that was a rhetorical question and didn't need a response. I decide that the best thing to do is to call Mum and Dad, fill them in about what's been going on and ask if it's okay to use their house as neutral ground tomorrow.

I call them and they agree. They are as keen to resolve everything as the rest of us.

I call Sarah. To say that she isn't pleased to hear from me would be an understatement.

"Sarah, I'd like to work out a way for us to get Rosie back home" I tell her.

"Bored with the role of cool Auntie Eve are we?" she asks.

Ignore, it, ignore it, just stay focused upon the reason you're having this conversation.

"I just think that it would be best for everyone if Rosie could come home and we can start to move forward," I say in the most reasonable tone I can muster.

"Well, thank you for that statement of the obvious. And how do you propose to achieve this?"

"I've spoken to Mum and Dad and they have invited us all to meet at their house tomorrow to talk everything through. Does that work for you?" I ask.

"Depends what time. Ronald and I are playing golf in the morning."

"We can be as flexible as you like. What time are you likely to finish? We'll fit around you," I say, hopefully sounding a lot more reasonable than I am feeling.

"We'll be there for 2pm but you'll have to bear with us if we are late: you never know how long a round will take," Sarah says.

"Absolutely fine, Sarah. We'll make sure that we are there for two, but we'll understand if you are a little later."

"Right then, tomorrow afternoon it is. Goodbye, Eve." With that, the phone goes dead. Goodbye to you too, Sarah.

I tell Rosie what has been agreed and she says, "So, only another twenty eight hours of freedom then."

I give her a sideways glance. She smiles and says, "I was only meaning that we'd better make them count."

I can go with that. Carl is out for the day, renewing his bromance with James, and so we plan a girly day of a trip into town for shopping and lunch. Over lunch, Rosie asks me a question which I wasn't expecting.

"You know how you told me that you have told people that you were going to kill yourself?"

"Yes…" I reply, wondering what it coming next.

"Did you really mean it? What happened?"

"You really want to know?" I ask, wondering just how honest to be.

"Yes, I want to know."

"Well, I've struggled with my mental health for years and years. When things turn black, I don't want to be here anymore. I don't want to have to think or to be." I find myself about to quote another Matchbox 20 lyric. I have no doubt that the reference will mean anything to Rosie, but I decide to go for it anyway.

"The best way I can think to describe it is to quote a song lyric that you'll probably never have heard of."

"Try me," Rosie encourages.

"It's me, and I can't get myself to go away."

"And is that how it feels?" she asks.

"Yes, when I'm in the depths I can escape from everybody else, but I can never escape from my own head."

"And that's when you wish that you weren't here anymore?"

"Yes. One of the things that I've realised, though, is that there is a big difference between not wanting to be here and wanting to be dead." Am I being too honest here?

Rosie thinks for a moment and then asks me, "Have you ever tried to kill yourself?"

"No, I've thought about it several times but never gone as far as actually planning to do myself in. I don't know if I'm too much of coward or whether the thought of the hurt I'd leave behind has stopped me."

"Wow, I never realised that things got so bad for you," Rosie said.

"I'm glad you didn't know because I don't really want anyone to know. I know how much it worries your Nan and Granddad and it's something I don't want anyone to experience. It would be selfish of me to put that onto anyone."

"But how do you deal with it and keep going on?" she asks.
"Not very well." I admit. "I cause a lot of hurt to Carl and to my Mum and Dad and I'm very ashamed of that. I'm trying to find some psychological support at the moment. I'm a mess, honey. I'm trying my best to be less of a mess because I can't carry on like this – for my own sake or for the sake of the people I love."

Rosie looks at me, searching for something to say.

"I think that maybe I've just been far too honest with you," I say, wondering if I crossed another line I shouldn't have.

"I asked you and you told me," she said simply. "Thank you for telling me."

"That's why it upset me when your Mum said that you'd talked about killing yourself. Believe me, even if you say it in passing, for whatever reason, it stays with people for a lot longer than it probably stays with you," I say with the voice of bitter experience.

"I understand. I didn't really want to hurt myself, you know. I just wanted to shock Mum into listening to me."

"I know, sweetheart. Just think about shocking her in a different way next time, eh?"

She smiles and the conversation moves on. She tells me about a pair of killer shoes that she's been after for ages and she's heard they're in the sale. We finish our lunch and start our killer boots quest.

When we arrive home, both somewhat jaded from our trudge around the shops but with Rosie triumphant (having found said boots at a truly knockdown price), Carl is home and watching the football results come in. I'm happy to learn that Spurs have won, keeping them in strong contention for the European places. Carl's happy too as Leeds scored a last-minute winner to keep them ahead of the relegation battle which is starting to hot up.

"So, lovely ladies, what's the plan for tonight then? Are you going to wine me and dine me?" Carl asks, playfully.

"Rosie?" I ask, "Want to head out again or have a night in?"

"Not sure my feet want to move again tonight, if it's all the same to you," she replies, wearily.

"A take-away, a DVD and a bottle of wine or two then?" I suggest to the nodding agreement of both parties.

Rosie chooses the DVD from Carl's vast collection, we order the food, open the wine and settle in for a night of lazy indulgence. We both find Rosie's company so easy and she wins extra brownie points with Carl when she insists on loading the dishwasher after we've eaten.

The next morning, the relaxed atmosphere of the previous evening has all but vanished as Rosie and I face the fact that we need to confront reality and meet Sarah. We spend the morning finishing her washing and gathering her things. On the journey over to Mum and Dad's, we talk intermittently but we're both preoccupied with our own thoughts. I'm not sure where Rosie's head is, but mine is firmly in the future, thinking about what I can expect from the meeting.

I run through what I want to get out of it – to start Rosie and Sarah talking and understanding one another. I also run through the best way to achieve this and how Sarah might be feeling. I don't know if Sarah has any doubts about what she wants for Rosie. I understand that she truly wants the best for her daughter. That's where the gap probably comes from: everybody wants what's best for Rosie – it's just what we think is 'best' differs. I try to imagine how Sarah might be feeling about the meeting ahead. It's difficult because I don't know how Sarah thinks. When I draw a blank here, I try to imagine how I would feel if the roles were reversed. I'd probably feel threatened and isolated because my daughter had nailed her colours to someone else's mast and was arriving with them, whereas I was arriving on my own.

If we assume that there might be some truth in this, what do I need to do to make Sarah more comfortable? I need to think about where I sit so it doesn't seem like it's Rosie and me against Sarah. I also need to use my words to emphasise what we have in common rather than where we differ. I think I also need to butt out and let them talk before adding my contribution.

As we pull into Mum and Dad's drive, I can feel the tension in Rosie. Before we get out of the car, I do my last-minute pep talk.

"So then, what's the main outcome we're aiming for?" I ask, feeling like the Consultant me rather than the Auntie.

"I want her to start listening to me and take me seriously. I want her to realise this isn't just some childish rebellion and I've really thought it through," Rosie answers.

"And what's the best way of achieving that?" asks Consultant Eve.

"By showing her I'm serious and that my arguments are sound. It's going to be tough, but I guess I need to try to keep my emotions in check, don't I?" Rosie looks to me for reassurance.

"Sounds like a plan to me," I tell her. "Ready to go?"

She nods and we leave the car and knock at the door. Mum answers and hugs us both.

"Are you ready for this, Rosie?" she asks, obviously as concerned as the rest of us about the outcome of what's feeling more and more like a high-level diplomatic summit.

Rosie tells her she's as ready as she'll ever be.

"Good girl!" Mum says, seemingly relieved that Rosie will play her part in what unfolds. "Your Mum isn't here yet, which gives your Granddad time to talk you through his ideas for the meeting. He's been giving it a lot of thought and thinks he's come up with a plan."

As if he has heard his name mentioned, Dad comes into the room, looking pleased with himself.

"I've been thinking about this conversation today and I want to try something I saw on TV," he tells us. "I think we should sit around the table and have just one person talking at a time. We need to have an object to hold - and only the person holding that object is allowed to talk. Now we just need to find a suitable object..."

I can't help but wonder what Dad has been watching, but his idea has a number of merits. We all seem to be prepared to go along with it.

Dad scans the bookshelves that line the dining room and selects the Peter Rabbit doll I bought for Mum years ago, probably while I was still at university.

"This'll do!" he exclaims, holding Peter Rabbit aloft like a valuable trophy. "Whoever has Peter Rabbit can talk and the rest of us will listen. Is that alright with everyone?"

We all nod our agreement and Dad moves on with his master plan.

"Let's move into the dining room so we can plan where everybody is going to sit."

We all dutifully move into the dining room and wait to be assigned our seats.

"I'll sit at the head of the table," Dad tells us, "So I can introduce what's going to happen and keep an eye on the Peter Rabbit rule. Rosie, you sit next to me on that side," he gestures to the side of the table nearest the wall, "You can sit next to your Nan and across from your Mum so that you can look at each other when you're talking. Sarah can go next to me on the other side and Eve next to her. Everybody okay with that?"

Again we all nod and all move to our designated seats. Dad really has thought about this and I'm more than happy to go along with his suggestion. For one thing, I think that it might actually work and, for another, it takes the responsibility away from me. Instead, I can focus on helping to keep the peace. Go for it, Dad! I have to smile to myself with the knowledge that we've only been talking for a few minutes and we've already invented the Peter Rabbit rule.

While I go into the kitchen to help Mum with drinks for everyone, Dad is talking to Rosie. I try not to eavesdrop (actually, that's a big fib) but I hear him coaching his granddaughter and I know that he's determined to make this work.

We've finished our drinks by the time Sarah arrives, slightly flustered and eager to exert her authority upon the situation.

"I did warn you that I might be late; Ronald was held up on the ninth green," she says by way of greeting.

"That's alright, Sarah. No harm done." Dad replies. "We've just been catching up and talking about how we're going to do things today. Let me bring you up to speed before we start. Would you like a cup of tea first?"

Sarah says that she's just had one so Dad ploughs on, introducing Sarah to his plans and the all-important Peter Rabbit rule.

"It all seems a bit excessive to me. Can't we just talk like normal human beings?" Sarah pouts.

"It's just that we've tried that before and it's got us nowhere," Dad tells her. "Everyone else has agreed to give it a go and I'd be grateful if you would too."

I can sense Sarah feeling that she's being backed into a corner and I expect her to come out fighting. However, she doesn't: she accepts it.

"We've saved you a place here," says Dad, indicating towards the vacant seat next to him. "Between me and Eve."

Sarah takes her place and the meeting is ready to start.

Dad takes Peter Rabbit and starts to talk. He has clearly rehearsed his opening remarks and it's important for him to say what he needs to say.

"I'm glad we're all here," he begins, "I like having my four favourite girls together, no matter what the occasion is." Good start, Dad, reminding us that we're all important to him and that we're all responsible for a part of his happiness.

"However," he continues, "It's really upsetting me that this situation is going on and on without any resolution. I think that, today, we should work together to find a way around this, so that everybody is happy with the direction we take."

I nod instinctively, both because I agree with what he's saying and because I want him to know that he's doing a good job. I look around the table and see Mum nodding too. Sarah and Rosie are avoiding one another's gaze, choosing instead to keep their eyes firmly fixed upon the table's shiny surface and the mugs scattered around it.

"Who is going to start us off?" Dad asks, offering Peter Rabbit around the group. I'd like to say my piece, but I know that mine is not the voice that needs to be heard right now. When he receives no takers, he says, "Rosie, how about you? After all this is all about you and your future."

Dad presents Peter Rabbit to Rosie and she starts to talk, a little nervously to start with but soon building in confidence.

"I want to start by saying that I'm sorry if I've worried you by disappearing, Mum, and by making some of those threats. I realise now that I didn't handle things the right way and I am sorry for that."

Good start, kiddo.

"I want you to know," she says, still looking straight at Sarah while she talks, "That I'm serious about wanting a career in social work. I want to help people and help the world to be a better place. It's important to me to do something meaningful. There are a lot of people out there who need help and I think that I could play a part in helping them."

Rosie looks around at the rest of us to see Mum and Dad nodding. I give her a wink of encouragement and she carries on.

"I've researched the best places to study and I've researched possible career paths for people in social work. It's not a dead-end job, Mum: there's potential to have a great career and a meaningful one. That's what I want."

With that, Rosie hands Peter Rabbit back to Dad.

In his role of facilitator and chairperson – of which, it has to be said, he is making a brilliant job – Dad takes back Peter Rabbit and says, "Thank you, Rosie, very well put. I think that really helps us to understand you a bit better. Sarah, would you like to reply to what Rosie has said?"

Before Sarah has a chance to comment, Dad hands her Peter Rabbit. It's funny how we have all so readily accepted the power of this little stuffed toy. Sarah takes Peter Rabbit and turns him over in her hands while she thinks about what she wants to say.

"I want the best for you, Rosie. That's all that your father and I have ever wanted and why we have worked so hard to make sure you can have the best. We had plans for you to go to Oxford or Cambridge and then join one of the professions – accountancy or the law. That's how we think you can make the most of your life. Social work seems like an easy option and something that anybody could do. We don't want you to be just anybody, Rosie."

At this point, she stops. We all wait to hear if there is more to come or if she has said her piece. I'm pleased that she handled it calmly and made it clear that she and Ronald want the best for Rosie. Sarah hands Peter Rabbit back to Dad. Dad looks around the table to see who wants to talk next. Rosie avoids his gaze, looking down at the table. If I had to hazard a guess, I'd say that she was working through her emotions and trying to put the words together for what she wants to say next.

In the absence of any other takers, I raise my hand as a signal that I'd like to take Peter Rabbit. My thinking is not to offer an opinion, but to express the common ground that we've established and make it clear that, while we may have different opinions, we all have the same end goal. I also want to give Rosie and Sarah some thinking time without an uncomfortable silence.

Dad hands me Peter Rabbit and says, "Eve, then, over to you."

"I just wanted to clarify that I think we've reached an important point: we've established that everybody wants the best for Rosie. It seems to me that we just need to understand what 'the best' means. Rosie used the word 'meaningful' a couple of times and that's obviously important, to feel as though she's doing something worthwhile."

Rosie sends me a brief smile and Sarah shoots me a look that I don't really understand: all I know is that she wants me to shut up. I don't have anything else to add and so I do shut up. I raise Peter Rabbit in the air to offer him up to the next speaker. Mum indicates that she'd like to say something and so I pass Peter Rabbit to her.

"We all need to remember that this is Rosie's life we're discussing and she needs to be comfortable with the decisions that she makes. Rosie is an intelligent and talented young woman with a great future to look forward to, and she needs to make sure her future is in something that will make her happy."

I could have kissed Mum for saying this. It's what I would have liked to have said, but was worried that Sarah would perceive it as me stirring up trouble.

Mum's words have triggered something in both Sarah and Rosie as they both reach out for Peter Rabbit. Sarah gets there first and so has the floor again.

"It's all very well for you to think about Rosie's happiness: in your positions, you can afford to do that. Ronald and I need to think about our daughter's financial stability and what is going to give her the best options. We want her to be able to enjoy the same high standard of living that we enjoy. We want her to look back on her life and know that she was successful. For that, she needs the financial security of a good profession."

I see Rosie wrestling with a number of different emotions and I'm worried that she is going to hit out. I think I'd be tempted to, given what she was hearing. She stays quiet for a minute and then signals that she'd like to talk. Sarah hands her Peter Rabbit.

"Mum, I appreciate what you're saying but there is a big thing you need to realise. I'm not you and I'm not Dad. Success for me isn't about a nice house and being a member of the golf club: it's about knowing I've done something to help people and about finding someone to share my life who gets what I do and why I do it. I know you don't approve of the way that Eve lives her life but, Mum, what you don't see is the way she helps people through her training and the difference she makes to how people think and feel about themselves. I want some of that: I want to know that I have left people in a better state than I found them. Can't you understand how important that is to me?"

Oooh, not quite what I was hoping to hear... bringing me into the conversation and holding me up as the example she wants to emulate will not go down well with Sarah. Sarah grasps Peter Rabbit.

"So you're telling me that you would rather be like Eve than like your Dad and me?" she spits in disbelief.

Rosie looks at Dad to see if she can take the rabbit and talks again. He nods and passes the toy to her.

"What I'm saying is that I want to find my own path and that path might not be what you and Dad think is the right one, but it will be right for me. Mum, there is more than one way to live your life. I know what you and Dad have given me and I'm grateful, but I know what I want to do and I know why I want to do it. I'll find a way to do it whatever you think but I'd like to do it with all of you on my side and supporting my decisions."

When she makes this last statement, she reaches out her hands to Sarah. Sarah ignores the gesture.

Rosie carries on. "Mum, surely you don't want me to spend years studying something I don't want to do and be miserable about it? Think of it this way: if I study social work and don't like it, I can still go into accountancy or the law. They hire people from all kinds of backgrounds. All I'm asking is that you let me try it my way. I'm not closing down too many options – apart from maybe medicine or something very specialised. But if I don't study social work, I'll be closing down that option and I really don't want to."

If this were a cheesy American film, this would be the moment when Mum, Dad and I whoop for joy and carry Rosie around on our shoulders. This last statement was so beautifully put that I can't help but feel torrents of pride in my niece. She stayed calm and thought about what she wanted to say and delivered a killer argument. I realise that I have forgotten to check out Sarah's response. Her mind seems to be racing to find a way of objecting to what Rosie said but drawing a blank.

Dad takes Peter Rabbit from Rosie. "I think," he says, "That Rosie has made an excellent case for herself and you have our support," he looks at Mum for confirmation and receives it, "To go out there and follow your dreams. What do you say, Sarah?"

Dad hands Peter Rabbit to Sarah, waiting for her response. I realise that this is going to make or break this, that she has to make a choice to about whether she listens to Rosie or dismisses the whole thing. Please make the right decision, Sarah. I look at her, trying to catch her eye, but I can't.

"If you can prove to us that studying social work could still lead to an offer from one of the big accountancy or law firms, we'll discuss it," she says. I feel a collective exhalation from the other people around the table. "That doesn't mean that we'll agree to everything you want to do, just that we'll talk about it."

Dad says, "Well, that's all we can ask at this stage. We just want you to keep talking to each other. So, Rosie, you're going to do some research into what the degree you want to do could open up for you once you graduate and Sarah, you're going to listen to what Rosie has to say. Is that fair?"

Rosie nods enthusiastically, Sarah less so. She played it well, but I guess that she had no real option. If I were her, I'd probably be feeling a little cornered, and I'm not sure that that would feel particularly good.

"And so," Dad says, "Is there anything else anyone wants to add before we adjourn this meeting and put Peter back on his shelf?"

Rosie takes Peter Rabbit and says, "Yes. I'd like to say one last thing. Firstly, I want to say thank you to Mum for listening to me. Secondly, I'd like to say thank you to Granddad for coming up with the Peter Rabbit idea – it really worked. Thirdly, I'd like to say thank you to Eve for taking me in and for helping me to get my thoughts straight. Finally, Mum, I'd like to come home now."

Smiles all round. I wonder if Rosie has, in fact, missed her calling and should be planning a career in international diplomacy.

And so, the Peter Rabbit circle, as it will now be forever known, breaks up, feeling that we've achieved our objectives. Rosie collects her stuff from my car and puts it in Sarah's. As the three of us leave, I hear Dad saying to Mum, "I think that worked didn't it?" and hear Mum saying, "You did a great job".

I hug Rosie goodbye and she whispers, "Thank you for everything."

I whisper back, "Sweetheart, you don't need my help, you nailed it all by yourself."

As I am about to pull out of the drive, Sarah knocks on my window. A chance at some reconciliation? I hope so. I smile as I wind down the window.

"Hi Sarah. How are you feeling now? It's good to be able to talk without Peter Rabbit in your hand eh?"

"There's no need to be so smug, Eve. You might be feeling as though you've won a victory today, but remember that I know just how selfish and manipulative you are. I know you staged all of this to get your own way."

What? Where did that come from? I wasn't feeling smug, I was feeling pleased that we'd moved forward.

"Now, please move your car so that I can take my daughter home, where she belongs."

With that, Sarah turned around, climbed into the driver's seat and waited for me to move.

I play those last words over and over in my mind. What had I done to make her think I was smug, selfish or manipulative? After five minutes' driving, when I was away from the house, I pulled the car into a parking area and turned off the engine. All of the warm and hopeful feelings I'd had as we left Mum and Dad's had been replaced by a sense of complete incomprehension. Had I missed something? Had I said the wrong things? I'd only spoken once and that had been a pretty neutral statement. I feel the tears well up in my eyes and then plop onto my cheeks. I didn't know what to do, what to say, what to think. I was at a complete loss. Had I really got things so badly wrong?

I sit in the lay-by for what seems like an eternity. I feel completely bewildered. Usually, I have an innate sense of mood and am particularly tuned into the negative things that I might be accused of. If anything, I invent negatives and make things appear worse than they actually are. I trust my inner sense and today, my inner sense told me that we had done a good job between us and should be slapping each other on the back in a celebration of that job well done. What had I missed? How could my behaviour be construed as smug, manipulative and selfish?

While I'm sat there, the voices in my head have their usual field day, persuading me that Sarah's right. I rake back through my memory and find examples of when I considered myself to be selfish and there are a lot of them – my explosions, times when I've caused hurt to other people, actions I've taken which served my needs rather than other people's. When I think of myself being smug, I think of examples of when I've had good news, won a piece of work or received great feedback from somebody on my course. The kinder voices might have described this as grateful rather than smug, but right now, the kinder voices have been drowned into silence. Manipulative I find more difficult. I know that, despite all of my many faults, I am too open for my own good. The idea that I could be perceived as manipulative by anybody horrifies me.

I pull myself together enough to continue the drive home. I try to distract myself by listening to music but it doesn't work: those three words just keep reverberating around my head. I'm deep in thought and halfway home when my phone rings. I see from the hands-free screen that it's Carl. I answer him, trying to keep my voice level.

"Hey, gorgeous!" he says. "I've just phoned your Mum and she said you left a while a go so I wondered where you were. Sounds like you played a blinder between you all: your Mum was delighted with what happened."

"Carl," I ask, "Am I smug?"

"Only when Spurs win," he quips.

"I'm being serious. Am I smug? Am I selfish? Am I manipulative?"

"What is this, Eve?" Carl asks warily.

"Sarah told me that I was smug, selfish and manipulative and I'm scared that she's right. Am I?"

"I don't understand. I thought that today's meeting was a big success. What am I missing?" he asks, unsure of what he's getting into. I realise that he was looking forward to a positive, hopeful conversation. Instead, he gets this.

I tell him what Sarah said as we were leaving Mum and Dad's. "She's right, isn't she? I'm all of those things and worse. She's probably just saying what everybody else is thinking." Those voices have done a spectacular job of winding me up into a state of utter self-loathing.

Carl stays quiet for a minute and then speaks. "Eve, I don't understand this and I don't understand why you're taking it so much to heart when everybody that I've spoken to is positive about what you did. You're listening to Sarah and no-one else, and that's neither accurate nor fair. Where are you now? Just get home safely and then we can talk."

I tell him I'm about forty-five minutes from home and promise I'll drive safely and get back as quickly as I can. I switch the radio on and hope that Radio Four can distract the voices for long enough to get me home in one piece. I watch my speed and pay extra attention and arrive home about fifty minutes later.

I open the door. Jess is there to greet me. She has no awareness of our emotions or mood: her drivers of food and cuddles transcend anything else. I stroke her as she wraps herself around my legs, making it difficult to take off my boots. I go into the living room, expecting to find Carl there, but it's empty. I hear noises upstairs and find him in the bath, reading. He must be well and truly lost in his book as he doesn't seem to notice I've come in. He jumps when he notices me.

"Hello," he says, "I must've lost track of time. I'm glad you're back safely. Give me five minutes to get out of the bath and I'll be all yours."

I go downstairs and wait for him. He comes down ten minutes later, dressed and carrying a beer. He offers me one but I don't want anything.

"So then," he says, "Tell me all about it. Start by telling me about the meeting and then about what happened with Sarah."

I tell him about the meeting and what we'd managed to achieve between us. He laughs about the Peter Rabbit rule and says that he thinks it all sounds very positive. Then I tell him what Sarah had said to me in the car.

"But that doesn't make sense after everything else you've told me".

"It didn't make sense to me either," I tell him, "But I obviously did something to make her say what she said. Maybe she's right, maybe I pretend to be as good as I can be, but maybe I'm selfish and manipulative. Maybe she sees through me in a way that no-one else does."

I run through all of the evidence that I've dredged from my memory banks to support Sarah's opinions.

After a couple of minutes, he holds his hands up and says, "Eve, enough! This is insane. Stop it."

"But she means it and I have to accept that. You want to see the best in me and maybe ignore some of the bits you'd rather not acknowledge. I'm not a good person, Sarah sees that and maybe you should too."

"I'm not listening to this," Carl says angrily.
"I'm not doing this again, Eve. I've had enough. Don't think that I have you on some kind of pedestal. I know your faults just as you know mine. Despite that, I know you're a good person and I love you. Eve, you have a choice to make: you can believe the spiteful words of one person and then think of everything that supports it, or you can listen to the rest of us. Your choice, Eve. You can listen to me or you can throw away all the support and positive stuff you get from me, Rosie and your Mum and Dad. Throw it away if you want, but you're going to be throwing away a lot more than you realise."

He stands up. "I'm serious," he says, "And now I'm going out. I'd suggest that you have a long think about what you want, Eve, because if you carry on like this, you're going to push all of us away." I hear the door slam and I am left on my own.

I think I've gone too far this time. I've listened to all of the negative crap in my head and put this above the opinions of the people who have stuck by me when most people would have given up. I'm scared that Carl has finally had enough. I don't blame him.

The evening goes by in a blur of self-pity. I take a bath and go to bed. I hear Carl come back - I have no idea what time. I'm hoping that he'll come into the bedroom and we can talk. He doesn't. He cleans his teeth and then heads for the spare room and spends the night there.

I can't sleep and just lie in bed, staring at the ceiling. The voices won't give me a break and I have nothing powerful enough to drown them out. So, this is me; this is what being Eve will be like for the rest of my days. I'm incapable of accepting the support I'm so generously offered because I don't believe I'm worth supporting. How can I expect anyone to love me or even like me when I can't find it within me to like myself? One phrase keeps echoing in my mind:

I've had enough.
I've had enough.
I've had enough.
I've had enough.
I've had enough.
I've had enough.
I'VE HAD ENOUGH.

Chapter Seven

The Incident

I'm up early the next morning to catch the 6.30 train to London. I look in on Carl in the spare room, hoping that he will be awake enough to give me a sign of how he feels towards me, but he is still flat out and I don't want to wake him. I'll just have to wait until later to learn my fate.

I really don't relish the thought of getting the train and being perky all day, but it's an important day which could lead to more work, so I have a little chat to myself and bring Work Eve out to play. At least it's a subject I know really well – Influential Communications – and the group I'm working with turns out to be lovely and very interested in the course.

As I work through the materials with them, I find my head flashing back to the previous day and wondering why I was completely inept when it came to using these Influential Communication skills on my sister. I still couldn't pinpoint the moment when I'd made such a serious mistake that prompted her to call me those things. I analyse and I analyse, but I can't identify that moment. Maybe, I reason, it wasn't about yesterday. Maybe they are a series of pent-up accusations that she's been building for a while. It can't be easy for her that her daughter relates to me more easily than she does to her. If the situation were reversed, I think I'd feel resentful too.

Whenever the group are doing practical activities, I sneak a look at my phone to see if I've had any communication from Carl. There isn't any. This worries me as he usually texts and emails me a lot. The growing sense of doom tells me that I have seriously blown it this time. I can't get my head around the thought of life without Carl. He's always been there for me, despite what I've done to push him away. Maybe this time, I've pushed just a bit too hard and he's had enough.

While I'm with the group doing my thing and being perky and interesting, I can keep going. Once they have all left for the day and it's just me, the panic takes over and I start to worry about the changes that might now happen in my life. I need to know how he's thinking and don't want to wait until I walk through the door to find out. When I'm on the train home, I text him to tell him I'm on my way back.

"Hi. I hope your day's been good. I'm on the 1640 train home so should be back by 7. I hope we can talk. I don't know how you're feeling about me, but I love you and I'm sorry xxx"

His reply takes about an hour to come through, by which point I've tied myself up in knots.

"Sorry, left my phone last night and only just got it back. I love you too but we do need to talk. See you later xx"

I start to analyse the text in great detail. Two kisses rather than three? I love you but? I convince myself that I need to prepare for a conversation which ends with us both going our separate ways. I start to dread arriving back home. I dawdle as I leave the train, stretching out the time that I have left before my world turns upside down.

When I can delay the inevitable no longer, I put my key in the lock and go into the house. Carl is waiting for me in the living room. He looks almost as nervous as I feel. I take comfort from the fact that he gets up to kiss me, and has made me a cup of tea. But can I take comfort from it? Is it a sign that things will be okay or is he softening the blow that's coming my way?

"Are you coming to sit down so we can talk?" he asks me.

I can't think of a good reason not to, so I sit and prepare myself. Carl has clearly thought through what he wants to say.

"Eve, I need you to listen to me. I need you to give me your full attention and switch off those voices which are probably already chattering away in your head. Okay?"

I nod. I don't think I've never known him so serious, so intent on his message. I try to stay in the moment and not give way to the critics in my head: I know it's important to focus on every word Carl says to me.

"I was angry with you last night," Carl begins, "And I'm sorry if that added to the way you were feeling."

I want to interrupt him and tell him that it's okay, try to make him feel better about what has happened, but I think better of it. I don't want to interrupt his flow.

"However, I am angry. I love the part of you that gives so much to so many people, but I'm as angry as hell with the other part of you that seems intent on destroying everything. That part of you pushes away all of the positive, supportive, loving stuff that you get from so many people and focuses only upon the negative baggage you get from a few. It makes me feel like everything I say to you – all of which I mean, by the way – is wasted because you just throw it away. Why is it that people like Sarah and Barbara have a higher priority in your head than me, your Mum and Dad, your friends? Why take everything they say to heart and throw the rest away?"

I don't know what to say. When he puts it like that, I can understand why he's so angry. I dismiss all the wonderful things that he and most of my family and friends give me. What, actually, is the point in them giving me anything when I spurn it so readily?

"Is it really so difficult for you to believe that we really love you?" Carl asks. "It's almost as if you can't accept it because it doesn't match what you think about yourself. Is that what it is? You don't think you're worth loving, so you can't believe that anyone does?"

Carl looks at me, as though indicating that it is my turn to speak. I hesitate for a moment to make sure I'm interpreting him correctly. He stays quiet and so I begin to talk.

"I've listened to every word that you have said and it makes so much sense. You're right, I don't think I do deserve love from you or anyone else, so I can't believe you actually care about me. I throw it all away because it doesn't match my feelings for myself. I spend so much time telling myself how useless I am that I guess I collect evidence – from Sarah, from Barbara – which supports what I'm telling myself. I don't know what to say to you except that I'm sorry. I love you and I don't know what I'd do without you. Please don't leave me."

Carl smiles and strokes my face. "I'm not going to leave you – not yet anyway. I do need you to get some help, though. If you carry on like this, you'll push everyone away so that you can prove your opinion of yourself is right. You're my love and it breaks my heart that you can't find the good in yourself when there is so much good to find. Please, Evie, please find a way to sort your head out and learn how to see yourself like we all see you. It's no accident, you know, that you have so much love around you: it's because you give so much to everyone else and so little to yourself."

These words set the tears flowing and, once they start, I cannot stop them. I cry and I cry, thinking about all of the pain I've caused to the people around me and all for what? As Carl says, so that I can prove that I am as worthless of love as I believe?

I feel so selfish and so blinkered, as though I've been focusing upon my thoughts and my feelings instead of truly listening to anyone else.

When I can form real words through the sobs, I promise Carl that I'll find help and that I'll no longer disregard the good things others give me.

"Baby, that's all I ask. I'll be here all the way with you. Now come here, Mrs Bug-Eyed Monster."

He folds me up into his arms and holds me tight. I don't think that I've ever been more grateful for anything. We sit together for a long time while my snuffles subside. I haven't lost Carl but I need to make some serious changes. I owe it to Carl, I owe it to Mum and Dad, and I owe it to my friends. What I need to do is to find a way of owing it to myself too.

Once we've finished our very prolonged cuddle, I do some practical things. I open my post and find that I have a letter from the Mental Health services inviting me to an appointment with a clinical psychologist the following Monday. I some ways, I'm very pleased because I want to get this sorted out as quickly as possible. In other ways, I'm nervous at what I might discover about myself and the strange workings in my head.

I tell Carl about the appointment and he is most definitely pleased, telling me that the sooner I talk to someone, the sooner I can start to heal myself. Nice way to put it. Maybe I need to find a way of evicting myself from my own head and letting Carl take up residence instead.

Over the next few days, Carl and I are a little tentative around each other. He seems to be watching me closely to make sure I'm stable and not going to do anything daft. I am watching him for signs that he's with me because he wants to be, not because he feels that he has to be. I'm not exactly sure what signs I think that I might find, but I keep looking anyway. I'm happy when he shows me spontaneous signs of affection and I gradually relax into the knowledge that he's still with me.

One annoyance hits me towards the end of the week. I'd planned to meet up with Alex over the weekend and had booked theatre tickets for us on the Friday evening. However, on Thursday afternoon, I receive a text from her:

"Eve, I'm SO sorry to do this, but I'm going to have to cancel. One of the kids is ill and I don't want to leave them. Can we rearrange? Xxx"

I know that she has a family and her commitment to them comes first, but this is the third time in a row she's cancelled on me: the first was the get together in Birmingham, the second, my birthday and the third, this weekend. I don't know whether I have the right to feel pissed off about it, but I do. I haven't seen her in so long and I was really looking forward to the weekend. I try to talk it through with myself and come to the conclusion that I'm being selfish and don't really understand the responsibilities that come with having children. So now I'm annoyed with Alex for cancelling and annoyed with myself for being annoyed – two for the price of one.

I ask Carl if he'd like to come to the theatre and he laughs so I take that as a no. I text George to find out whether he's free and he says that he'd love to come with me. We have a great evening together, dinner first at a nearby Chinese restaurant then off to watch the play. George always indulges my desire for Chinese food. Carl doesn't like it, so I take any opportunity when I'm out without him to eat it.

The play is wonderful - a modern-day take on one of my favourite Shakespeare plays and it works perfectly. It's at the Royal Exchange Theatre which I've always loved. The theatre in the round always makes me feel as though I'm truly part of what's going on. Afterwards, George raves about how they have made such an old play so relevant to us today. He's always been a bit sceptical about Shakespeare, but I think he's now a convert.

The rest of the weekend is low key but fun. We spend our Saturday at the cinema taking in two films, with a trip to the Spice Valley in the middle. It feels a little self-indulgent but I think that Carl deserves a little indulgence after the stressful week before. On Sunday evening, I can feel myself getting tense, thinking about the trip to the psychologist the following day. I find myself snapping at Carl when he spends two hours poring over one of the Leeds United fan sites. He looks at me and frowns.

"Is this Eve talking or Eve who's strung out about what awaits her tomorrow?" he asks.

I can't defend myself as I know that he's right.

The next morning, I am nervous but ready. As he goes out to work, Carl kisses me and tells me to make the most of the experience.

I arrive at the Health Centre ridiculously early (a sure sign of nerves) and sit in the car listening to the radio until ten minutes before the appointment. I wait until the allotted time and then a man comes to greet me. He introduces himself as Hugh and makes some small talk about the weather. He takes me into his office and indicates for me to sit in one of the chairs. Although his approach is welcoming and laid back, I feel my nerves beginning to rise. I hear myself talking absolute rubbish as he continues to talk about the weather. When I'm nervous, I babble.

When I finally shut up, Hugh tells me what will happen next. He tells me that he's read the notes from my meeting with Jackie, but wants to hear from me in my own words about what has brought me to see him. Then, once we've established what I want to achieve, he'll suggest the best course of action and we'll set up future appointments to work together.

I describe to him about the explosions and how they scare me. I tell him about the most recent one after Sarah's anniversary lunch and the impact that it had on Carl, Mum and Dad. He listens intently, stopping every now and again to ask me a question. I answer him as fully and as honestly as I can, determined to do whatever I can to help myself. The questions Hugh asks give me confidence that he's genuinely listening and trying to understand. This spurs me on to talk more and explore the situation. Unlike my conversation with Jackie, it feels as though he is keeping an open mind and not trying to steer me down a specific path.

We talk for about forty five minutes. Hugh takes notes throughout. At this point, he starts to bring the session to a close by summing up. His summary is accurate: it feels a bit weird to hear it all said back to you, almost as if it's happening to someone else. After his summary, Hugh tells me that he thinks it best to try something called Cognitive Analytic Therapy. He explains that we'll try to map out what happens around the explosions and work on my relationships with the people around me. He asks if this sounds okay to me and I tell him that he's the expert and I trust him to choose the right path forward. We arrange a session for the same time the following Monday.

When I come out, I try to work out how I'm feeling. Although I didn't expect an instant cure – if, indeed there is one – but I thought that I might feel different and have more to tell people about what happened. At least I've taken the first step and started the process. Now, I should be heading in the right direction.

I phone Carl from the car and then, when I've arrived home, I call Mum and Dad. The general consensus seems to be that I've done well in taking the first positive step and that they're pleased I've found someone who seems willing to help.

So, I guess so far so good, but we really are only at the beginning.

The following week's session seems to come around in a flash. It only feels like two minutes since I was last sitting opposite Hugh in this magnolia-painted room. Nothing much has happened in the previous week. I was away for a couple of days with work and Carl had a bumper number of people passing their driving tests. He's found a new sci-fi series to download and has been almost permanently glued to that every spare moment that he's had. I've had a couple of texts from Rosie and she appears to be making some progress with Sarah and Ronald. Although I'm really pleased, I'm also cautious about being too effusive in my replies as I don't want Sarah to have more reasons to come down on me.

Hugh tells me he'd like to start by mapping the process of one of my explosions. It's soon apparent that he's a visual thinker. I struggle with this a bit because I really don't think in pictures, so I suggest that he adds words to his drawings. I'm comfortable with words and they help me to understand his pictures.

He asks me how I like to be when living my normal life. I think about this for a minute because everything I want to say sounds cheesy. I tell Hugh this and he advises me to go with what's in my head. And so we start the cheese-fest. The words that I have in my head are: respectful, giving, welcoming, supportive and inclusive. I share these with Hugh. He adds these to his diagram.

"And what are you like when you're in the middle of an explosion?" he asks me.

That's a difficult one because I don't really have any memory of these times, and so I have to go on what those who've witnessed the explosions tell me. These words come to me a lot more easily and I don't feel the need to self-edit or check for the cheese factor. The list tumbles out: disrespectful, out of control, manic, screaming, self-absorbed, shameful, hurtful... the list goes on. I think about what Carl, Mum and Dad have said to me and add another word – suicidal.

"Do you think that you are suicidal when this is happening?" Hugh says with a tinge of concern in his voice.

"I don't know. I don't think so, but I talk about it. I talk about wanting to escape and, last time it happened, I talked about throwing myself under a bus. Regardless of whether I really do feel suicidal, I hate myself for worrying people and leaving them with the fear that I am going to harm myself."

"It's almost as if you become the exact opposite of what you want to be," Hugh offers and he's right. It's as if everything I stand for is dismissed and replaced by everything that I abhor.

"Help me to understand what leads up to an explosion... How do you feel before it happens?" Hugh asks.

I think about this, trying to work out the series of events and feelings that precede the explosions, trying to find the patterns.

"I always feel a lot of pressure before I explode," I venture.

"And where does that pressure come from?" Hugh asks.

"Sometimes, there are outside influences, but most of it comes from me." This is something of a revelation as I always assumed the pressure was external. In that moment, however, I realise that it is almost exclusively self-imposed - pressure I put upon myself.

"And what is this pressure telling you to do?"

Again, I think for a moment before answering; he's asking me questions which delve right to the heart of what's happening.

"It's more what the pressure is telling me not to do," I answer. "Not to behave badly or inappropriately, not to say anything which other people may misinterpret, not to do are say anything in anyway hurtful."

"That's an awful lot of pressure," Hugh observes. "Must make it difficult to relax."

"It makes it pretty much impossible to relax," I concede, "I feel like if I relax, I'm in danger of making a mess of things. I miss out on so many things because I can never quite be in the moment and just go with the flow. It's like I have to make a choice – should I relax or should I behave myself?"

"As well as the pressure that you're feeling, what else is going on?" Hugh asks.

"I have this overriding feeling that I'm being judged by everybody, like everybody has an opinion about me and like everybody's talking about me."

"And what do you think they're saying?"

"It's never positive. They're always picking up on the bad parts of my character and my behaviour."

"Do you think that this is an accurate assessment of what is really happening?"

"It feels real at the time, but I don't know for sure. Carl says that I think that everybody is judging me because I'm judging myself and so assume that everybody else is doing the same. Whether they are or not, my head is convinced that everybody is against me." I must sound absolutely crazy. I look at Hugh to see if he's thinking how crazy I am, but he continues to scribble his notes, his face totally impassive.

"So we've talked about how you feel before an explosion, but what about afterwards?" Hugh asks me.

Again the words tumble out easily.

"Ashamed, vulnerable, out of control, angry with myself for the damage that I've caused, needing to make amends."

Hugh stops for a moment to sketch out the finished diagram – the visual representation of my journey through an explosion from before it happens to the moment itself and then how I feel afterwards. He shows me when he's finished and I agree that this encapsulates it pretty much perfectly. The picture helps me to understand the process and I can start to see the transition from acceptable me to unacceptable me.

"Are there ever times when you don't explode but you worry about your behaviour?"

I think back to times when I've allowed myself to relax and then start to worry about the impact that I've had. Whenever I go out and have a glass of wine or let myself talk, I spend the next morning analysing every detail of the occasion and finding examples of what I said that could be misconstrued or what I did that might leave people with a negative impression of me. Like everybody else, there are times when I make a total arse of myself – like when I fell downstairs after a night out with Anna. I assumed that she would think less of me for being clumsy; she was worried that she should have done more to catch me.

I break out of my thoughts to find Hugh looking at me, expecting an answer. How long had I been in my own little world?

I explain what I've just been thinking about to Hugh.

"It sounds like that pressure again," he says to me.

"Yes," I agree, "Pressure to be perfect – or whatever 'perfect' means in any given situation."

"When do you relax?" Hugh asks me.

Another insightful question.

"I relax when I'm with Carl and it's just the two of us," I tell him.

"And what is it that you think makes it okay to relax when it's just you and Carl?"

"I guess that it feels okay to just be me when I'm with Carl. I guess that it doesn't feel as if he judges me. He's seen me at my best and at my worst and he still loves me."

When I think about it, I also realise that, most of the time, I relax around Mum and Dad too. This, I think, is dependent upon the conversation. If we keep it away from stressful topics, I can be okay being me.

We are nearing the end of the session and so Hugh summarises what we've covered. We go through the diagram that he's drawn and talk about the pressure that I feel and the judgement that I feel is coming my way.

I think about this a lot on my journey home. When I was talking to Hugh, it all seemed so obvious. I described it all in such a matter of fact way that it must be something that I was aware of. The more I think about it, the more real it becomes. I'm useless at relaxing and useless at allowing myself simply to be. It's as though I'm caught in a perpetual dilemma – relax or behave. Are the two states really mutually exclusive? Can I not have one without the other?

Am I really acting upon the belief that if I'm relaxed I can't be behaving myself? I think back to my recent social interactions and that's just what I do seem to do. I allowed myself when I had coffee with Rosie and I ended up blabbing about Call Me Babs and the football manager. I had a few drinks at the Uni Girls' get together in Birmingham and I lost the plot. I don't trust myself to be myself. I believe that being me leads to trouble.

I think back to when I was last truly relaxed and it was when Carl and I were in Marsa Alam. How come I could do it then? Because (although there were other people around) we were on our own and not trying to build any other relationships? Because there were no other outside influences that gave me any sense of pressure? Probably both.

Thinking about being in Marsa Alam makes me smile. I remember the freedom of whizzing in and out of the coral formations, the warming feeling of the sun on my skin and the sense that we could be exactly who we wanted to be because nobody else's opinion mattered.

While my mind is wandering back to Egypt, I make myself laugh as I recall our first night. We were still getting used to the place and hadn't quite figured it all out. After dinner, we decided to have a glass of wine on the terrace outside our room to watch the stars. I was sitting peacefully outside when Carl came out to join me. As he came out of the sliding patio doors, he noticed a cat and was so caught up in watching it that he shut the door behind him, inadvertently locking us out. The room keys were inside and the patio door had locked itself.

As usual while I'm on holiday, I had nothing on my feet. Carl had on his flip flops but not his trousers – he'd taken them off after eating an extra portion of cake and they were feeling a tad too tight. So there we were – locked out of our room which was about as far as you could get from Reception, one of us with no shoes and one with no trousers. The fundamental question was, how do we find help? I offered to go but Carl's flip flops were so big on me that they tripped me up with every step. The only solution was for Carl to borrow my jeans and go to Reception.

I sat outside gazing at the stars and listening to the wind rustling through the fronds of the palm trees and waited. And waited and waited. At one point, I thought I heard somebody trying the door, but when Carl didn't appear, I assumed I must be imagining it. At least half an hour went past – in which time I'd polished off my own wine and half of Carl's – and then Carl appeared at the patio door looking as white as a sheet.

"What happened?" I asked after he had opened the door and let me in to rush for a pee.

Carl told me the whole sorry – but not unamusing – story. He'd gone to Reception and braved the laughter when he told the man what had happened. Or could the laughter have been because he was wearing a very girly pair of white jeans? He'd been given a new key card, walked back to the room to try the key but it wouldn't open the door. So, he trudged back to Reception to explain the problem, braved a second bout of laughter and was given yet another key.

He'd told the man at Reception that this new key had better work because his legs were tired from walking to and from Reception.

"My friend," said the man, "I can help you and your legs. Please wait here."

So, Carl waited as instructed and, two minutes later a golf buggy drew up outside the hotel entrance.

"My friend," said Mr Receptionist, "Here is your transport to your room."

This, Carl tells me, is where the terror started. What had started as a nice gesture turned into a white knuckle ride and the golf buggy sped across the hotel complex at speeds that a golf buggy really shouldn't reach. According to Carl, he nearly fell out several times as the buggy careered around corners and went up and down dunes of sand on its way back to our room. He poured himself another glass of wine and downed it in a single gulp.

For the rest of the holiday, every time we went near Reception, Carl was greeted with the cry, "My Many Keys!"

Bringing back these memories reminds me that life is good at times. But it also reminds me that, when I'm not in carefree holiday mode, I struggle to be that same person who finds the fun in situations and laughs wholeheartedly. I'm so serious most of the time because I'm trying to keep myself under control. I don't trust myself. Where on earth does that come from? Partially from experience when I explode but there must be something else.

I'm still pondering what this 'something else' might be when I meet Hugh for my third session the following week.

"How have things been over the past week?" Hugh asks me.

"I've been thinking about everything a lot and working very hard at relaxing," I tell him. He looks at me quizzically and I realise that what I have just said is utterly absurd. Working hard to relax? The perfect definition of an oxymoron!

"And have you been able to relax?" he asks.

"Not a lot, no. I can't switch off: it feels as though I'm constantly trying to find answers but I don't always know the question I'm trying to answer," I tell him.

"What answers have you been trying to find?" he asks.

I tell him about the 'something else' I'm trying to find to explain why I don't trust myself to behave appropriately.

Hugh tells me that this may fit in with what he wants to cover today - thinking about the relationships in my life and their influence upon me.

"Tell me about the people who have the most influence on you," Hugh says.

"Carl, my Mum and Dad and my closest friends are all so supportive," I tell him. "I often wonder why they care as much as they do."

He asks me to describe the influence this group of people have on me and the word that immediately springs to mind is 'enriching'.

"They sound like people that are good to have around," Hugh offers. I nod my agreement.

"Is there anybody that doesn't feel so enriching?" he asks.

Now we're going into rougher terrain, territory that has a HUGE warning sign at the entrance. As though he can sense my reticence to talk about this, Hugh tells me that it's okay to say what I'm thinking. It may be okay to say it, but is it okay to think it?

"My sister, Sarah," I tell him after a long pause.

"And what makes your relationship with Sarah less enriching than the other people you have spoken about?" Hugh asks.

Blimey, where do we start with answering that one?

"I feel as though she is always judging me and always finding me wanting," I tell him. "It's been the same since we were kids, I was the silly little sister that just got in her way and annoyed her. I wonder if that's how she still sees me; I'm not sure she's realised that I've actually grown up and am an independent woman in my own right."

Hugh takes this in, makes a quick note for himself then asks me, "What do you want from your relationship with Sarah?"

That question stops me in my tracks. What do I want? I spend so much time moaning about what I don't want in my relationship with her, but I'm not sure that I've ever flipped it on its head and articulated what I do want. Maybe because I'm constantly focused upon the stuff that I want to get rid of, I just keep getting more of the same. Now there's an interesting thought...

"I would love to have an easy relationship with her," I tell Hugh.
"And what would 'easy' be like?" he asks.

"Easy would be two people coming together because they choose to be together; two people who can talk without any agenda and without any preconceptions of one another."

"What preconceptions do you have of Sarah?"

Wow, these questions really aren't getting any easier. I have to stop and think: in all the time I've spent thinking about Sarah, I've never thought about it this way.

"I expect her to be down on me, I expect to have to justify myself and I expect her to be disappointed in me and in the choices I make. I expect her to be holier than thou and disapproving and to think that I'll never measure up to her expectations. I guess I perceive her life as far too straight-laced, unimaginative and, in the grand scheme of things, unimportant."

"So, you perceive your sister's life choices as being unimportant?"

Hearing my words being reflected back to me is harsh. Here I am complaining about the judgement I get from Sarah when all the time I'm judging her decisions and choices as being unimportant. This hits me - hard. I think about all the times I've taken the piss out of Sarah for the importance she places on her position at the golf club and her seniority at work, the times I've sniggered at her matronly dress sense and her sensible car choices. For somebody who prides herself on being non-judgemental, I am one hell of a judgemental bitch.

I feel totally floored. Is this really me? I start to wonder how many other people for whom I've created equally damning preconceptions . Call Me Babs comes to mind.

Hugh sits in silence until I am ready to continue. "I'm wondering," Hugh begins, using the same approach to softening language that I've encouraged Carl to use with his learner drivers, "How these preconceptions you have about Sarah help you?"

Another excellent question, Mr Hugh, and one for which I have no ready answer. How do they help me? Do they actually help me or do they just create another barrier to prevent Sarah and me from understanding each other?

"I suppose that making fun of her helps me by stopping me from feeling quite so useless. If I can undermine Sarah's way of thinking, her perception of me doesn't hurt quite as much." Did I really just say that? That's almost profound.

I continue. "I've never felt as though I measure up in Sarah's eyes. Because the things that are important to me are not important to her and vice versa, I feel like she doesn't rate who I am and what I've achieved."

"Is it important to you to have Sarah's approval?"

"It must be... because I always hope for it and am always disappointed when it doesn't happen," I say, surprising myself with the words. "When I was little, I always wanted her to take me seriously but she never seemed to. After a while, I stopped trying and even went out of my way to court her disapproval."

"And now?"

"I accept the fact that Sarah and I have chosen very different paths and aspire to very different things but that doesn't stop me wishing she could occasionally let me into her world and try to enter mine." Once again, I surprise myself. I would have laughed if someone had told me I was so keen for Sarah's understanding and approval. But there's no disputing that those words just left my lips.

Hugh glances at the clock and I do the same. I'm amazed to notice that the session is all but over: I hadn't realised we'd been talking for so long. Hugh summarises what we've talked about and then tells me he's away on holiday for the next two weeks. For a moment, I want to tell him that he can't go, that he can't leave me with this huge issue hanging over me. The panic doesn't last for long: I remind myself that the responsibility for sorting this out lies with me, not Hugh. He asks the questions but I give the answers and work out what to do about it. Of course, it would be easier if he just told me what to do. He never does though; in the three sessions we have had together, he has never offered an opinion or made suggestions. I realise that even if he did, the pig-headed part of my character would refuse to accept them anyway. We arrange to meet in three weeks' time and I leave, my head whirring with thought and questions.

I feel an overwhelming need to talk to someone and try to make sense of the jumbled mass of thoughts in my head. I know that Carl is busy with lessons all day and I'm not ready to talk about this with Mum and Dad. I call Anna. She is dashing off to a meeting but promises to call me as soon as she's free. She calls back a little over half an hour later. Anna knows that, when I'm in thinking overdrive like I am just now, the it's best to let me get it all out. Some of the time I work it out just by saying it out loud. Today is not one of those days. As much as I love Anna and am eternally grateful for her positive support, I sometimes wish that she wasn't so completely on my side. There are times when I know that I need a good hard kick up the arse, yet Anna always finds reasons to explain and support my actions.

"Evie, you make fun of Sarah so the hurtful things that she says don't hurt quite so much. You're protecting yourself and that's what you need to do. You've said yourself that she doesn't understand your world and makes no attempt to find out about it and that's absolutely true. You're not a judgemental bitch."

"It's okay to tell me when I'm wrong, you know," I tell her.

"And when you are, I will do," she tells me. "By the way, do you still want some company at Guy's video thingy next week?"

Guy's video thingy is a big deal for him. He's VJing at a club in Manchester and, if it goes well, he's been promised a regular slot at their weekly garage night. Garage is definitely not my kind of music, but I know that Guy is nervous and that having some friendly faces there will boost his confidence. He's so creative with his video stuff that I am completely in awe. I don't understand it and have no point of reference but I know that it's good.

"I'd love you to come and I know that Guy will be really pleased," I tell Anna, grateful that I don't have to be the only fish out of water. "I'm not sure where it is yet, but I'll let you know as soon as I do."

With that, Anna has to dash into another meeting. We say our goodbyes and she asks me to keep her posted about Sarah.

Keeping Anna posted about Sarah implies that I'm going to do something about everything that's come out of the session with Hugh today. I'd rather avoid it, but then I remember the promise I made to everybody about the explosions. I don't know what I need to do, but I know I must do something.

When Carl comes in from a long day of 'teaching fuckwit teenagers how to drive someone who isn't a maniac or a getaway driver', I tell him about the day's events.

"What do you think you'll do about it?" he asks, as I knew he would. Carl is much more comfortable being in solution mode than listening to whirring emotions.

"I guess I need to talk to her. I need to persuade her that I need some of her time. That's not going to be too easy. Maybe I could tell her that I promised Mum and Dad I'd sort my head out and I need her help to keep that promise."

"Ah," Carl muses. "Nothing like a good bit of emotional blackmail eh?"

"Maybe, but at least it's emotional purpose with a positive intention," I reply.

"Ah well, in that case, emote and blackmail away," he says with a smile.

Is that what I'm trying to do, emotionally blackmail her into talking to me? I want to open up the channels of communication and for that, I need a strategy. I think that she's unlikely to want to talk to me of her own volition.

Carl doesn't seem to be taking this whole issue as seriously as I'd like, so I decide it's time to talk to the wisest woman I know – my Mum. I call her and talk her through what I've learnt that day during my session with Hugh. She listens intently and only when I have finished does she offer an opinion.

"You and Sarah are certainly very different. That doesn't mean that either of you is always wrong or always right. Sitting in the middle, we understand both sides."

I tell Mum that I want to talk to Sarah, to apologise for the judgements I've made and to find a way of moving closer together. We agree that I need to make an initial approach to Sarah and tell her that I'd like to talk without giving her the details straight away. We discuss whether this is best done by email or phone and agree that an email would be better to give her time to absorb things and respond in her own time.

"What will you do if she mentions it to you?" I ask.

"Encourage her to talk to you," she says simply.

As we're coming to the end of the call, Mum says, "You're doing the right thing, Eve. It won't be the easiest conversation you've ever had, but I think your bravery does you great credit. Just understand though that you don't have to be the only one who apologises and shoulders all the blame. Mistakes have been made on both sides and I don't want you to take all this upon yourself."

My Mum has this amazing knack of giving support and finding exactly the right words without showing any bias or favouritism. A rare skill and I tell her so.

I resolve to sleep on it and contact Sarah tomorrow. My natural inclination is to rush in and do things straight away, but I've learnt to my cost that this is not always the best way forward.

To my surprise, I sleep well that night. I wake up early as I am working in Birmingham and need to catch my train. I decide that I'll have the time and space to work on my email to Sarah on the way. I buy myself a big paper cup of Earl Grey tea and settle into my seat on the train. The training course I'm running today is one I've done many times before, so I don't really feel the need for any last minute preparation. I know that as soon as I start, it will all flow.

So, my only responsibility on the ninety-minute journey to Birmingham is to compose my email to Sarah. I go through about eight iterations before I am completely happy with my composition:

"Hello, Sarah,

This email has taken a great deal of thought as I want to get the words right and find a way for us to move closer together. You are my sister and I love you and it would mean the world to me if we could be closer than we are right now.

I'm not sure if Mum and Dad have told you, but I've been having some support from a psychologist to help me understand some of the things that happen in my head and my responses to them. It's vital for me to find answers so that I can make the most of the relationships that are most important to me. One of these is my relationship with you.

After my last session with the psychologist, I realised that I've been making a lot of assumptions about our relationship without really understanding whether they are true and I'm sorry if any of these have hurt you. I'd really like to talk to you to understand your perspective and find ways of understanding each other better. I know this would mean a lot of Mum and Dad, too.

Can we find some time to sit down and talk to one another with nobody else about? I'm quite happy to come over to you if this helps.

Sarah, I hope we can do this. Please know that my aim is not to attach blame or justify anything: I simply want to talk to my sister.

Love,

Eve xx"

I hit the send key as we are pulling into Wolverhampton station and then spend the remaining fifteen minutes of my journey preparing for the day ahead.

I don't really expect to hear from Sarah until that evening at the earliest as I know she will be at work. However, at lunch time, there is an email from her:

"Saturday morning at 11am at our house. Ronald and the children will be out until lunchtime."

That's all it says, no acknowledgement of the words that I've written and no sign off, but at least it's an email from her and at least she's agreed to meet me. I call Mum when the training group are out for lunch and tell her. When she asks me how I feel about it, my initial response is elation, quickly followed by trepidation.

I drive myself completely potty over the next few days, rehearsing what I want to say. In the end, I give this up as a bad job in the knowledge that whatever I say will depend on what Sarah says to me. I try to plan for every alternative, but decide that the likelihood is that whatever happens will be the one scenario I haven't even considered.

When Saturday morning comes around, I'm up far too early and change my outfit at least five times before I'm happy that I've set the right tone – conservative enough for Sarah, yet still feeling like me. I drive over to Sarah's, arriving so early that I have time for a stop at a nearby coffee shop. I know that to arrive early would be just as frowned upon as being late. I finally ring the doorbell at 11:58.

I've prepared myself for a mildly frosty and overly formal Sarah and this is exactly what I get. She opens the door and shows me into the living room where she has a cafetière of coffee waiting. Oops, first awkward moment. I've never taken to coffee and feel like I'm being difficult by asking for tea instead.

Sarah comes back with a cup of tea complete with milk. I can't bring myself to tell her that I don't take milk and so I accept it with thanks.

I'm wondering who is going to talk first when Sarah breaks he silence.

"You wanted to talk?" she asks.

"Yes, I did and I'm grateful to you for finding a time for us," I say. When I hear the words coming out, it sounds like the way I talk to a prospective customer that I am meeting for the first time, not the way I'd expect to talk to someone I've known all my life. I realise just how nervous I am but I'm also sad that my relationship with Sarah has reached the point where we talk to each other as strangers.

She looks at me and I know she's expecting me to start. Where do I begin? I've rehearsed my opening line so many times, but each opener now seems inadequate. I decide to start with a bit of drama. Sarah probably won't like it, but it might get us to a place where we can talk openly.

"I want my sister back in my life," I tell her, surprising myself by what I'm saying. Do I really want her back in my life or do I simply want an end to the current hostilities? Well, I said it so let's go with it.

"We've drifted apart over the past few years and I'd like us to be closer. I know that we're very different people with very different lives, but I'd really like us to understand each other a bit more and be comfortable in one another's company."

Time to shut up now, I think and let Sarah have her say. I find myself steeling myself for whatever comes my way next. It strikes me again how strange it is for two sisters to have reached this point.

"I don't understand you and the choices that you make," she says. "You were always celebrated as the clever one who could do whatever she wanted, yet you've never taken the opportunities and created a worthwhile life with the social standing of which everybody obviously thought you capable."

Do I notice a touch of resentment there? Is this something that she's been holding onto for all these years? I think back to when we were growing up and I was bright and I did excel at school. Sarah, meanwhile, did okay but never really set the world on fire.

"You had the chance to do something really important with your life and make a career that we could all be proud of, but you didn't. You dropped out and wasted it all. When you started your career and rose through the ranks so quickly, I could tell people about what you'd achieved. Now, what can I tell them? My sister who had the whole world at her feet has set up a little business that no-one has ever heard of and travels around the country delivering training courses that no-one ever uses and no-one ever remembers."

Ouch! That smarts. I want to defend myself and the work I do and the difference it makes to people. I want to but I don't. At this precise moment, I think that it would fall on deaf ears.

"You could tell them that I'm happy in my work and feel as though I'm doing something worthwhile to help people?" I offer.

"Oh the same kind of hippy ideals with which you've been filling my daughter's head," she snaps.

Now I understand why she was so disappointed in Rosie's choices, because she thought that she would make the same bad decisions as she thought that I had.

"Is there a chance," I ask, not expecting any form of acceptance for my argument, "That there is more than one way of bring successful? Success for some people might be climbing up the corporate ladder but it wasn't for me. I realised that I was doing what other people expected of me, not what I wanted for myself. Success for me is about doing what feels right and doing things that help other people to do what feels right. Maybe that's how Rosie's feeling."

In retrospect, this last statement is somewhat of a risk and potentially inflammatory, but it's out of my mouth before I can censure it.

I wait for a response from Sarah, but none comes. In fact, she doesn't say anything for a long time. When I can bear the silence no more, I start to talk again.

"I've felt for a long time that you are disappointed in me and I guess I'm starting to understand why," I say. "When I was talking to Hugh, my psychologist, he asked me about the relationships that were important to me and we talked about you. I realised that I assume that I will disappoint you and that makes me sad. I think I have reached the point where I simply act as if you will be disappointed. That's hard for me. It's not that I desperately need your approval, but that I don't want your constant disapproval."

"So trying behaving in a way I won't disapprove of," Sarah says.

"How can I do that?" I ask, genuinely wanting to know the answer.

Sarah thinks for a moment. "Try being committed to making the most of your life. Ronald and I have worked hard to get where we are and it annoys me that you don't appear to even try to achieve the same. You're throwing away all the things that have been handed to you on a plate – things that most of us have to work very hard at."

Resentment again? I'm learning a lot here. I never for one moment thought that Sarah thought I had talents. I thought she just perceived me as a waste of space.

"I do work very hard to be where I want to be," I say in response. "I think that we just value different things. I know that I have poked fun at your world at times and I am truly sorry for that. I think that it's because I don't recognise value in the same things that you do and I realise that I need to step out of my world and into yours more often to understand."

Surely that admission of culpability has to win me some credit.
"Poke fun?" Sarah asks scornfully. "You have been positively rude about it in the past. I'd like to know what is so wrong with us aspiring to be respected in our community."

"Nothing at all," I concede. "I really am sorry if I have made you feel like that. However, Sarah, you've made me feel the same way about the choices I've made and the decisions that I have come to. I think that we're both guilty of dismissing one another because we aspire to different things."

It is important for me to say this because, although I do want to apologise for my past mistakes, I do not want Sarah to think that the guilt is all on one side and that she has a perfect right to criticise.

"The truth is," Sarah says, "That I am disappointed in you. You have no ambition and you seem hell bent upon throwing everything away. All this talk about not wanting to be here and thinking about throwing yourself under a bus – yes, Mum and Dad do talk to me about it you know. They call it your mental health problems. I just think that it's selfish and attention seeking, typical Eve. How dare you worry them so much? If it's all talk, stop it and have some thought for the people around you that you're hurting. If you mean it, just bloody do it so that the rest of us can get on with our lives."

These words pull me up sharp. Does she actually mean this? I have to take a very deep breath before I talk again as I really want to rant and rave about the insensitivity of what she has just said. I don't as I know that this would just play into Sarah's opinion of me.

"If you've never experienced mental health problems, I'm glad for you" I say. "I can imagine that it's very hard to understand if you've never been there. Believe me, I wish I hadn't. I agree with you that it is selfish and I hate myself for the pain I've caused to Mum and Dad, and to Carl. I wish I could find a way to explain it, but I can't. There are times when I wish I wasn't here, but that's not the same as wanting to be dead. I've explained that to Mum and Dad and I think they understand as best as they can. That's exactly why I'm trying to get some help."

"And so you should. You're not a teenager any more, Eve and you need to realise that. Start taking responsibility for yourself."

Ouch again. I think that I do take responsibility for myself and am also too eager to accept the blame when I'm not the only one at fault. I'm not convinced that telling Sarah this will have a positive effect and so I change tack a little.

"You're right, I'm a grown up woman. I sometimes feel as if you don't really see that. Sometimes I think you still treat me as the little sister I used to be. I'd really like you to accept the me that is here today, not the memory of the little girl who needed her big sister to fight her battles and fix her mistakes."

"So you're saying you don't need a big sister anymore?" Sarah asks.

Is that what I'm saying?

"What I'm saying is that maybe neither of us has completely moved on from where we used to be. Maybe you're still taking the role of big sister who needs to guide and admonish and maybe I'm still taking the role of the little sister who feels that she can never quite do the right thing. I don't know. What I do know is that I'd like us to meet as equals, accepting the choices each other has made and wanting to be in one another's lives on that basis."

The voices in my head stop in stunned silence for a minute. They very rarely praise anything I say or do, but for a moment I swear that I can hear them chanting, "Go Evie, Go Evie, Go Evie!" That last statement summed up perfectly what I have wanted to say for so long and, in the moment, I've found precisely the right words to articulate years of wanting.

"I need some time to think about all of this," Sarah says, suddenly rigid and formal again. "I think that this might be a good time for us to stop this conversation. You have said what you wanted to say and I've listened. I think that's more than enough to ask of me for one day, don't you? Besides, Ronald and the children will be back soon and I'd rather you were out of the way for that."

With that, I'm somewhat unceremoniously ushered out of the door. As I leave, I catch hold of her arm which causes Sarah to flinch: however, I persevere.

"Thank you for listening, Sarah, and for giving me your thoughts too. It's helped me to think about things differently and I'm grateful for that. I hope we can do this again soon."

Sarah makes no response but walks over towards my car – a sure sign that my time is up and it's time to stop talking.

When I get back in the car, I check my phone. There is a text from Mum asking how it went. I call her from the car and recount the whole conversation. After I've finished telling her – deliberately missing out the bit when Sarah told me that if I wanted to kill myself to get on with it - Mum asks me how I'm feeling now. How am I feeling now? We've made some kind of progress, well I have anyway. I understand more about why Sarah seems to disapprove of so much that I do, but I'm not sure that I feel any more positive. I tell Mum this.

"Sarah probably needs some time to reflect," she says. "You've always been able to assimilate information quickly whereas Sarah needs a bit more time. Just give her a while to take in what happened and what was said. It sounds to me as if you did a good job, so give yourself credit for that. Sarah's response will probably come later."

I would have loved the interaction with Sarah to end in a warm, sisterly hug and mutual promises to make things different from hereon.I knew that I wouldn't get that, though. I did what I could and I'm happy with the way I handled it and maybe that should be enough for now. It has to be enough because I'm unlikely to get anything else. Can't my performance (not quite the right word, but the only one that comes readily to mind) be enough for me to feel okay about what just happened? I resolve to try and make it enough for the time being.

I'm still thinking about my encounter with Sarah when I go to meet Anna for dinner several nights later. Guy's gig doesn't start until late and so we have decided to have dinner beforehand to catch up properly. It's been a while since we've seen each other.

As soon as we sit down, Anna is keen for a Sarah update. I recount the events of the big meeting and Anna immediately rushes to my defence and tells me how unfair some of Sarah's comments were.

"They are how she feels," I tell her, "And I need to respect that. I don't agree with everything she said but it helped me to understand where some of her hostility comes from and that's useful."

I tell her about my closing comment and Anna cheers, loudly. That's very unlike her: one of the things that I really like about Anna is how understated she is. Still, the cheer makes me feel good about what I said.

Once she's asked me all the questions about Sarah that are on her mind, I'm ready to move the conversation on. I haven't completely processed what happened between us and I'm not really ready to discuss it in too much depth. Anna seems satisfied with what she now knows and satisfied that I have held my own.

I ask her about her world and she tells me what a tosser her new boss is – her words, not mine.

"What makes him so bad?" I ask, intrigued as Anna isn't usually so strong in her distaste for anyone.

"I know that we accountants aren't exactly renowned for our social skills," she says in her usual way of doing herself down at the same time as every other member of her profession, "But this guy is unbefuckinglievable!"

Must be bad if Anna is swearing.

"Last week, he asked me why I wasn't married and if I couldn't have kids. Cheeky fucker. What's it got to do with him how I live my life?"

I know that this was not the best thing to say to Anna. I always imagined her having children and being a wonderful mother, but it's never quite happened.

"What's more," she continues, "He has absolutely no idea of what we all do. Yesterday, he asked me what's happening in Accounts Payable. I don't bloody know; I'm a management accountant, not a bloody Accounts Payable clerk."

Not being up on the inner working of an Accounting Department, I can't fully comprehend the insult, but from the way that Anna is talking, it's obvious that he made a huge *faux pas*.

"They all think he's some kind of golden boy, but at this rate, it won't take long for the powers that be to realise he's just a tossbag in a sharp suit with a grossly inflated opinion of himself."

Rant over, I think. Having got all that off her chest, Anna changes the subject.

"What have you sorted out for Carl's birthday next week?" she asks. "Will you be able to top what he did this year for yours?"

Absolutely not, I think to myself, not even going to try because his efforts were so spectacular.

"No," I tell her, "My efforts will pale into insignificance by comparison. I've bought him tickets for the Feeder gig later in the year, the Game of Thrones books he's been lusting after and a pile of rare DVDs he's wanted for ages."

As Anna knows, our mutual love of the band, Feeder, helped us to connect. Before we met, he'd been a bit of a dance fan, doing the clubs and the drugs that went with the scene. I'd always been an ardent rocker and indie kid and never got my head around dance music. There was a period in the mid-nineties when I thought I was the only person not to have bitten by the dance bug.

"I asked him if he wanted a get-together," I continue, "But he told me he'd much rather the two of us went out for dinner somewhere instead, so that's what he's getting. I've booked us a table at some swanky French place in town with a wine list that will make him dribble. The day after his birthday, he's going buggy racing with James and some of his friends. Not sure I could begin to compete with that. Still, I have my own ways of making sure it's an occasion that he won't forget."

I give Anna a lascivious smile.

"Lucky boy," she says.

As our main courses arrive, conversation turns to the night ahead of us. Anna wants to know what to expect.

"I have absolutely no idea," I tell her. "To be honest, I don't really know what garage music is. I'm thinking of it as an opportunity to broaden my horizons before retreating to safer ground with proper music and lyrics that actually mean something."

"So, no preconceptions then? " Anna smirks. I'm so glad that you're keeping an open mind."

I smack her arm playfully. She has no room to talk. My self-affirmed indie kid friend has her musical boundaries just as I have mine. The main difference is that she can be swayed by the reviews of an album in Q magazine whereas I am resigned to the fact that music journalists in the know seem to hate with a passion most of the stuff I like.

"Do you think we're going to stick out like a pair of sore thumbs?" she asks, already knowing the answer.

"Yes, I expect so, but what the hell? I'm not gangsta enough for the crowd that's probably going to be there and I'm okay with that."

"It always fascinates me how Guy can blend into any crowd," Anna says admiringly. "He's basically an old hippy but he doesn't seem to be phased by where he is – he just goes with it and carries on being Guy. I really respect that."

Me too. To be so comfortable in your own skin that you just keep on keeping on, regardless of where you are or who you're with, must be a great feeling. My intuition is that Guy isn't even aware of it. I admire it too and could really learn something from his approach.

We forego dessert; neither of us has a particularly sweet tooth and we don't lust after chocolate or other sweet delights. Anna has arranged to get a lift home with Guy and all of his VJing equipment, so she's caught the train into town. She's hoping that the venue we're heading for will allow her to indulge her passion for real ale. I'm not convinced: I imagine it to be all European bottled beers. I have driven. I have this self-imposed rule about drinking on a school night and, although I haven't got to deliver a training course the following day, I have a stack of design work to do and I'll need all of my faculties intact to get through it. My own fault for leaving it until the last minute.

Given that I don't think that Anna's desire for real ale is going to be sated at the club we're going to, we stop *en route* at one of the micro-brewery pubs springing up around Manchester. I feel wrong for ordering a Diet Coke. The beer's no temptation: the only place I have the occasional beer is in Egypt where it doesn't really taste like beer. It's funny that I choose to drink it there: I always hear the voice of my uncle (who spent many years in Cairo), ringing in my ears and telling me it's not proper Egyptian beer unless it's had a dead donkey floating in the vat.

After Anna has indulged in a couple of pints of real ale and I've had my fill of Diet Coke, we head for a previously uncharted part of Manchester to find the venue where Guy is playing. Do you call what a VJ does 'playing'? It'll do as I can't think of a better word.

Guy has already told me that he has put Anna and me on the guest list and that feels pretty good. Okay, it's only a small club in the arse end of Manchester, but being able to say, 'we're on the guest list' still makes us feel kinda rock and roll! We walked in and immediately felt out of place. Number one, we were obviously unfashionably early as there was hardly anybody else there and number two, nobody else was dressed anything like we were. 'Think of it as a learning experience', I said to myself. 'You're just visiting a different world and increasing your knowledge.'

Those wise words did nothing to make me feel more comfortable. We searched for Guy for about five minutes and both breathed a collective sigh of relief when we spotted him. He was near the stage, setting up his computer. He gave us a huge grin when we saw him. However cool he appears on the outside, I know that Guy suffers badly from nerves. It made me glad that we had gone there to support him. He gave us both a big hug when we walked over to where he was setting up.

"So what can we expect tonight then?" Anna asked.

"Oh, you know, just your usual garage set," Guy answered. No, we really didn't know but neither of us wanted to draw attention to our un-cool ignorance.

"There's a couple of beat box guys doing a set too: should be awesome," Guy continued. Still none the wiser, we nodded.

"Are you on from the beginning?" I ask.

"Yeah, been working on a whole new set of visuals for this," Guy tells us, "Even been filming some stuff with that old fruit machine, that you helped me to track down. Looks pretty cool. Got to concentrate now, I'm on in ten."

The mention of the old fruit machine takes me back to a night about six months ago when Guy had taken me to a drumming jam night at another obscure place in Manchester. When we met, he asked me if I wanted a tour behind the scenes at the old BBC building in the centre of the city. Never one to pass up a new opportunity, I said yes and he sneaked me in with an old employee pass. After this adventure, he asked if I could take him to see a friend of his who had an old fruit machine he wanted to borrow. We got in the car and he took me to a very grim-looking council estate on the other side of town. We went up to the fourth floor of a tower block, knocked on the door and had to avoid the very vicious dogs who greeted us when the door was opened. Guy chatted to the owner of the flat for about five minutes and was then taken to see said fruit machine. He was in raptures and proclaimed that it was exactly what he wanted. He loaded the fruit machine into the boot of my car and off we went.

We leave Guy to make his final preparations and find a seat where he can see us and we can keep up the encouragement. Anna's hope for real ale is firmly dashed, as is her second choice of a good glass of red wine. She settles instead for a vodka and tonic.

The gig leaves us in a state of utter bewilderment. I find the music loud and unintelligible. I try to find some kind of rhythm that I can hang onto, but even that escapes me. We can hardly hear ourselves think and, for one of the first times in my life, I feel decidedly middle-aged.

Despite music which is definitely not to my taste, Guy's visuals are brilliant. I'm astounded by his ability to get into the music and make the rhythm of the images on-screen sync perfectly with the music. I know nothing about what I'm witnessing, yet I have no doubt that Guy is great at what he does. I feel a swell of pride in my lovely friend's talents.

When there was a break in the cacophony – sorry, the music – Anna leant over to me and asks, "On a scale of zero to minus ninety nine, how cool do you feel right now?"

"Off the scale," I reply, "And not in the right direction."

And then, while all around us are topping up on their designer beers and waxing lyrical about the 'banging' set that they had just experienced, Anna and I embark upon a philosophical discussion about music appreciation.

"What is it, do you think," Anna asks, "That makes us favour one form of music over another?"

I have a long-held theory about this and now is hardly the time to hold forth about it, but I do so anyway.

"Have you ever come across Howard Gardner's theory of the eight different forms of intelligence?" I ask her.

Anna looks at me blankly and says, "Err, accountant here, I doubt it."

I ignore the self-deprecation and continue on with my quest.

"Gardner's research," I inform her, "found that there are eight distinct forms of intelligence and, of those eight, every individual tends to favour two or three and be positively turned off by one or two others."

"Ok," Anna says, "And the link between this and musical taste is…?"

"I'm just getting to that. I think that your preferred forms of intelligence have an impact upon the music that you like. For example, I'm very hot on verbal and linguistic intelligence and you know me, it's all about the lyrics."

"That's true," she agrees, "Always an obscure lyric for every occasion. So that explains you, but what about everyone else?"

"Well, people who are into physical intelligence are probably influenced by how they can move to music, people with auditory and musical intelligence by the quality of the music itself and those with intrapersonal intelligence – they're people who like to understand how experiences fit into their map of the world – are probably influenced by music they can relate to and songs that define things they've encountered."

There are huge holes in my theory, such as how intelligences such as logical and mathematical or naturalist relate to music, but I don't dwell upon these.

Just as Anna is about to ask more questions for which I probably have no answers, the music starts up again and we're introduced to the wonderful world of beat box. I have to admit that the things that these guys can do with their vocals is impressive, but I can't help giggling. It might be clever, but why would you want to do it in the first place? I see Anna stifling a giggle to and we smile at each other conspiratorially.

After the best box guys, it's time for Guy to go into action again. Again, to the untutored eye, his skills seem mightily impressive. To my relief, the second set is shorter than the first set and is over quicker than I'd expected.

We wait for Guy to pack up his equipment and watch him receiving a number of slaps on the back from people with far more knowledge than us who are obviously similarly impressed. Just as we are about to go over to him, a man with an air of authority approaches him. Neither of us can hear what is being said, but from the expression on Guy's face, it looks like good news.

When the man has moved on and Guy's equipment is safely stowed in his huge holdall, he comes over to find us.

"Did you see that bloke talking to me just now?" he asks excitedly. We nod. "That was the guy that owns the place," he says, "And he's asked me if I want a regular gig here."

"Brilliant!" Anna and I both exclaim at the same time.

"You did say yes, didn't you?" Anna asks.

"Bloody right I did!" Guy tells us. "I start next week."

We both take turns in hugging him and congratulating him on doing a cracking job. We talk as knowledgably as we can about what we saw and how it worked so well with the music.

We are still talking when the club stewards tell us it's time to leave. We go outside and get ready to say our farewells. I'm parked a couple of streets away, but Guy has been able to park at the back of the club.

"Want a lift over to your car?" Guy asks.

"No, it's fine," I tell him, "It'll only take me a minute or two to walk over there.

I say goodbye to both of my friends and wander back to the car, pleased for Guy yet still trying to make sense of the evening and the new experiences I've had. I decide the call Anna first thing tomorrow to dissect it properly.

I'm not far from my car, fumbling in my handbag to find my phone to let Carl know that I'm on my way back when I hear loud music and the screeching of tyres. This is the last thing I remember before everything goes black.

CHAPTER EIGHT

The Questions

When I wake up, I have absolutely no idea where I am. I try to move my arm
and feel an excruciating pain shoot from my wrist all the way up to my shoulder.
I am suddenly aware of a tube in my nose, something clipped to my finger and
my leg hanging in the air, covered in a plaster cast. I seem to be hooked up to
various monitors making intermittent bleeping sounds.

I open my eyes and feel a blinding pain in my head. As the world comes back
into some sort of vision, I see that Mum and Dad are sitting by my bed. I smell
the sanitised smell of hospital. I try to sit up but can't. My Dad notices me first.

"I think she's awake," he says urgently and shakes my Mum's arm to make
sure she's noticed.

"Hello, sweetheart," my Mum says, folding my hand into hers. "You gave
us such a fright. We didn't know if you were going to wake up."

None of this makes any sense.

"Where am I?" I ask weakly, trying to piece together what on earth is going on.

"You're in hospital, love," Dad tell me. "You've been here for four days now. You had some kind of accident but nobody quite knows what happened. You were picked up by an ambulance after a police woman found you lying in the road near that club you went to with Anna".

Anna? I remember walking out to my car after I'd left Anna and Guy. My head is pounding and I can't quite focus upon my surroundings. Then I panic – does Carl know I'm here? I try to ask, but the only word that comes out is 'Carl'.

"Carl's here," Mum said. "The hospital called him when you were brought in and he called us. He's just gone to get a drink. He's been here since he got the call and we've been here every day."

Dad goes to find the nurse while Mum sits and holds my hand.

"What happened, Evie?" she asks.

"I don't know," I say and I really don't. How the hell did I end up here? I remember the loud music and the screeching tyres and then no more.

The nurse comes in and calls for the doctor. The doctor asks Mum and Dad to leave for a few minutes while she examines me. She shines a light into my eyes and it makes me want to close my eyes. She tells me to keep my eyes open and follow the light as she moves it. I struggle to do as she says but my eyes don't want to follow and my head hurts.

"How are you feeling?" the doctor asks.

"Pretty ropey," I tell her, trying to smile but it hurts too much.

"Do you remember what happened?" she asks. Why does everybody keep asking me this? No I bloody don't! I try to think back and remember but there's nothing: my memory seems to have wiped it all. I remember leaving the club, saying goodbye to Guy and Anna, searching for my phone, hearing music and tyres and then nothing.

"I'm sorry," I tell her, "I really don't. I'm sorry, I'm trying to, I honestly am but there's nothing there." I feel the tears well up in my eyes and within seconds, they are falling fast. Why can't I remember? My fear is that it's something so awful that I don't want to remember.

The doctor puts her hand on my arm in an attempt to calm me down.

"Don't worry about that now," she tells me, "Let's just be pleased you're awake again."

After further prodding and poking, Mum and Dad are allowed back into the room and Carl is with them. He rushes over to the bed and tries to cuddle me, but I let out a yelp of pain.

"Hello, baby," he says, his voice cracking with the emotion of the situation, "I'm so pleased to see you."

"Hello," I say, trying and failing at another smile. I want to tell him how pleased I am to see him too, but the words just won't come. I'm willing him not to ask me what happened and, to my relief, he doesn't.

For the rest of the day, I drift in and out of sleep. Mum, Dad and Carl stay with me. Every time I wake up, I can see the relief on their faces. I try to stay awake so that they don't worry, but I can't.

One time, as I wake up, I remember what Dad had said to me earlier in the day. I've been here for four days? I panic, thinking about all of the things that I was supposed to do. What about work? Has somebody told people that I'm here? I hate the thought of letting people down.

I must have said something because Dad says, "Don't worry about work. Anna has sorted that. She went through the diary on your phone and found the contacts from your emails. It's all sorted and she has found people to cover the work. Everybody has sent you nice messages and hopes that you're okay."

I settle back into the bed, glad at least that my work is covered. Thanks, Anna, I owe you one.

Mum tells me I've had a stream of visitors – Anna, Guy, George, Gill and Alex have all been here. I smile to myself in my head – the one time Alex turns up and I'm not conscious. I ask if Sarah has been. She hasn't, but Rosie and Harvey have. I think about all the worry that I've caused so many people and find myself saying sorry to anyone who will listen.

That evening, the doctor comes to see me again. She asks how I've been and Mum, Dad and Carl tell her about the day, some of which I remember and some of which I don't.

"The good news," the doctor says, "Is that she's unlikely to fall back into a coma. We just need to keep a careful eye on her now."

Coma? I've been in a coma? I suppose I must have been to have been here for four days and remember nothing.

I see Mum and Dad hugging each other and then Mum turns to hug Carl. I really have frightened them all.

"Maybe," the doctor continues, "It's time to go home and get some rest. We'll call you if anything at all happens. Eve is going to need you all over the coming weeks, so you need to stay strong. Go home and get some proper food and sleep, then come back tomorrow."

The three of them look at one another, clearly reticent to leave me. I smile and nod to them. They all look absolutely exhausted.

"I'm okay," I tell them. "Go."

Reluctantly, they follow doctor's orders and pack up to leave.

As soon as I am alone, the fear kicks in. Fear of what, I'm not absolutely sure. All I know is that when I had people around me, I felt safe. Now I don't. The throbbing pain in my head grows more and more pronounced, and the beeping of the machines I'm hooked up to seems to get louder and louder. I don't even know what the machines are for. I'm assuming that a regular beep is a good thing. Several times, I am convinced that the beep has stopped and I panic.

I try to assemble my thoughts as best as I can. In the time that I've been awake, I've established that nobody knows what's happened to me except that I was found on a Manchester pavement and brought to hospital, and I've been in a coma for four days. Do I know what's wrong with me? Has anyone told me? There's a fair chance someone has, but I either didn't listen or I didn't take it in. It's obvious from the plaster cast and the traction contraption that my leg is broken. My head and my arm hurt too.

I try to find a better answer to the questions about what happened other than 'I don't know' but the truth escapes me. I guess that the question isn't going to go away, but my current answer sounds feeble to say the least.

I sleep fitfully that night, waking up regularly after weird dreams. In one of them, I'm in a court room being cross-examined and asked to give a full account of the night of my accident. When I explain that I can't, I'm held in contempt of court. In another, I'm confronted by the angry mother of a brood of fluffy yellow ducklings who wants to know why I have taken them to the cinema to see a 15-rated film. Every time I wake up, I have to tell myself it was only a dream and that it's okay to go back to sleep.

When I wake up properly, I see the sun flooding through the blinds and assume that it's morning. I scan my room, reacquainting myself with the still unfamiliar surrounds, when I see something wonderfully familiar – my Dad.

"Good morning, sunshine," he says to me. "We've decided to take shifts today in keeping you company. You get me first, then your Mum and Carl for the evening. So what are we going to this morning? Fancy a quick jog?"

I laugh despite the fact that it hurts.

"Dad," I ask, "Have they told you what's wrong with me?"

"Yes, love. You have a broken leg (but I imagine that you've already worked that bit out), a badly sprained wrist, several bruised ribs and some kind of head injury. They're not quite sure what yet. Sounds like you whacked your head on the pavement and knocked yourself out. The doctor is doing more tests to find out what kind of damage it's caused. That's why you have two such fine shiners"

I didn't know I had black eyes. In fact, I have no idea how I look. Finding a mirror wasn't my number one priority yesterday.

"Do I look really scary?" I ask him.

"You're not looking your best, love, but I think we'll let you off – extenuating circumstances and all that.

I'm not sure why, but I burst into tears and cry as if my heart will break. I see tears well up too in Dad's eyes. He takes my hand and holds it tightly.

"Oh Evie, my little girl, we thought we'd lost you," he says.

"Not yet, Dad," I tell him, "Not yet."

"I've brought you something," Dad tells me, fishing in the bag that he has on the chair next to him. He brings out a cube of plasticine with a cocktail stick poked into it.

"A splotty!" I exclaim, as though he had just handed me a precious jewel.

Let me explain, when I was little, my Dad used to make me a splotty whenever I needed cheering up. There is no significance I know of for the plasticine or the cocktail stick and where the name came from I have no idea, but a splotty was always a highly prized gift. This is my first splotty for over thirty years and I love it.

For the next couple of hours, Dad reads the paper, reading interesting articles to me. He tells me that Spurs won over the weekend and when he investigates the day's share prices he's pleased to discover that most of his stock has had a small rise over the past week. The doctor comes in and does her usual prodding and poking. She comes in about four times during the day, making notes every time but not venturing any opinion about my wellbeing. I have a little snooze – during which time I suspect that Dad does too – and wake up to find that his place has been taken by Mum.

Mum tells me about progress in the herb garden and the marvellous new book she's found with Victorian recipes for the herbal lotions and potions of which she's so fond. I ask her about Sarah and she goes quiet.

I ask her what she is not telling me and she shakes her head.

"I'm not sure what is going on with your sister," she tells me. "We called to tell her about your accident and tried calling yesterday to tell her that you'd woken up, but she doesn't seem to want to talk to anyone. Rosie asked if she and Harvey could come and see you again, but Sarah told them no. I don't understand it. Did the two of you have a falling out that we don't know about?"

I shake my head. "I haven't spoken to Sarah since I went over to their house for our big conversation," I tell her.

"It's very strange," Mum says, "But don't you worry, I'll get to the bottom of it."

I have no doubt about that: Miss Marple has nothing on my mother.

I sleep again and awake as Carl comes in, ready to take over Operation Eve from Mum. Mum kisses me on the head and tells me that she'll see me tomorrow.

Carl tells me that Jess is missing me and keeps sleeping on my pillow in my absence. Strange, when I'm there, she hardly ever comes near our bed.

"I bet she's missing the prawns I secretly buy and feed to her when you're not looking," I tell him.

"Worst kept secret ever," he tells me. I nick half of them – I'm damned if a cat is having fancier food than me!"

"I'm sorry, Carl," I say.

"Sorry for what?" he asks.

"I don't know. For whatever happened and for making you all run around like headless chickens."

"Have you remembered anything else?" he asks. To my surprise, this is the first time anybody has asked me this today.

"No," I sigh. I keep trying but there is nothing there.

He looks at me with an expression I can't interpret. Usually, I can tell exactly what's going on in that overactive brain, but right now I draw a blank.

"What?" I ask him.

"Nothing," he says, "Don't worry about it."

Somebody telling me not to worry always makes me worry. Luckily, I doze off before I can create too many monsters in my head.

I wake up again after a fairly dreamless night to find Dad there, present and correct for his morning shift. This routine continues for the next couple of days and I like having Dad, Mum and Carl with me. I wonder why no-one else has been in and when I ask, I am told that they have been asked to wait a few days until I'm stronger.

On the third or fourth day, I wake up to find not Dad there but a nurse looking slightly concerned.

"Is everything okay?" I ask her, a little worried that Dad isn't there. "Is my Dad not here today?"

"He's waiting outside," the nurse tells me. "There are a couple of police officers here to see you. D'you feel up to talking to them?"

This takes me by surprise. "Okay," I say, "I can talk to them."

The two police officers, a man and a woman, come into my room, ask how I am and whether they may sit down. They sit and the female officer introduces them both. She tells me that they would like to know what happened on the night of my accident. She says that they have already spoken to Guy, Anna, Mum, Dad and Carl and would like to hear my version of events.

I tell them that I can't remember a lot and the female officer asks me to take my time and tell them everything that I can. I run through the events as I remember them again – leaving the club, saying goodbye to Guy and Anna, looking for my phone, hearing the music and the screeching tyres – but still have nothing new to share with them.

The male officer notes down everything that I say, puts down his pen and asks me a question that shocks the hell out of me.

"There is no CCTV in the area where you were found and no accidents have been reported. We've been told that you've been depressed recently and have talked about doing yourself harm. Did you try to kill yourself?"

Now I know that I've complained before about people tiptoeing around the suicide question, but that was a little too in-your-face.

I am too shocked to speak for a minute and look at him as though he has just slapped me round the face.

"No!" I tell him.

"But you can't tell us what happened?" he asks.

"I can't tell you because I don't remember. I've told you everything I know and I'm sure that it fits with what I've told other people too. Do you think I just jumped out in front of a car or something?"

The female officer indicates to the male officer to keep quiet and she takes over.

"We're just considering it as a possibility," she tells me, "So far, we have little to go on and no evidence that might help us, so we need to follow up every potential avenue. We were hoping that you might remember something more."

I can feel the anger boiling inside me. How dare they? I don't know what did happen but I'm damned sure it wasn't self-inflicted.

"Yes, I struggle with my mental health," I tell them, "And yes, there are times when I would like to be able to escape, but never like that. Now, if there's nothing else I think I'd like you to leave."

To give them credit, they do just that, telling me that they will be back if anything else comes to light. I'm still fuming when Dad comes into the room. I tell him about our conversation and he nods, as though he'd been expecting it.

"You knew that they wanted to ask me that?" I ask. "Why the hell would they think I tried to kill myself?"

"Evie," Dad says in as measured a tone as he can muster, "We have all wondered if that's what might have happened. You know that you talk about things like that when you're upset, so you can't blame us for wondering. You've told me yourself that people are most likely to kill themselves when they seemed to be coming out the other side, that they don't have the energy to do it when they are down in the depths."

Damn me for sharing my Samaritans teachings with other people.

So that's why everybody has been asking me to remember what happened. It's not just the police, it's my family too. To say I feel indignant would be the understatement of the year. The indignation must show on my face because Dad tries to soothe me.

"Love, think about it from our point of view. When you're upset, you become someone else, someone we don't recognise and that person seems hell bent upon doing herself harm. We didn't want to believe it, but we had to consider it."

I think about this and realise it was a reasonable – if unpalatable – conclusion. They have seen me lose the plot many times and, from what they have told me, this version of me seems capable of a lot of things that I wouldn't even countenance.

"If you could just remember what happened, it would help us all to make sense of it all and put the worry out of our minds."

"Dad, I'm trying to remember. I keep thinking back, trying to recall even the smallest detail and there's nothing. I can't tell you with 100% certainty that I didn't jump under a car, but I don't think I did. I'd had a lovely night with Anna and Guy and I was feeling better than I have for quite a while. I know I had that uncomfortable conversation with Sarah, but even that feels like a step forward. Dad, please don't think that, please."

I cry again, feeling desperate that I can't put everyone out of their misery and desperate that I don't know what happened.

After a while, Dad says he's going to find us both a cup of tea. When he comes back, without tea, he tells me he's called Mum and Carl, told them about the conversation with the police and told them about the our conversation too.

"I just wanted them to know," he said, "I didn't want you to have to keep bringing this up and upsetting yourself. We all agree that if you say that you didn't try to do anything daft, we believe you. We just wish we understood what has happened to you."

Me too, Dad, me too.

Later that day, the hospital's resident psychologist pays me a visit. No prizes for guessing why, I think to myself. She is a nice lady and very well-meaning, but I want to scream when I have to cover the same ground again. No, I don't think I tried to kill myself, no I can't be 100% sure because I have no real memory, yes I do have mental health problems and yes, there are times when I would rather not be here. I wonder about getting these statements printed on a T-shirt for whoever turns up next.

We have a long discussion about suicide and I reiterate my belief that there's a big difference between not wanting to be here and actually wanting to be dead. We talk about my sessions with Hugh and whether they've been helpful. I tell her that they have.

She talk to me about the 'other person' who seems to come along during my explosions and she asks whether I think this other version of me could have done something to hurt me. I tell her once again that although I can't be 100% sure, I don't think so. I tell her that I can usually sense an explosion coming and, this time there had been none of the usual tell-tale signs. She explores these tell-tale signs and I repeat that I've experienced none of them in recent weeks, despite the uncomfortable conversation with Sarah.

After an hour, she tells me that she has to go and asks if she can call by to see me again. I think to myself that I can't really stop her, given that I can't move from the bed, but decide that this would be churlish given that she is genuinely trying to help me. I tell her this would be fine and she leaves.

True to their word, Mum, Dad and Carl don't mention the 'jumping under a car' theory again. Over the next few days, they continue to take it in turns to sit with me and do their best to entertain me. I find that I'm nodding off less frequently, so at least I'm a little more companionable. I must be getting better as I'm starting to find the indignities of bed pans and bed baths more and more degrading. I'm allowed other visitors too. George comes to see me, bringing the traditional grapes as well as a big bag of my favourite crisps.

"Thought you might like a change from all that healthy nonsense they feed you in here," he tells me. We talk about his latest fight with Salford Council, the political party he's helping to found and, inevitably, we end up on the sordid story of his permanently complicated and fascinating love life. He tells me about the new dating site he's joined, the people he 's met and the stalker who's been following his every move since their one and only date.

"Totally mental!" he tells me, "Needs to see a psychotherapist to work out some deep-seated issues."

He stops in his tracks and apologises profusely, telling me that there's nothing wrong with having mental health issues, it's just that his stalker is clearly insane.

"It's okay, George," I say, trying not to laugh because he's obviously mortified by what he's said. "For the record, we're 99% sure that I didn't try to do myself in and I'm no crazier than I have ever been.

He seems to be reassured and changes the subject.

"What a shame, you missing Carl's birthday," he says.

Carl's birthday! I had forgotten. I'm not even sure what day it is but I have to have been in here for long enough for Carl's birthday to pass.

When he comes to see me that evening, I beg for forgiveness.

"No worries," he tells me, "I think it's fair to say that you've had a few more pressing things on your mind than the fact that I'm yet another year older."

"Even so, I'm so sorry. I've wrapped your presents and I'd booked us a table at that new French place in town. I know I forgot but I hadn't forgotten. That sounds ridiculous, but you know what I mean."

"The scary thing is that I do know what you mean, even though what you said makes very little sense. And by the way, I have to admit that I found your presents – you always hide them in the same place which you think I don't know about but I do so it was easy. Thank you. I'm using the fact that you're not home to watch all of the DVDs I know you'd hate."

"Thoughtful to the last," I say, "I'll make it up to you when I'm out of here."

"Make it up to me by getting out of here."

The following day, Mum tells me she wants my help with a cunning plan. I love the fact that she still quotes Baldrick from Blackadder. She tells me that Rosie and Harvey have been forbidden from coming to see me for reasons still unknown. Mum doesn't think this is right and so she's been conspiring with Rosie to smuggle her in under the pretence that the two of them are spending the day together in Manchester.

"Mother!" I exclaim in mock horror. "Conspiring with your granddaughter to deceive your own daughter? What is the world coming to?"

"I know you're teasing me," she says, "But this hasn't been an easy decision. I don't like going behind Sarah's back, but this situation is ludicrous. You could have died and she won't even talk about it."

"I was teasing," I tell her, "And I'd love to see Rosie."

Mum brings Rosie in the next day and, to start with, she's shocked at the sight of me. I've no idea just how shocking I look as I have yet to look in a mirror and all of my visitors have been too polite to pass comment.

"You think I look bad," I tell her, "You should see the other guy."

She giggles and this breaks the ice. Mum steps out on the pretext of going to buy us all a drink and leaves us to it for a while. I ask Rosie about what's going on and she tells me about the universities she's planning to apply to.

"To do social work?" I ask. She nods. "Result!" I say.

"That's the weird thing," Rosie says, "Before you ended up in here, things were getting better. After your visit to see Mum – which I'm not supposed to know about but overheard her talking about it to Dad – she sat down with me and we really talked for the first time in ages. She asked me about social work and said she'd help me look into the best universities. I thought we'd turned a massive corner and then wham – you have your accident and she goes completely off her rocker."
"How so?" I ask.

"We can't talk about it; she bawled Harvey out the other day for even mentioning your name. It's like she's pretending that it didn't happen and that you don't exist."

"Weird" I agree. It does worry me and I wonder what on earth I did wrong this time, but I don't dwell on it too much; I'm too happy to have Rosie here with me.

"Harvey wanted to come too," Rosie tells me, "But we thought it might be too difficult to smuggle us both out at the same time. He sends his love and asked me to tell you that he's recorded his new Dubstep compilation for you. You're his hero after having your post-gig accident!"

"So probably best not to tell him that I hadn't got a clue what was going on and that every track sounded the same to me then eh?"

"Probably not," Rosie agreed.

Mum comes back into the room, carrying drinks for us all and a caramel shortbread for Rosie. Rosie coos in appreciation and devours it in thirty seconds flat. We spend a happy hour together, talking about Rosie's university choices, the grades she needs to achieve, her hunt for an organisation to sponsor her through her degree and her thoughts on her future student life. I'm really sorry to see them leave. Rosie vows that she'll be back very soon – with or without permission.

As they're heading out of the door, Mum suddenly remembers something that she was meant to tell me.

"Carl wanted me to tell you," she says, "That he's not coming in tonight. Anna wants to see you and tonight is the only time she can do for a couple of days. Carl thought that the two of you would probably want to chat on your own, so he'll be in tomorrow as usual."

I'll miss Carl's visit but it will be great to spend time with Anna.

When she arrives, straight from work, Anna hugs me as best she can.

"I feel awful," she says, "If only Guy and I had walked you to your car, this might never have happened".

"Or alternatively," I say, "It might have happened to you instead and then I'd be feeling awful that I let you walk me to my car. It's not your fault, honey, honest."

I think that she just about accepts this. She asks how I am and I tell her that I am getting better every day. We talk about the stream of doctors and nurses that attend me daily, the lack of privacy and dignity I feel with the bed pans and my general frustration that I can't do anything for myself.

"Have you heard about what Guy's doing?" she asks me. I tell her that I haven't.

"He's fed up with the police doing nothing so he's launched a campaign on Facebook and Twitter, asking anybody who was at the gig if they saw what happened. He's told everyone that he can't offer a reward, but will do a free VJ set for anybody coming forward with useful information."

"Wow, I didn't know anything about that, no," I tell her, "That's so good of him. Has he found out anything useful yet?"

"A few complete cranks but some that might sound hopeful. One person even talked about a friend of theirs having videoed it on their phone. He's talking to them again tomorrow."

This is an unexpected move forward. Maybe I can actually find out what happened and stop torturing myself with the many questions that keep charging around my head.

"Talking of Guy…" Anna said to me in one of her overly-rehearsed I-want-to tell-you something-but-I'm-not-quite-sure-how-to moments".

"Yes?" I ask, innocently as though I have not noticed the script she needs to deliver. The words come out quickly.

"We both came to see you when you were in a coma and both felt wretched about it. We went for a coffee afterwards and talked and talked. Since then, we've been out for dinner together and we're going out again tomorrow night. I just wondered if you'd mind.

Guy and Anna. At first thought, not the most obvious coupling. However, on reflection, they both always enjoyed one another's company. They live in very different worlds but always seem to enjoy visiting the other person's world. Guy has crippling self-doubt most of the time and Anna is the most enthusiastic supporter that anyone could ever hope for. Yes, I get it and, what's more, I like it.

"Mind? I ask, "No, of course I don't mind. I think it's fantastic. Now come here and give me a hug, just make sure that you avoid my dodgy leg and arm. Oh! And try not to pull any of my cables out like Dad did the first time he hugged me – that one always brings the nurses running!"

We hug and I can tell that she is relieved. I could never resent Anna for being happy. She deserves the best in life and I want her to be happy all the time.

I tell her this and she says, "I was just so nervous about telling you, what with everything you've been though. I really like him, Eve and I think he likes me too."

I can clearly see the glint in her eye and the soppy smile that now greets me. Guy and Anna, I think again. So some good has come out of this mess. I sleep soundly that night, occasionally grinning to myself about the good fortune that has come the way of two of my dearest friends.

When Dad arrives the next morning I'm still eating my breakfast and having my daily debate with the nurse about the fact that I can't stomach eggs first thing in the morning. On the whole, the food isn't bad, but breakfast always seems to be eggs and the tea is always very stewed. By the time my first visitor of the day arrives, I am gasping for a decent cup of Earl Grey. Dad always brings me one, making me even more pleased to see him.

This morning, he has news of an unexpected visitor later in the day. He tells me that Mum was feeling very guilty after smuggling Rosie in to see me the previous day. The guilt reached the point where she phoned Sarah and, as Rosie would say, she fessed up.

Sarah's response was not what Mum was expecting. She said she would like to talk to me in private. Mum suggested that she took her slot this afternoon and Sarah agreed. So, no Mum today, but Sarah instead. I am intrigued and more than a little nervous. What had sparked this desire to talk to me after apparently denying my existence for the past week or so? I ask Dad if he knows anything about her intentions, but he is just as much in the dark as I am. We are both feeling a little lazy this morning and so we watch a little daytime TV. I wonder how people survive on a diet of the tripe that graces our screens in the morning? When Jeremy Kyle comes on I insist that we change the channel. Dad agrees.

I'm not quite sure when to expect Sarah so I prepare myself from the moment I have finished my lunch. I rack my brains for what I could possibly have done this time, but can't think of a thing. In my mind, while the last conversation we had didn't exactly end warmly, it was constructive.

Sarah arrives just after 2pm. She sticks her head around the door and asks if she can come in. There is something different in her demeanour. She takes a seat and asks me how I am. I give her what has become my stock response – I'm getting better every day, thank you.

"That's good," she says.

I realise what is different. Sarah is being deferential, sheepish almost. The plot thickens. I ask her how she is and the floodgates open. She tells me that she hasn't been able to get my accident off her mind and that she's been worried sick. Not what I was expecting.

"Can I ask you something?" she asks me.

"Whatever you want," I tell her.

"Did you try and kill yourself because I told you that if you were going to do it, you should just get on with it?"

So, Sarah has been beating herself up because she believes that this is all her fault. I guess that explains why she hasn't wanted to talk about it. I need to let her know that it isn't true. I need to stop her from torturing herself.

"Absolutely not," I tell her. "Sarah, I don't remember what happened but I don't believe I did anything to try to hurt myself. I was in a good place and talking to you helped me because I felt as though we had moved forward. You had no part to play in this, please trust me about that."

"Honestly?" she asks meekly.

"Honestly and truly," I tell her.

She breaks down and weeps uncontrollably. I reach out my good hand to her and catch hers with it. Whatever has been going on in her head, it has obviously taken her through hell. I feel a depth of compassion for my sister that I've not felt for a very long time.

When she can talk again through the tears, she says, "I thought you'd taken what I said to heart. I thought you'd decided that, if you were going to do it, you should do it quickly. I didn't mean what I said and I feel such an awful person for saying it."

That depth of compassion gets deeper still. She has driven me mad over recent years, but I hate the thought of her suffering like this.

"You've been very angry with me recently," I tell her, "And when we're angry we sometimes say things we don't mean. I never once thought that you actually wanted me to hurt myself. I took what you said as a sign that you were unhappy with me."

"And how did I deal with that?" she asked, although I had a feeling that the question was rhetorical. I was right, as she quickly followed it up with, "When you knew that things weren't right, you tried to talk to me to find a way through it. When I thought that things weren't right, I blamed you and tried to push you further away still."

Fair point, actually, but maybe now is not the time to say so.

"And what do you want to happen now?" I ask.

"I want you to try and find a way to forgive me for what I said and I want my little sister back in my life."

"The first bit is easy: you're already forgiven. The second bit will work with a minor adjustment. How about you ask to have your sister back in your life and drop the word 'little'?" I ask. "I think that we're both old enough now to be equals, don't you?"

Sarah nods, trying to deal with the tears and runny nose with the back of her hand. I allow myself a fleeting moment of naughtiness by wondering what the ladies at the golf club would think if they could see Sarah with mascara half way down her cheeks and a hand covered in snot. It's only a fleeting moment and the thought soon gives way to compassion.

When she regains some of her composure, she tells me that she has been thinking about our previous conversation at her house.

"I think you're right when you say that I act as though I've been disappointed in you. I've found it very easy to judge you and blame you. If I'm honest, I think that I always wanted you to do all the things I couldn't. You went to university and I didn't because my grades weren't good enough. I thought that you could do whatever you wanted - and I wanted you to do so much."

"But did you want me to do what you'd have liked for yourself or what was going to make me happy?" I ask her.

"That's the problem, isn't it?" Sarah says, "I wanted you to do all the things I felt deprived of, all the things I thought I'd never have access to. It didn't occur to me that the things I valued didn't have the same value for you. I should simply have wanted you to be happy. That's what Mum and Dad have always done for both of us and it's why they've found it much easier than me to be proud of you."

"On the whole," I tell her, "I am happy. Admittedly not right now, with my leg up in the air, my face probably looking like I've been caught in a Friday night brawl in the rough end of town and having to ask permission to pee. But if you forget the past few weeks, I'm happy with the choices I've made and the life I live. I love Carl, I love my work, I love my family and I love my friends. I'm not sure it gets much better than that."

"But what about the depression? You say you're happy with your lot, but there are times when you clearly are not. How can you go from being content with what you have to wanting to not be here?"

If I knew that, I think, I would have saved myself a lot of strife over the years.

"I'm grateful for what I have," I say, "But there is one thing that I am not happy with and that's the hard time I give myself. I put so much pressure on myself that I don't have a cat in hell's chance of achieving my self-imposed benchmarks. I fail everything, then berate myself for it and then I spiral downwards."

I look at Sarah and she's listening intently: I have the feeling that she wants to understand.

"When I say I don't want to be here," I continue, "What I think I really mean is that I don't want to be inside my own head anymore. It's exhausting and I'm on a hiding to nothing because my expectations of myself are sky high and often contradictory. I can't possibly achieve everything because to succeed in one area would always lead to failure in others. That's why I'm trying to get some help from the psychologist, because I can't live like this anymore."

And, with that, so many things click into place. I had never thought about the contradictory nature of my expectations…'relax but be perfectly in control' is a prime example. How can I possible achieve I expect of myself when the very nature of what I'm expecting is at odds with itself?

Over the next couple of hours, Sarah and I talk like we haven't done in years. We talk about Ronald and the kids, her work, their home and lots more besides. She asks me about Carl – something she has never wanted to know about in the past. She asks about our plans together and I tell her that neither of us wants to have a family and we don't have any particular desire to marry, but we know we want to be together. For the first time, she seems to accept this.

Sarah and I are still talking when Carl arrives. The look on his face when he walks into the room and finds us talking like the best of friends, was priceless. Sarah stays and talks to Carl for a while, then announces that it's time for her to head off before Ronald thinks she's been abducted. She hugs me and kisses my forehead.

"I'm so glad you came," I tell her "And I'm so happy we've been able to talk like this."

"Me too," she says, "I'll be back to see you very soon."

She blows me a kiss at the door and is gone.

Carl still looks flabbergasted. "You going to tell me what happened here today?" he asked. "Has the hospital branched out into personality transplants?"

I try to hit him, but he ducks. I tell him the whole story and he sits there open-mouthed. When I'm finished, I can see him searching for something to say.

"Well, er, good then, I guess. Bit of a surprise but good."

I have to stay in hospital for another two weeks before I am pronounced free to go home. In this time, I continue to be prodded and poked by the doctors and thankfully, an MRI scan shows no signs of brain damage.

The psychologist comes to see me every other day: I think I'm high on her 'at risk' list. It takes me three or four sessions before I think she's convinced I'm no danger to myself. I talk to her about my conversation with Sarah and the good that it has done for both of us. I also tell her about my moment of revelation when I realised about the contradictory nature of the pressures I pile on myself. That was a huge moment for me and one that I've been pondering ever since.

I'm visited twice by Guy and Anna. I have to smile when I notice them holding hands and looking to the other for approval of what they are saying. I ask Guy if there is any progress in his quest to find out what happened to me that night.

"Still working on it," he says, "Still trying to get hold of the guy who thinks he can give me a video of it. I'll find it."

The policewoman I've met before also comes back, this time on her own. She's a little tentative when she arrives, not really surprising after she and her colleague were abruptly evicted on their last visit. She introduces herself as Sharon and apologises for the heavy-handed questioning last time.

"He always gets nervous when he has to handle anything sensitive," she says, "And the problem is that, when he gets nervous, he tends to jump in with both feet and say the first thing that comes into his head. It's never the right thing to say."

She asks me if I've remembered anything else and I tell her I haven't. She tells me there's nothing new at their end either. I tell her about Guy's Facebook and Twitter mission and she's interested to know what's happening. I explain that Guy thinks someone has a video of the event but that, so far, he hasn't managed to track it down. She asks me to let her know if anything at all is found and gives me her card. She also asks for Guy's phone number.

Before I'm allowed home, I have to prove that I am able to get around and take basic care of myself. I am provided with a wheelchair. I would have preferred crutches but, as my arm is also in a bad way, I have no real way of using them. Once I've demonstrated that I can wheel myself to the loo and cope alone, and when Carl, Mum and Dad have been interviewed about the support available at home, I'm told I can leave the next day.

Carl, Mum and Dad congregate around my bed and we have small celebration with the lime cordial that has recently become my tipple of choice.

"Well whatever you said to them obviously worked," I said raising my glass in salute to them all.

"We told them," said Mum with her best don't-mess-with-me-or-else-young-lady expression on her face, "That your Dad and I are going to move in with you for a few weeks while you get yourself sorted and that is precisely what we are going to do. Carl needs to go to work and you need help all the time. Carl has already made you a temporary bedroom in the dining room. It's all sorted and all agreed."

She nods her head at the end of her final statement to indicate that she will not be argued with.

In the morning, we're all called into a 'patient conference'. The doctor who has been looking after me and the psychologist are both there. I have the feeling of being back at school and being called into the Headmaster's office.

The doctor begins. "Eve you have made good progress and we are not expecting you to relapse, but we do still need to keep an eye on you. I have spoken to your GP and arranged for you to visit the surgery once a week as well as weekly telephone consultation. We need to check that your progress continues and there are no signs of problems form your head trauma. You plaster cast will stay on for another three weeks and you'll need to keep your arm strapped up for that period, too. Before you leave, the nurse will issue you with a sling so you can keep your arm movement to a minimum. Does all this make sense?"

I nod dutifully and repeat what she's said to confirm that I've heard and understood.

"Now, in terms of support, who is going to be with Eve?" the doctor continues.

Mum speaks up to tell her that she and Dad will stay with us to help Carl take care of me.

"Good," says the doctor. "For the first week or so, Eve will probably need someone there all the time as she gets used to being back at home. I have the feeling that she'll try to do too much too quickly; please don't let her. Her body has been through a lot and needs time to heal properly." The three of them assure the doctor that I'll be kept under close scrutiny and won't be allowed to lift a finger.

Now, the psychologist adds her piece.

"I have spent a lot of time with Eve and I don't believe she meant to harm herself. However, her recent mental health issues may be influenced by both the physical trauma to her head and the mental trauma of the whole experience. Watch out for signs of changes in mood and call me if you have any cause for concern. Eve, you've made a lot of progress, but I'd like to arrange a series of sessions with a psychologist to make sure you do not slide backwards. Is this okay with you?" I get the feeling that I don't have a choice, but I'm not tempted to resist.

"It's fine," I say, "Is there any chance that I could continue to see either you or Hugh? I don't really want to have to start again from scratch.

The psychologist says that she won't be able to take the sessions with me as she is attached to the hospital, but she will try and arrange for me to see Hugh.

An hour later and issued with a bagful of medication, a sling and appointment cards to come back to the hospital for a check-up, I leave the hospital and return to the big wide world. The noise of car engines gives me a start and I am tempted to scuttle back into the security of the hospital. However, with the help of my three carers, I am hoisted into the car and taken home.

Chapter Nine

The Truth

Over the next week, Carl, Mum, Dad and I settle into a routine. Mum helps me to wash and dress in the morning while Dad does breakfast. We spend the morning reading the paper and doing a range of puzzles. I've really missed my nerdy puzzles while I've been in hospital. It pleases me that, while my body is a complete wreck, my brain is still sharp and I can devour puzzles just like I used to. Mum and Dad make me laugh: they spend ages sitting next to each other on the sofa with their phones like a pair of anti-social teenagers. I've been so used to being without my mobile in hospital that I keep forgetting to turn mine on.

Jess seems alternately happy to have me home and put out that there are suddenly two extra people in her domain. She is fascinated by the plaster cast and keeps sniffing it. At night, she sleeps with me in my makeshift bedroom in the dining room. The only problem is that she regularly wakes me up, yowling if any other cat dares to show itself at the dining room window. On several occasions, I find her trying to headbutt the intruder through the window. It's amazing how fierce and brave she is when there is a sheet of glass between her and her foe.

After a few days, the doctor's premonition comes true and I start itching to contribute to the running of the household. I haven't been using the wheelchair at home as space with four of us in the place in a little tight and the chair is somewhat unwieldy (no pun intended). I have learnt how to hop into the kitchen and even, with a little practice and concentration, hop upstairs and slide on my bum back down.

I'm not good at being looked after and waited on and feel guilty that everything is being done for me. I want to do something as a thank you for all that everyone is doing for me. While Carl is at work, Mum is out at the shops and Dad is having a quick pre-lunch snooze, I decide that the least I can do is to get lunch ready. I hop into the kitchen, get some tomatoes and mozzarella out of the fridge and begin to assemble some bruschetta. Having only one good arm makes it difficult to chop the tomatoes, but I manage it. However, when reaching over to find the bread, I lose my balance, send several baking trays clattering and end up in a crumpled heap on the floor. What's worse, try as I might, I cannot get myself upright again.

The clattering wakes Dad up and he comes rushing into the kitchen. He finds me still in my crumpled heap, covered in tomatoes. I think that he is going to tell me off, but instead, he bursts into fits of laughter. Thanks, Dad.

"Eve, my girl, you always have to learn the hard way, don't you? Now do you understand why the doctor said you have to rest and not start doing anything?"

"Yeah, yeah, yeah," I say, "She never said that if I did, I might end up with tomatoes dripping down my face – that might have been enough to discourage me."

Between the laughter which still has a firm hold of him, Dad manages to hoist me up and put me back on my feet.
"Now, do as you're bloody well told," he tells me, "Hop back into the living room and accept the fact that you need help."

Feeling both contrite and frustrated, I do as I am bloody well told and sit down. After a few days, the frustration outgrows the contrition and I find myself becoming irritable and short-tempered. I'm so used to being fiercely independent that having to rely upon other people for even the simplest tasks is getting to me. I have a little talk to myself and remind myself how grateful I am for all the love and support I'm receiving and tell myself that it would be good if I could show that gratitude a little more clearly.

Carl adapts to the new living arrangements with good grace, although I know that he's missing his space and his usual TV viewing. At night, he often sneaks down to sleep with me when Mum and Dad have gone to bed and we share the single mattress even though neither of us can sleep comfortably with my plastered leg in the way. The intimacy of having him so close to me is very important. I'm worried that he'll begin to think of me as his patient rather than his girlfriend. He has been very tolerant with me and I want him to know that it's not going to be like this forever.

On the second Thursday that I'm home, Mum tells me that she and Dad were thinking of going home over the weekend to check on the garden and give us some space. I bet they wanted some time on their own too. I told them it was a great idea and that Carl and I would be fine on our own.

We were fine. I'm learning to navigate the house with slightly more grace and Carl is learning that the washing fairy and the tidying fairy who he obviously thought lived with us are, in fact, figments of his imagination. I feel a bit smug when he tells me that he hadn't realised all that I normally do around the house. Bet you're learning very quickly now, matey.

We have an indulgent weekend of take-aways and DVDs. We enjoy just being together and, on the Saturday night, I manage to hop upstairs and sleep in our bed with Carl. I'm just about able to wash and dress myself and so Carl no longer needs to be my glorified home help. I can also make a cup of tea; the only problem is that I have no way of transporting the cups full of hot liquid with me from the kitchen. Carl suggests a thermos flask and I suggest where he can stick his thermos flask.

By the time that Mum and Dad arrive back on Sunday night, I think that he's had more than enough of his Florence Nightingale act and he welcomes them back with open arms.

"She's all yours," he says, "Been a bloody nuisance all weekend."

I know that he's joking but I can't help feeling that I am indeed being a bloody nuisance. I feel like a baby bird in a nest, constantly squawking for something and unable to do anything for itself. I keep thinking about what I can do to repay their generosity but nothing seems adequate.

The following day, I have a session with Hugh. I'm pleased that he's been able to arrange to work with me and I tell him so. He asks me how I am feeling.

"Mentally or physically?" I ask him.

"Whichever you want to talk about," he tells me.

I don't really want to list my ailments and tell him that my plastered leg is so itchy that I'm using one of Mum's knitting needles to attack the itch when no-one is looking. I decide to answer the question from a mental point of view. After all, that's probably what he's most interested in.

"I am a little frustrated by the fact that I can't do anything for myself and have no way of demonstrating my gratitude to everyone who's taking care of me," I tell him.

"Do you think that you need to demonstrate it?" he asks me.

"I feel as though I should, yes," I say. "I've caused so much disruption to so many people and I feel guilty that they can't get on with their lives. Every day, I'm expecting that they'll have had enough of me and start to resent all the attention they're giving me."

"If the situation were reversed, would you resent having to take care of one of them?"

"Not at all, but that's the problem. The situation is never reversed: it's always me causing the problem and always them picking up the pieces. The accident, the explosions - it's always my doing."

"Let's talk about the accident," Hugh says, "Do they think you caused it?"

"If you mean do they think I tried to harm myself, I don't know. We've talked about it, but because I can't tell anyone what happened, I think there's still a shred of doubt."

"Is there any shred of doubt in your mind?"

Very subtly done, Hugh, I'm impressed.

"Most of the time, no, but when I am awake in the night thinking it all through, I do start to doubt myself. What if the other Eve is becoming more powerful and more influential? What if I did try to do something to myself? That would explain why I don't remember it, because I blocked it out, just like I do with the explosions."

"It must be very distressing that you can't remember," he says.

"Yes, for me and for the people who want to know what happened. I wish I could tell them something that would put their minds at rest, but there's nothing to tell."

For the rest of the session, we talk about my mental state before the accident. I tell Hugh about my conversation with Sarah and the way it left me feeling. He asks me to think about any signs that might warn me I was becoming depressed at the time. I can't think of any.

The next morning, I have an excitable phone call from Guy.

"Where have you been?" he asks me, "I've been trying to get hold of you since yesterday."

"Sorry," I tell him, "I keep forgetting to switch my phone on."

"I've got it," he tells me and then waits for a response, as though I know what 'it' is.

"That's great," I tell him, "Got what?"

"The video," he says, "The video of your accident. I know what happened."

This is huge news and I can't quite take it in.

"Tell me?" I ask, suddenly hungry for the facts.

"I thought it would be better if you see if with your own eyes," he tells me, "I was going to just email it over, but I thought that it might come as a bit of a shock if I didn't warn you first. Watch it and then give me a call so that we can decide what to do."

I tell him that I will and I open my emails on my laptop. When I find the email from Guy, I am suddenly very nervous. I am about to find the answers I've been searching for ever since that fateful night and, now that the time has come, I'm not sure I want to know. I shout Mum and Dad and tell them what's happened. I ask them if they'll watch it with me as I don't want to be on my own. The three of us sit together on the sofa. I open the email and press 'play'.

The video is quite shaky, but we can clearly make out two men getting into a car, fumbling for a couple of minutes with the keys to get the car started and then setting off, hitting the car in front of them in the process. They turn their music on full blast and the thump-thump-thump of it is so loud that we have to turn the volume down.

We watch as they swerve along the road and come close to a figure walking along the pavement. It takes me a moment to realise that this figure is me. The car swerves, as if the driver has over-steered it and careers onto the pavement. We watch as the car ploughs into the back of me, knocking me flying. It hits the back of my legs, stops, reverses then speeds off. I, meanwhile, fall to the ground and hit my head hard on the pavement. The person filming this obviously comes to take a look at me as the camera homes in on my prone body. We see blood running from my nose. Then the camera cuts away, the person runs away and the film ends.

We are all too shocked to talk when the film finishes. It feels quite surreal to watch the events unfolding, events which until now I'd known nothing about. My Mum cries softly and reaches over for me. My Dad comforts my Mum while keeping one had firmly on mine. We sit there like that for what feels like an eternity, each of us trying to process what we have just witnessed.

My Dad speaks first.

"Bastards!" he says, "Rotten drugged-up bastards! They are so loaded that they can't drive in a straight line, they knock you over then they scarper so they don't have to face the consequences. Cowardly, drugged-up bastards!"

Neither Mum nor I can think of anything to say, just as well really as Dad's rant isn't over yet.

"And what about the bastard taking the video? He's no better. Coming up to take a look at you and then running off, leaving you in that state. Another cowardly bastard!"

Mum tries to soothe my Dad who is working himself up into a frenzy.

"I know it's horrible to watch and I understand exactly why you're angry, but let's think about this for a minute. We now know that Evie didn't try to hurt herself and we also know who did hurt her. The car's registration number was clear to see on the video."

This does the trick and calms Dad down. He regains rational thought and manages to form a sentence without the word 'bastard' in it.

"What do we do with this?" he asks. "Has Guy sent it to the police?"

"I'm not sure," I tell him, "I told him I'd call him when we'd watched it. Maybe I should do that now."

They both agree that this is the best thing to do and so I call Guy.

"So what do you think?" he asks, understandably proud that his detective work has paid off.

I didn't really know what to say or, indeed what I thought. Everything was still sinking in.

"I'm glad that I've found out some answers," I tell him, "But it's really weird watching that happen to me."

"That's exactly what Anna thought," he tells me. "Got 'em banged to rights, eh? You can see how out of control they both were and the registration number is clear."

I agree and ask him who else he's shown the video to.

"Just Anna," he tells me, "I didn't want to do anything else with it until you'd seen it."

I'm not sure why, but I'm grateful for this.

"Are you going to send it to the police?" I ask him.

"Hmmm, I was kinda hoping that you'd do that," he says.

"Okay, any particular reason why?"

"Well, it took me ages to persuade the bloke who took it to hand it over to me because he's scared that he'll be in trouble for not reporting the accident. He only gave it to me when I promised that I wouldn't hand it over to the police."

"But surely you're going to break that promise?" I ask, "Because we have to give this to them."

"Well," Guy says,"If YOU give it to the police then, technically, I haven't broken any promises, have it?"

Slightly twisted logic, but I'm quite happy to go along with it if Guy feels as though this way will keep his honour intact.

"Do you know why he took the video in the first place?" I ask, wondering at the chance in a million which lead to someone filming it.

"I asked him that," guy says. "He told me he'd seen them keying a couple of cars in the car park and he thought that they might have a go at his, so he decided to film them in case they did."

I call Sharon, the WPC who came to visit me in hospital and tell her what has happened. She gives me an email address to send the video to and tells me that she'll be in touch when she has watched it and has a better idea of what will happen next.

Next, I call Carl to update him on the day's events. He's delighted. He promises to be home as soon as he can.

When he arrives home, he asks if he can watch the video. I'm a little reticent as I don't want to see it again and I'm not sure that he'll really want to see what happens to me. However, I know that this is not my decision and he's adamant he wants to watch it. Knowing that Mum and Dad won't want to see it again either, I suggest that he takes the laptop upstairs and watches the video there.

We wait for him to come back down, anxious to know how he's doing after watching the film. He comes down about fifteen minutes.

"Are you okay?" I ask him, expecting him to react like Dad who is still seething all these hours later.

"I can honestly say," Carl says, "That I never thought I'd be so pleased to see a video of two idiots knocking my girlfriend over."

"Thanks very much," I tell him, not sure to make of what he has just said.

Realising what he has said, Carl jumps in to put the record straight."No, I don't mean I enjoyed it," he says, "I hated watching you go through that and I hated seeing you lying there injured with no-one to help you. What I mean is that I'm glad we have the video. For two reasons, actually: one, because it means that the Police have the evidence that they need and two, because we all now know beyond a shadow of a doubt that you didn't do anything to hurt yourself. I think that makes me happier than anything else. Crazy Eve didn't take over."

I didn't realise the Carl had named my alter-ego. I wonder if he calls the normal version of me 'Sane Eve'. Probably not.

"I just hope that they have enough to get that pair of miserable little fuckers," Carl says.

I don't think that Carl has ever used language like that in front of my folks, but they let it pass. In fact, my Dad says, "Yeah!"

Later, Mum and I are sat together on our own.

"I was thinking," she says, "With all the drama of today and all of us dealing with our own feelings, I don't think that any of us have asked you how you're feeling. I'd like to know, if you're happy to tell me."

I hadn't really stopped and taken stock of my feelings, so Mum's question gives me pause for thought.

"Lots of different things all at the same time," I tell her. "It was the weirdest thing watching myself being hit by the car, totally surreal. I'm angry at them for doing it, not just for what they did to me, but for all the stuff that they have put you all through as well and the disruption that they've caused to so many lives. Strangely, I think that I'm angrier at the guy who filmed it and then just left me there. What would have happened if no-one had found me?"

"It doesn't bear thinking about," Mum shudders.

"Despite the anger, I can't begin to tell you how relieved I am that I now know for certain it wasn't me trying to hurt myself. I didn't think I had, but I also know there was always a chance I did. I feel like I've taken back some control over myself."

Mum takes my hand and I see the tears in her eyes again. "Me too, sweetheart. I can feel our Eve coming back to us and we've been waiting for her for a long time."

There was nothing to say to that. I lean over and kiss Mum. What should have been the tenderest of moments was slightly spoiled by the fact that I lost my balance and ended up in Mum's lap. We laughed, she set me upright again and we went to join the boys. We find them watching one of Carl's sci-fi series, one which I've never really understood. Dad is clearly having trouble with it too, as we find Carl trying to explain the plot and back story. Dad murmurs understanding, but I'm not convinced that he's any clearer.

Although Carl and Dad are still very angry – Carl planning his own kind of justice for the two men and Dad regularly muttering, "Bastards!" under his breath – the atmosphere in the house changes noticeably. The video has proved that, as Carl said, Crazy Eve didn't take over. Also, it felt to us all that we'd moved out of limbo and onto a path with a clearer way forward.

Mum starts to talk about when they should go back home. I know that this is partly because I'm now slightly more mobile, but I think that it was also much to do with them feeling free to stop watching me for signs that I might harm myself. Carl tell them he's arranged for a friend to cover his driving lessons for the next week so he can take care of me.

We are meant to be going to Liz and Dina's civil ceremony on Saturday, so we suggest Mum and Dad stay until then. This idea meets with unanimous approval.

"Are you sure you'll be okay?" Mum asks me.

"We'll be fine," I tell her. "It just means that, if all the household fairies don't come back, Carl might have to learn how to use a few more domestic appliances."

He shoves me for that last comment, but I think this has been a good lesson for him in what keeps our home ticking.

When Saturday comes, it feels like the end of an era. I'll be sorry to see Mum and Dad go: I've loved having them around.

Over the past few days, I've accepted that I'm not going to be able to make a grand entrance at the civil ceremony - well at least, not the kind I'd want to make. I've grudgingly accepted that the wheelchair will have to come too and even more grudgingly, that I can't wear the beautiful new shoes I bought especially for the occasion.

"You could always wear just one of them?" Carl offers, "That way, we can all visualise what you would look like with both of them on and no pot on your leg."

The idea sounded crazy at first, but it grows on me. Maybe having the wheelchair could actually be an advantage. The shoes were truly beautiful but so high that I hadn't a hope of walking around in them all day. Yes, one shoe it would be. I could start a trend – call it the 'Cinderella Look'. Shoes sorted, I started to think about the outfit. I needed to find something that would look demure and ladylike in a wheelchair. Too short a skirt and I risked showing everything I've got to all and sundry. With Mum's help, I had raided my wardrobe and found a long floaty dress that just happens to tone perfectly with the shoes.

The ceremony is just beautiful and Liz and Dina look so happy. Even better, Gill and James and Alex are there. They cheer when the chair and I make our appearance and then delight themselves by telling me how wheely, wheely good I look...

After the ceremony, we lose Carl and James for quite a while, eventually finding them outside sharing a joint and talking about zombies. It's good to know that the bromance is well and truly intact. It gives me a chance to catch up properly with Gill. She wants to know everything about everything and wants to know what the police are doing now that they have the video. The truth is that I don't know: I haven't heard from Sharon since she emailed to say she'd received the video.

It's good to be back in the real world again and spend time with people I care about. At last, even Alex and I have actually managed to be in the same place at the same time. When we talk, I find out more about why she has been so flaky over the past year: she and her husband are having problems and she thinks it's heading for the divorce courts. That explains why she's here at the wedding on her own. Alex, however, is determined to let her hair down and have fun. She tears up the dancefloor with whoever wants to dance with her, dancing alone if she gets no better offers.

Towards the end of the night, I realise that one of the Uni Girls is missing: there's no sign of Call Me Babs. I ask Gill about it and she tells me the whole sorry tale of Barbara's eviction from the group.

"We were all having doubts after what she did in your room at Christmas," she says, "But she put the final nail well and truly in her own coffin when Liz and

Dina invited her to the ceremony. She told them that it wasn't a proper marriage and that they should know better than to engage in such a tasteless charade."

"Wow," I say, "Crass even by her standards".

"So, the vote was taken and we all agreed that she is now *persona nongrata*. We would have asked you to vote too, but you were in a coma at the time and we didn't think we could rely on you to use your vote wisely!"

"So then, no more Call Me Babs lauding it over everybody with her distinct fashion sense, no more grossly inappropriate comments or pimply-arsed conquests?"

"I'm afraid not, no."

"I think I can live with that. It'll be interesting to see if she keeps up her friendship with Sarah," I say.

"Now then, Sarah," Gill says, "What's been going on there?"

I start on another story to update her on all of the comings and goings with Sarah, happy that the story finishes on a positive note.

"Well, good on her," Gill says, "I always knew that, deep down, she wasn't a complete bitch."

"Oi!" I say, "That's my sister you're talking about."

CHAPTER TEN

The Future

When we return from Liz and Dina's day and find that we have the house to ourselves again, it is as though a new chapter is beginning.

On our first night together, completely on our own, Carl and I cuddle up in bed.

"I know this is a stupid thing to say," he says nevertheless, "But I've missed you."

I know exactly what he means. Although I've loved every second of having Mum and Dad with us and I'll be eternally grateful for the love and care they've shown me, I've missed Carl too. I've missed our little life for two people – and one cat – and I've missed the togetherness of us being in our own home, just the two – sorry, Jess, the three – of us.

"Do you know what's worried me the most?" I ask him.

"What?" he replies.

"I worry that you will think of me as someone to be cared for and, if I'm honest, not someone to lust after. I want you to know I'm still your girlfriend, with everything that entails."

"Is that a come-on?" he asks me playfully.

"Play your cards right and it could be," I tell him.

He reaches over to me and we make love for the first time in weeks. It's all the more special, all the more intense because I know that I still have the same place in his thoughts.

Afterwards, he won't let me go and I don't want him to.

"I love you, relatively normal Evie," he says.

"I love you too," I tell him.

That night, we sleep soundly, never quite breaking the contact with one another but allowing each other our own space. I wake in the middle of the night and can't stop looking at him. He looks like an elegant red squirrel when he's asleep. It might not sound like it, but that's a compliment. I turn to him several times and kiss him. I can't believe my luck that he's still here and seems happy about it.

For the first week, Mum and Dad call every day to check that everything's okay. I look forward to their calls. I miss them. I try to keep up with the routines we established when they were with me. Each day after the BBC Breakfast News, I watch Heir Hunters and discuss it with Dad later in the day.

I still feel a real urge to do something that shows how grateful I am for everything they've given me. Every day, I think about what I could do and, every day, it never seems like enough.

Later that week, the plaster cast is removed from my leg. I'm horrified by how hairy my leg has grown under its plaster armour and I go straight upstairs to shave it as soon as I get home. The joy of being able to have a proper bath without one appendage sticking out awkwardly is immeasurable.

My mobility is still questionable and I'm careful not to put too much pressure on my newly-exposed limb. I hop around still, as though the cast were still in place. Over time, I tentatively learn to put some pressure on my leg and start to walk in a more balanced way on it. Carl says I still look slightly drunk, wheeling from side to side, but for me it feels like progress. I stick to flat shoes and try to walk a little further every day. By the end of the week, I'm able to make it to the end of our block of houses. A couple of days later, I can make it back, too.

On the advice of the hospital, I try to build up the power in my legs through swimming. I start with a few lengths at a time, but by the end of the week, I can manage half a kilometre. Given that I used to swim two or three kilometres a day before the accident, this may not sound much, but I greet it as a triumph.

I continue to have my weekly sessions with Hugh and they bring a welcome opportunity to reflect and take stock of where I'm up to. In a weird way, they provide some normality in a very abnormal world. They help me to hold onto the me I was before the accident, the whole me.

This week, he starts by asking me where my head is at the moment. Good question, as always, Hugh.

The fact is that my head is in a relatively good place. I'm grateful to everybody for everything that they've given to me.

"I'm interested in the use of the word 'grateful'," Hugh says. "Does that imply that you think that people have given you over and above what you should expect from them?"

"Yes," I tell him, without a moment's hesitation. "They've put their lives on hold for me and given me more than I could ever hope for. I'm unbelievably grateful."

"Yet you've said before that you would do the same for them, 'in a heartbeat', I think was your phrase?"

"And your point is?" I ask him.

"I'm interested to know why you would give the same without a moment's thought, yet you seem unable to believe that other people would do the same for you."

"I'm not sure that I've earned the right for this level of support; I'm not sure that I've ever done enough to warrant it," I tell him.

"I've noticed," he observes, "That you use the word 'enough' a lot. You use it to express that you've had enough and don't want anymore and to quantify what you give to people. Is the word important to you?"

Ooh, shame on you, Hugh, for making a sick woman delve into the depths of herself and think hard about things.

"I just want to be enough for people and to feel I'm giving them as much as they give me."

"Does life work on a bartering system, then? You have to put in so much before you are justified in taking something out?"

Bugger, he's well and truly got me there.

"I need to feel okay in myself that there is a balance between give and take," I tell him.

"And who is determining where that balance lies?"

"Me, I suppose. It's all based upon whether I feel as though I have done enough to earn taking something out."

"Do you ever share your judgements about what 'enough' means to the people around you?"

"Okay, okay, you've got me. I'm basing this entire premise on my own thoughts and perceptions of what 'enough' actually is. Happy?"

The session is coming to a close and, as usual, Hugh summarises what we have discussed and brings the important issues back into sharp relief. Then he tells me that we're going to start thinking about relapse planning - planning what I can do if I feel myself starting to move towards an explosion and spiralling down again. He says that he'd like to begin by spending next week's session considering what I've learnt and how I can use that knowledge.

This question – what have I learnt? – plays on my mind before my next session with Hugh. I talk to Carl about it and he encourages me to start making a list.

I tend to think about it before I go to sleep at night so I keep a pad and a pen next to my side of the bed to note down any revelations that come to me. After a couple of days, the list covers two pieces of paper. I review what I've written to try and find some semblance of order in my thoughts.

My reflections on what I've learnt are interrupted the following day by a phone call from WPC Sharon.

"We've caught them," she says, "The two men who ran you over. We tracked one of them down using the car registration in the video and, when we showed him the video he gave us the other man. We've charged them both."

"That's good news," I tell her, knowing that it is but feeling everything connected with that night being stirred up again and finding the same sense of horror building inside me. "What happens now?"

"They've both denied involvement despite the clear video evidence, so it'll probably go to court. We've handed it over to the Crown Prosecution Service. Oh… One other thing, the guy who took the video has come forward and confirmed that the two guys were in the club that night. Your friend Guy has identified them too. I don't know why they don't just plead guilty and save us a lot of time and expense."

When Carl gets in, I tell him what's happened and he's delighted. He asks me if I've told Mum and Dad yet. In all the drama, I hadn't thought about that. I call them straight away. The news gives Dad the opportunity to use the word 'bastards' again, combined with various other insults. Mum is quieter and not as sweary and wants to know what happens next, so I tell her what I know.

Given what's happened and the feelings that it's stirred up, my session with Hugh this week takes us in a slightly different direction than planned. It's probably just as well, as I haven't finished my homework and can't really rely upon the excuse of Jess eating it. We discuss my feelings about what happened and those that have emerged since Sharon's phone call. As we talk, I register that I'm no longer angry. The anger has been replaced by fear.

"Fear of what?" Hugh asks.

Until that point, it had been an unnamed sense of dread that was just swirling around. His question helped me to pinpoint the nature of that fear.

"Fear of seeing the men that put me through all this," I tell him, "And fear of having to live it all again in court. What if they don't believe me? What if they twist it around and make it my fault?"

"So, a fear of being judged, a fear of being to blame and a fear of not being believed?" he asks.

"Yes."

"We've come across these fears before, I think."

He's right, we have. Even with all the evidence stacked against the two guys who've been charged, I'm doubting myself and wondering whether what I have to say will be enough.

"It might be useful," Hugh says, "To add these feelings to your thoughts about what you have learnt. Is that okay?"

It is okay and I think that he's right that it's useful.

Later that day, I tell Carl about my conversation with Hugh and the things I fear. He's understanding, yet adamant that the two men don't have a leg to stand on. I make a joke about this, referring to the leg that has recently shed its plaster cast. While he laughs, the joke isn't enough to sidetrack him.

"You may very well have to face them in court," he says, "But you won't be on your own, you'll have us with you every step of the way. And think about it this way – would you rather be in your position witnessing justice being done or their position having justice done to them?"

A well-reasoned, rational argument, but it doesn't stop some of my irrational fears slipping back in. I imagine being in court and coming face to face with them. I imagine the arguments that they could make in their defence. I had all of my faculties on the night - I was stone-cold sober – so they can't use that one. Going through it in my head is uncomfortable, but it leaves me feeling a little more reassured. I decide there is nothing I can do about it until I know what's happening, so I put it in a little box in my head, marked 'To be dealt with at the appropriate time'.

I turn my attention back to my homework: what I have learnt? I remember that there's another important question to add to this: what am I going to do with this knowledge?

I review my previous list and consider Hugh's suggestion of adding my learning about my response to the men's arrest. After trying to answer the whole question in one go and tying myself up in knots, I decide on two lists – one entitled 'What have I learnt?' and one entitled 'How will I use my knowledge to move forward? Having agreed the titles of the lists, I can start to populate them. I go through numerous iterations, asking Carl, Mum and Dad for ideas. After all, they've lived through it with me and have probably noticed things that I've missed.

When I see Hugh for the next session, I present the lists to him, as proud as a small child bringing home her painting from school. I almost want Hugh to promise to take a copy home and put it in pride of place on his fridge.

This pride, I realise, is not about fulfilling the assignment, but more that I think that I've created something very valuable, something I can use to make a real difference to my life and the lives of those around me.

"What drove you to add the second part?" Hugh asks .

"There seems little point in learning if you're not going to do something positive with the knowledge that you've gained," I tell him.

Hugh asks me to talk through the points on each list.

The top ten things that I have learnt, in no particular order of significance, are:

1. I judge myself far more harshly than others judge me (if, indeed they are judging me at all): I then transfer my harsh judgement onto them and presume that's what they're thinking
2. Because I judge myself and find myself wanting, I automatically assume that others do too
3. Although I understand the difference between wanting to escape from myself and wanting to be dead, it's not as easy for other people to understand and it scares them
4. I set myself impossible goals and standards, many of which contradict: therefore, I can't possibly achieve them
5. My perception of what I need to do to be 'enough' is unattainable and out of line with others' expectations
6. Because this perception of being 'enough', is unattainable, I assume that I am not enough
7. I set myself up for failure through my demands upon myself and then compound the failure and disappointment by beating myself up when I don't achieve them
8. I am not always (or even usually) accurate in my assessments of what people are thinking about me
9. People actually love me because of who I am and what I do: if they feel this way, maybe it's okay to be me
10. Just because I don't feel worthy of love at times, it doesn't mean that this love stops: as a very wise person once said to me, 'just because you can't feel it doesn't mean it's not there'

The top ten actions that I'll take as a result of this knowledge, in no particular order:

1. Identify the patterns that precede an explosion and become more aware of my early warning signs so I can deal with the situation before it becomes explosive
2. Reach out to people when I feel myself heading downwards instead of isolating myself
3. Allow myself to be vulnerable and 'incapable' in order to talk about the things in my head

4. Question the assumptions I make and check their validity without the bias of my warped sense of reality
5. Check out these assumptions with those involved to get their perspective
6. Be more inclusive in my search for 'evidence' about myself instead of simply focusing on anything that confirms what a terrible person I am
7. Consider the demands I place on myself and check them out for contradictions
8. Consider whether I'd make similar demands of others – maybe imagine myself telling somebody important to me that they must fulfil the demand and check my response
9. Tell myself, particularly Crazy Eve, to get over myself and come back into the real world
10. Allow myself to feel the love and support that's so generously offered to me

When I finish my list, I feel wonderfully energised and I'm grinning inanely.

Hugh asks me about the list of actions and how confident I feel about living up to them.

"It's not going to be easy," I tell him, "Because it'll require some complete mind shifts. I want to do it, though."

He asks how I will deal with myself if I 'fail' in one of the actions. Good question, what do I do if I can't live up to my benchmark?

I ponder this before replying because it's a crucial question.

"I think it's all about how I frame these things in my head," I tell him. "If I think of them as a set of unbreakable golden rules, I'll come down on myself hard if I mess up. If I think of them as a journey or a learning experience, then it'll be okay to mess up because it's part of the learning process."

I think that I must have said the right thing because Hugh smiles.

"We seem to have come a long way," he says, "With a few unexpected dramas along the way. How would you assess where you are now, Eve?"

More pondering; Hugh's questions are not to be answered lightly or flippantly.

"I feel mentally stronger than I have done in a long time," I tell him.

"Where do you think that this strength has come from?"

Yet more pondering required.

"I think I've actually been able to feel proud of myself in some situations, such as the way that things have worked out with Sarah. Plus the accident and incapacity meant that I've had to allow others to take care of me and be the capable ones."

"So you've actually allowed yourself to congratulate yourself on some things well done?" Hugh asks.

"Yes, I guess I have. One of the main things that's made a difference is that I feel I'm moving forward again. I'm not trapped in my own destructive world with only Crazy Eve for company. I've been able to talk more openly to people and they haven't condemned me for being wrong."

"And are you enough?"

Ooh, the biggie!

"I'm more 'enough' than I was. I'm learning it's okay to be me and that people care about me for who I am, not what I think I have to them to compensate for my inadequacies."

Hugh tells me that it might be a good idea for us to meet in about three months to check on where I'm up to. I agree.

I need my new-found strength soon afterwards when I find out that the court date has been set and that the prosecution needs to talk to me and prepare me to give evidence. I have a little wobble, but quickly right myself and prepare for the job in hand. It all seems quite straightforward because there's only so much that I can say and I've said it so many times that it's become second nature.

I hear that Guy has been called as a witness. I call to find out how he's feeling about this.

"If it gets those two banged up where they belong," he says, "It's a small price to pay. Besides, I have Anna holding my hand through it all."

"Still going well, then?" I ask him.

"Blissful," he says, "She's one in a million. Not only is she beautiful and charming, but she's also sorted out my tax return."

Fantastic. I reflect upon the fact that, while I wouldn't want to live through the experience of the accident again, it has brought about good: Guy's relationship with Anna, my relationship with Sarah and my relationship with myself.

In the end, the court appearance turns out to be a non-event. We – that's me, Carl, Mum, Dad, Sarah, Guy and Anna – all turn up at the allotted time, ready to do our bit when we find out that the two guys have both changed their plea and pleaded guilty. They are sentenced the following week and both sent down.

"Good!" says Dad, "Got what they deserved."

"Yes, pair of bastards," Mum says with a glint in her eye, gently teasing her husband.

The following weekend, it's Dad's birthday so Mum invites the whole family over for a celebration lunch. As Sarah and I greet each other warmly, I can sense Mum and Dad watching us and smiling to one another.

Harvey makes a beeline for me, wanting to know about the gig that led to my accident and the VJing that Guy did. I told him all about it and he kept saying, 'Whoa! Cool!' I think that my street cred went up enormously in his eyes just because I happened to be in a place where cool stuff was happening.

Before lunch, when we have all been handed a glass of champagne and made a rousing toast to Dad, Rosie and I find a few minutes to talk.

"So, how are things?" I ask her.

"All I can say is what have you done with my mother and who is this new woman in my life?"

"Good then, eh?"

"It's like she really listens to me now and tries to understand who I am. We even went shopping together last week which was a total first."

Dad is clearly having a high old time and loving having his family around him. Over lunch, the wine flows – a lot of it into his glass – and so does the conversation. The mock politeness and stiffness that has surrounded recent family occasions has gone and we enjoy being together.

After dessert, Dad bangs his wine glass as a sign that he would like to say a few words. As it turns out, he'd like to say a lot of words.

"It's such a pleasure to have my family around me, to hear all the laughter and feel the warmth."

This is greeted with a chorus of 'here, here' from his assembled audience.

Turning to Mum, he says, "Thank you for arranging today and for cooking such a splendid meal: as always, you've done us proud."

Turning to Sarah and me, he says "My two girls, how good it is to see you together again and happy in one another's company. I've wished for this for so long: thank you for making it happen."

Sarah and I respond with mock curtsies and then each blow him a kiss.

"This family," he continues, "Has been through more than its fair share of drama over recent months but we've come through it. Eve is well on the mend and those two 'nasty gentlemen' are now behind bars. Cheers to us all and let's do this far more often!"

With that, he raises his glass and we all join in with his toast. He's right: it's lovely to be together and so easy and relaxed in one another's company.

Later that evening, as I'm lying in bed with Carl, I reflect on the day and the events leading up to it, and I give thanks for the distance we've all travelled.

I think about the wonderful people in my world, the differences in myself and the journey that I've made and I realise that this life is well and truly enough.

Lightning Source UK Ltd.
Milton Keynes UK
UKOW04f1515191114

241866UK00001B/192/P